Dames Fight Harder
Maggie Sullivan Mystery #6

M. Ruth Myers

Published by Tuesday House

ACKNOWLEDGMENTS

Thanks to my daughter, Jessica Myers, for sharing her insider's knowledge of the commercial construction business, albeit in the twenty-first century with its many changes since Maggie Sullivan's day.

Ongoing thanks to the Dayton Police History Foundation for its wonderful window into an important element of Dayton's past, and to the organization's secretary-treasurer, Stephen Grismer for patiently answering my questions.

Any errors in the story you are about to read are entirely my own.

Late March
1942

ONE

Spring fever is a dangerous malady for a private eye. It blinded me to signs a hit man was waiting for me.

In the four months since Pearl Harbor we'd had nothing but defeats in the Pacific. The elevator in my building was on the fritz. But spring had come to Dayton and it was glorious. My head was so stuffed with daffodils and discovering the hat I wore matched the lacy pink of redbud trees that I didn't notice the door to my office was unlocked.

"Don't go for your gun," a man's voice warned as I entered.

I froze, my arms around a bag of shoes to take for resoling and my Smith & Wesson in my purse. I was pretty sure the man the voice belonged to was a friend, but events can cause people to change on a dime. His unexpected appearance here, and the way he'd been lying in wait, kicked every nerve in my body to full alert.

"Pearlie, you just about scared me to death. Okay if I turn on the light?"

Reaching from his spot behind the door, he did it for me.

His razor-thin body, with its economy of effort, flowed into view.

"Didn't want to wait in the hall and I had to see you first thing. Rachel's in jail."

"For what?"

"Murder."

Ditching the bag of shoes, I sank into my chair and stared.

Rachel Minsky, the woman he worked for, was my one close woman friend. On the outside, she was a pampered and pretty. Underneath, she was tough enough to run her own construction company.

"Did she do it?"

Pearlie walked to the pair of windows overlooking Patterson and opened one an inch or two. He lit a cigarette.

"She says she didn't."

Rachel had a gun. She could use it very effectively. She wouldn't kill someone in cold blood, but like me she knew the law couldn't always be counted on for justice. Pearlie turned to face me.

"They've got her at Ford Street. She wants to see you."

"Me?" I stopped swiveling side to side in my chair. "Look, Pearlie, I'll help her any way I can, but her lawyer may not want a private eye traipsing in to see her. He may think it makes her look guilty, he may have his own gumshoe on retainer—"

"She wants to see you. As soon as you came in, she said. I don't think she's talked to a lawyer. Anyways, she was real specific I wasn't to contact her brother."

One of her brothers was a lawyer. Maybe more than one. Rachel had several, and she'd mentioned them a few times, but she didn't talk much about her family. They were well off, I knew that much. She'd joked that she was the black sheep. I didn't think it was because of money, though. Rachel was plenty successful as a businesswoman. It was probably the businesswoman part they didn't like. Most likely they thought she ought to be married with kids.

I already was on my feet.

"What if they won't let me?"

Pearlie didn't frown the way most people would, but I could tell by the way his eyes had stilled that he was thinking. Without warning he flicked his half-smoked cigarette out the window and came toward my desk. Leaning across me, he picked up my pencil and wrote on the pad by my phone.

"I'll be at that number til noon. Mid-afternoon I got a piano lesson. You know how to reach me there. I'll check in."

"Keep trying."

"Yeah. Line of work you're in, you ought to get yourself an answering service."

"Pearlie, wait." He already was halfway to the door. "Give me a dollar."

He pulled a money clip out and peeled off some bills.

"If you're running short, I got plenty."

I chuckled. "No shorter than usual. Just a dollar. That way I can say I've been hired to have a look at things in Rachel's behalf."

For the first time that morning, his lips drew back in the hint of a smile. It was how I imagined a wolf looked preparing to feast. He put his money clip away. At the door he paused and gave the jamb a soft tap with the side of his fist.

"Rachel don't always ask for help when she needs it. She keeps things to herself."

I thought I understood what he was trying to say between the words.

"If there's anything I think you should know about, I'll let you know. In any case, I'll keep you posted."

He nodded, satisfied. I locked the door, wondering what kind of mess I was going to find when I talked to Rachel, and whether, if necessary, I'd be willing to lie to get her out of it.

***

Dayton had two main police stations, the fancy one downtown for the brass and detectives, and the not-so-fancy one for everyone else. The workhorse station, variously referred to as Ford Street, CPS, or on rare occasion Central Police Station, was a sprawling two-story building. It housed the jail, the booking desk, the motor pool and other day-to-day functions. Before the new dispatch center opened on Monument, it had housed that, too.

I parked my DeSoto on Sears and walked down the alley-like street in front of the station's front entrance. My fingers were crossed that silver-haired Seamus Hanlon wasn't on desk duty. He and another cop had been my late father's closest friends and were my godfathers. When I'd hung out my shingle seven years earlier, we'd made a pact: I wouldn't ask for information or favors where their work was involved and they wouldn't stick their noses into my cases. If it came to a tussle over whether or not I got to see

Rachel, I didn't want it to be Seamus I had to argue with.

A kid so green looking he had to be a trainee was running the desk. Seamus, who came in early, must have gone to breakfast. Or maybe he was filling in on street patrol or in a cruiser. As was the case everywhere, men were leaving the force left and right as their draft numbers came up.

"I'm here to see Rachel Minsky," I said. "You booked her early this morning."

"Are you her lawyer?" His tone conveyed doubt.

"I've been hired to help with her case."

He looked around for someone else to give input, but no help was in sight. Pulling a list toward him, he hunted her name. Then he slid the visitor's log toward me.

"You need to sign in. Put the time. And, uh, you need to show me identification."

Opening my purse gave me time to weigh pros and cons. I showed him the Special Detective license bearing the signature of the chief of police. His manner became more official.

"Okay. Follow me. I'll have someone take you back. You've got five minutes."

TWO

I'd been to see people in Ford Street lockup before. Its two dormitory-style women's cells were upstairs. The dimly lighted aisle looked bleaker than I remembered. The smells were worse, too, and the echoes. Or maybe it was just different when you were going to see somebody you knew.

Rachel Minsky reminded me of an expensive doll in Rike's department store. Her skin was creamy; her face a perfect oval. A wealth of black hair fluffed in a cloud around it. Her suits were as fine as they came, invariably enhanced by furs and a tasteful touch of expensive jewelry, which usually included garnet earrings.

Not this morning.

The woman who sprang to her feet at sight of me looked washed out. Her plain wool dress had a stain on one sleeve. Instead of stockings and high heels she wore anklets and lace-up shoes. Bereft of any hint of makeup, her skin looked pale and faded. She strolled toward me with her usual swagger, though.

"You need lipstick," I said.

"What I need is a double martini."

"How'd you get the bruise?"

It was small, at the edge of her eye, as if someone had taken a swing without much success. She gave her head a careless toss.

"One of my fellow denizens mistook me for a powder puff."

"Bitch," snarled a woman hunkered defensively on one of the bunks.

She was listening with interest, trying to size up my pink hat and wavy brown hair. So were several in the neighboring cell. Beckoning Rachel closer, I lowered my voice.

"Rachel, what happened? Make it fast. We've only got five minutes."

I stood five-foot-two and Rachel was shorter. I'd seen her stroll into a roomful of men who had guns pointed at her and not bat an eye. Now, despite her squared shoulders, she looked small and vulnerable. Her hands gripped the bars between us so tightly her knuckles were white.

"Two things first, in case we run out of time. As soon as you leave here, go see my brother."

"The lawyer?"

"Yes. His name is Joel. He's in the Lindsey Building. Sixth floor. If he's not in court, the receptionist there will say you need an appointment. Tell her his sister sent you with a message and you're to wait for an answer. Have it written out so she can take it to him."

"What exactly should I say?"

"'Truffle's in jail.'"

Truffle?

"And if he is in court?"

Her jaw jutted sideways.

"Then you'll have to wait." Tiny lines of tension fanned out from her eyes. She ran a hand through her hair. "I don't suppose you thought to bring me cigarettes."

"No. Sorry."

"No, you're not." She managed a smile.

"What's the other thing?"

"I need you to get rid of something so no one else finds it." Her husky voice had dropped even lower. Her dark eyes stared at me defiantly. "It's nothing to do with what happened last night. It's personal."

"What is it? Where do I find it?"

"An envelope. With papers inside it. It's in my office. The upholstery on my chair has half a dozen tacks that are loose. On the seat, at the back. Pry them up and replace them after you've removed the envelope. Then find a fire somewhere and burn it."

It went without saying I wasn't to look at the contents.

"You going to fill me in on the murder part now?"

"The s.o.b. they found had it coming, but I didn't do it. They found his body at one of my construction sites."

"But you knew him?"

"Oh, yes. That's how I know he was an s.o.b."

"I take it he was killed last night?"

"I assume."

The guard who'd led me to the cells began to walk toward us.

"Where were you?" I asked quickly.

"I keep a place downtown. I was there in bed."

"Any way of confirming it?"

Her sudden grin made her look like the old Rachel.

"The man who was sharing my bed tried to. The cops didn't seem to believe him. Tell Joel I want you in on this."

"Time's up," said the guard.

* * *

There were things from my conversation with Rachel that I'd have preferred to clear up before meeting her brother. The business about the envelope I was supposed to burn bothered me. She said it had nothing to do with whatever the mess was she'd landed in. I wanted to believe her, but a gnat of doubt kept whining at the back of my brain.

Her comment that she kept a place downtown had startled me too. I'd always had the impression she lived with her parents. Now that I considered it, though, that was pure supposition on my part. From time to time she'd mentioned family matters in passing, so they weren't alienated. Yet learning she kept a place of her own didn't really surprise me. At core, there was an elusiveness to Rachel.

Considerably short of all the answers I wanted, I sailed into The Lindsey Building, a tall, skinny place on South Main. Her brother's law firm had two names on the door and a reception area paneled in walnut with a dark green rug in front of couches where people could wait. When you stepped on that green rug, you were walking on money. A middle-aged couple sat on one of the couches, so deep in whispered conversation that they didn't so much as look in my direction as I made my way to the receptionist's desk.

"My name's Maggie Sullivan," I said leaning in and speaking quietly. "I need to see Mr. Minsky."

She gave a courteous smile. "You'll need to make an appointment."

"I have a message from his sister. I'm to wait for an answer."

I handed her a folded up sheet of lined paper from the legal pad I kept in my car. It had the message Rachel had dictated. After looking at it for a moment, the receptionist took it with reluctance. She rose and gestured toward the couch across from the whispering couple.

"Sit down, please. I'll see if he can be disturbed."

She disappeared through a doorway to the right of her desk. I'd scarcely had time to cross my legs before a man in a pinstripe suit that fit to the nth degree barreled through the same door.

Since Rachel was small, I hadn't expected him to be large. Or strikingly attractive. Coal black hair. A generous nose. The only real resemblance to his sister was the bottomless darkness of his eyes, which at the moment were very, very angry. He flew toward me like an arrow, seizing my elbow as he reached my side.

"I don't know what your game is," he began in a low voice. "If you think for a minute you can shake me down—"

I flicked my business card up between two fingertips.

"I'm friends with... the woman who sent that message. She dictated the exact wording."

Joel Minsky stroked his mouth as he read the card. He crushed the handwritten note he still held.

"Let's talk in my office."

The receptionist had returned to her desk.

"Tell my next appointment I'm running a few minutes late," he said shortly.

He wasn't inclined to small talk as we followed more green carpeting back to his office. Neither was I. Closing the door to his office, he waved me toward a chair.

"I've heard your name," he said as he took his position

behind as pretty a walnut desk as I'd ever seen. "I don't recall if Rachel's mentioned it. She keeps her personal life to herself. But I've heard it from business associates." His hands spread outward across the note that lay on his desk. "I take it this means what it says? My sister's in jail?"

"Yes."

"Why didn't she contact me?"

"I don't know."

"What's the charge?"

"I'm not sure she's been officially charged yet."

"What did they arrest her for then?"

"Murder."

He leaned back. His eyes closed. His well-manicured hands curled into fists.

"Who? When?"

"Last night. A man she knew. They found him at one of her work sites. That's about all I have in the way of particulars. They only let us speak for a couple of minutes. She says the police woke her up in the middle of the night."

"The little *fool*!" He shot to his feet.

I twisted to see him. He was donning his hat, preparing to leave. I rose to trot after him.

"Look, Rachel's helped me more than once. Anything I can do—"

"Our firm employs its own investigator."

"Mr. Minsky, I wasn't implying I'd charge you."

"Thank you for delivering her message, Miss Sullivan. That will be all."

He took me by the elbow and hustled me out, just in case I'd missed the hint.

THREE

Minsky Construction, identified by a sign in front of the single-story wood building, was in an industrial area. Its neighbors across the street were a warehouse and a coal yard. One side of the building had a fenced-in area filled with construction equipment and tarp-covered stacks of lumber. There weren't as many machines parked there as I remembered, and the stacks of lumber looked smaller. A waist-high redbud tree had sprouted to add a splash of pink next to one of the stacks.

"Maggie! How good to see you!" Cecilia, Rachel's secretary, hopped up from her desk behind a long counter and came to greet me. Usually three male clerks sat at battered desks behind the counter, writing in ledgers, spindling paperwork, coming to help supervisors who arrived from a project needing something. Today there were only two clerks. The third desk had the cleaned off look of one that was vacant.

"Isn't it a glorious day?" smiled Cecilia.

"Yeah, I have a touch of spring fever. How's Donnie?"

"Doing fine, thanks."

Cecilia had a boy who wasn't right and needed constant supervision. A few years earlier, she'd been out of work, on the edge of trouble, and worrying how she'd provide for him. Rachel at the time had an officious male secretary whose loyalty went about as far as spit. Things had worked out.

"Rachel isn't in, I'm afraid," Cecilia said.

They didn't know yet.

"I saw her just awhile ago. She's going to be late. She asked me to do a couple of things in her office." I dropped my voice and leaned across the counter. "She has me working on something minor."

Cecilia's lips formed a small 'O' of understanding.

"I'll show you back."

"That's okay. I know the way."

I hesitated. Cecilia was an excellent secretary. She was also sharp. She'd be less likely to pop in to check on me and offer help if I gave her an inkling of what was happening.

"The truth is, I'd feel better if you stayed out here to answer the phone. You may get a call from the newspaper. Rachel's in a spot of trouble. With the police. With luck no one's going to get wind of it, but you never know."

She'd defend the woman she worked for like a tiger. She'd probably do the same for me. She crisped to attention.

"I'll man the gate. If you need help finding anything, buzz."

"Thanks. I shouldn't be long."

Reasonably certain Cecilia wouldn't abandon her post unless I called her, I went around the counter and followed a familiar hallway walled with rough-cut plywood to Rachel's office. Its decor was just a cut above the hallway. Apart from a mid-sized cherry-wood desk and the leather swivel chair behind it, wall maps of the Dayton area, one showing the water table, were its only decoration. An open cabinet held blueprints. On the desk, tidy stacks of paperwork and an ashtray attested to Rachel's habits.

I went to work on the chair.

Precisely as Rachel had described, at the back of the seat cushion where the leather lapped down to meet the wooden frame, half a dozen tacks were looser than the others. Not loose enough to yield to my tugging or to the only prying tool I happened to have in my purse — my nail file. I swore at my lack of foresight.

I couldn't exactly waltz out and ask if anyone had a tack puller handy, or even a hammer or screwdriver, without stirring curiosity. I looked through Rachel's desk. The flat drawer held a nice brass letter opener that looked as if it might be strong enough. I'd try not to damage the leather with the sharp edge, but as much importance as Rachel attached to what was hidden in the chair, it was worth the risk. If the leather got cut or scraped, she could replace the upholstery. Or the chair. In case the letter opener wasn't as strong as I thought, I hoped it wasn't some sort of antique.

Holding the blade of the letter opener in two places, I wiggled one edge under the outermost of the brass upholstery tacks. Then I seesawed it up and down. The tack rose enough for me to grip it with my fingertips. It pulled right out. A bit more work and I had all six.

Even trickier than getting the tacks out was getting my fingers far enough into the access created to feel anything. I could just touch paper. Not sufficiently to pull it toward me, however. I sat back on my heels.

The metal tip of the letter opener was just as likely to make the edge of the envelope pop a fraction farther away as it was toward me when I applied pressure. My nail file and the crochet hook I carried for picking locks wouldn't even reach it, not with me retaining enough of a grip on them to do any good.

The human fingertip made contact with things far better than a hard surface did, though you might have to moisten it with your tongue when skin was dry. What could I find in an office, and a bare-bones construction office at that, which came anywhere close to making contact enough to keep the envelope inside the chair from slipping free?

A pencil.

Of course.

Specifically, the eraser end of a pencil.

Still kneeling, I straightened enough to peek over the top of Rachel's desk. If Cecilia or anyone else happened in, it was going to be hard coming up with a reason why I was crawling around on the floor. My eyes swept the desktop. The only writing implement in sight was the pen in a desk set.

I opened the flat drawer where I'd found the letter opener. Sure enough, one of the compartments at the front held pencils. Several were brand new. Choosing one of those, I rubbed the side of the eraser vigorously against the linoleum floor where I knelt. It came away dirty, but roughened now.

I eased my left index finger back inside the seat to pinpoint the envelope. Then I slid the pencil I was holding in beside it. The surface of the pencil's eraser nabbed the surface of the envelope.

Five minutes later, the upholstery tacks were back in place, maybe not as flush to the surface as they had been, but enough that only someone hunting evidence of tampering would notice they'd been loosened. I wiped the back of the chair with my hanky to make sure I didn't leave fingerprints. With the five-by-seven envelope I'd removed tucked in my purse, I exchanged a few parting words with Cecilia and walked out the front door of Minsky Construction.

Now to find a pay phone and check in with Pearlie.

***

Whoever answered at the number Pearlie had given me didn't identify himself or the establishment.

"I talked to Rachel," I said when Pearlie came on. "She didn't tell me much. They only gave us five minutes. They found the stiff at one of her building sites."

"Yeah. On Drinkwater."

"She knew him."

"Yeah. Guy named Gabriel Foster."

"You know him? Know anything about him?"

"No."

"Rachel says he was an s.o.b. and had it coming but she didn't do it."

Silence.

He hadn't known that part.

"You have anything else that might be pertinent?"

"Only the Who and Where part. That's all she had time to say over the phone before the cops caught on she had one in her bedroom. Is she okay?"

"Complaining she doesn't have cigarettes." Pearlie wasn't the sort to chuckle, but I hoped it eased his mind at least.

"They woke her up and hauled her downtown without letting her primp. Other than that, she seems okay. She wanted me to go and talk to her lawyer brother as soon as I left, so I did."

"And?"

"He was plenty shaken about the jam she's in. I offered my services. He declined — said they had their own investigator. He seems smart as they come and plenty successful. He took off barking at his secretary to cancel his appointments for the rest of the morning. Rachel's in good hands."

"No she ain't. Not without you involved."

"Oh, I intend to be involved. Rachel asked me to be."

"What can I do? Find out about this Gabriel Foster character?"

Wow. Pearlie was taking marching orders from me now?

"That would be great, Pearlie. Frees me up to tackle the cops. I need to find out how they found the body and that."

"You got some magic spell that makes Freeze share information with you now, do you?"

"Just my sunny personality."

Lt. Freeze was head of homicide. He didn't like me much.

FOUR

The skeletal structure rising from bare ground on Drinkwater Street made me think it was a fitting place to find a body. Not a fresh one, though. There wasn't so much as a scrap of wood with the street number on it, let alone a mailbox, but two patrol cars and an unmarked one with a strong resemblance to one I'd seen Lt. Freeze drive assured me I'd found the right place.

Freeze was lean with salt-and-pepper hair. I was pretty sure he smoked in his sleep since I'd never seen him without a cigarette in his fingers or between his lips.

"Stop right there," he said catching sight of me. "This is a crime scene."

"I kind of figured it was. I didn't think you went to many meetings of the Ladies Aid Society." I kept on sauntering, my hands in my pockets.

His eyes, which had a hint of squint from the smoke curling up from the stub in his mouth, narrowed further.

"Unless you've got some authorization to be here—"

"I do, as a matter of fact. I had a nice chat with Joel Minsky this morning." The absolute truth, although it perhaps wiggled around his implied question. The nuns who had sent me to the office so frequently in my youth had been more adept at spotting how I embellished answers than Freeze was.

"I know the stiff was named Gabriel Foster. I'm

assuming you found him somewhere over there."

I'd been observing the slow steps of two uniforms and a plainclothesman as they moved methodically around an upright girder at one corner of what looked as though it would eventually be a two-story building. Their eyes were glued to the ground as they moved.

Freeze was silent. He didn't like to admit I was every bit as good at my job as he was at his. He was a good cop in his way, but limited in imagination. It rubbed him the wrong way that several times in our acquaintance I'd come up with leads that he refused to follow only to have them pan out. No matter how many times I proved myself, he clung to the stubborn idea it was pure luck, or results from batting my eyes at susceptible men, when I beat him to a solution.

This time I didn't have time to play his games.

"Come on, Freeze. The department's losing men to the draft left and right. You've always been shorthanded and it's going to get worse until we rid the world of Hitler and his chums. I can be as useful to you as you can to me. How about we scale back the arm wrestling?"

In the nick of time to avoid burning his fingers, he flicked his cigarette nub onto bare earth packed down and marked by the tracks of construction vehicles and ground it out with his foot.

"I guess you'll get most of it from the lawyer anyway. He's not going to take No for an answer. The body was lying next to that corner beam. Could been leaning against it and toppled. Hard to tell."

"How long had he been there?"

Freeze hesitated.

"Couple of hours."

That explained the cops waking Rachel in the dead of night. It made me wonder why they'd promoted her from owner of the property where a body was found to suspect in the death of that body, though. And why they'd made that leap so quickly. In fact, it made me wonder a lot of things.

"How'd you happen to find the body at what, one o'clock? One-thirty?"

"Something like that."

"A construction project's not exactly the place for a midnight stroll."

"A guy was out walking his dog. Fido found it. The man called it in."

I pulled my notebook out of my purse.

"Name?"

"Hung up before they could get one."

"Doesn't that strike you as awfully convenient?"

Freeze shrugged. "Some people are funny that way. Don't want their name connected with anything bad."

"Maybe so, but I find somebody walking their dog out here at that time of night hard to buy too."

"If a dog's got to go, a dog's got to go, I guess."

"Maybe, but wouldn't you let them out in the yard? Or at least stick close to home on a sidewalk?"

"Why ask me? Sounds like you have all the answers."

"I don't, but Boike might."

"Boike?"

His expression puzzled, he half turned to look at the blocky blond who was usually one of two detectives helping him. I was mostly sure the men were allowed to breathe without permission from Freeze. What they didn't do was voice an opinion or volunteer information without being asked.

"Boike's spent a lot of time around dogs," I said. "He knows things about them. Can we get his input?"

My stab at diplomacy paid off. Or maybe Freeze felt more agreeable when he was lighting a cigarette.

"What's your two cents, Boike?"

"Miss Sullivan's right. If Fido wants out in the middle of the night, most dog owners let him go in the yard and come right back in. Or they go a little ways on the sidewalk, or down the lane. If they had trouble sleeping I guess they might walk farther."

"Across a construction site?" I prompted.

"Well..." Boike stole a look at his boss, who was listening intently. "Wouldn't be very smart. Not with debris and construction materials you could trip over. Not in the dark."

Freeze grunted. "Maybe he had a flashlight."

"Do any of the neighbors across the way have a dog?"

Across the street from us were houses, simple wooden structures that were taller than they were wide. They'd been kept up and looked as though they dated from the turn of the century. Either Freeze's men or cops in uniform would have questioned them by now to ask if any of them had seen anything or heard anything the night before.

"Not the ones I talked to, except for a little old lady whose dachshund is so arthritic she probably has to carry him down the steps to do his business in the yard," said Boike. He looked at his fellow underling. "You?"

"Didn't ask."

Freeze gave a grunt of displeasure at that answer and glared at me.

"What about where the dog scratched?"

"What?"

Their moment of incomprehension gave me a chance to slip around them and trot closer to the spot where the body had lain.

"Miss, you need to stay back," cautioned one of the uniforms putting his hand out.

I stopped obediently.

"When dogs find something that gets them excited, they jump around and scratch at the ground. Right, Boike?"

"Sometimes," he said dubiously.

Squatting isn't exactly a modest pose in a skirt, so I settled for bending to peer at the ground while I chattered on.

"I don't see any sign of little paws digging the dirt up. In fact I don't see any sign of little paws at all."

"Hasn't rained in a while. There weren't any footprints either, before you ask."

Or signs of a struggle. Or blood. Or... I wasn't sure what else I was hoping to see or not see.

"Not much blood," I observed.

If the homicide squad had been summoned, the late Mr. Foster hadn't fallen and broken his neck after getting drunk and having a midnight climb on the beams above us. The obvious choices left were shot, stabbed or beaten.

"Small caliber," Freeze said. "Twenty-two. Dead aim, too. One shot in the back of the head."

Not Rachel's style, I thought again.

She was innocent.

"Boss." The taut voice of one of the uniforms combing the area made us all turn. "Look."

Coming toward us he held aloft something he'd picked up with tweezers. The sun hit it sending shafts of color out like a prism.

It was an earring, the kind with a pear-shaped dangle. A diamond earring.

I'd seen Rachel wear a pair like it.

FIVE

Joel Minsky was unlikely to be back from straightening things out for Rachel yet, or to be up to the pleasure of my company twice in one day if he was. My best course was to give him a call from my office to alert him about the earring, so I did. Sure enough, he was still out. At least that's what his receptionist or secretary or whatever her function was said.

"Tell her they found Truffle's earring," I said when she offered to take a message.

She repeated it, her tone suggesting it was odder than the messages she normally took.

I hung up and swiveled from side to side. My inability to act, to do anything I saw as productive, frustrated me. The forced inactivity started me wondering how committed Joel Minsky was to helping his sister. More than once Rachel had said Joel was the one member of the family who believed her capable of intelligent thought and with whom she could have an actual conversation. His initial reaction at news of her predicament had been one of anger, though. Was the bond she felt with him reciprocated?

What if Rachel's family considered her such an embarrassment they'd be glad to see her out of their lives? What if they thought it would serve her right to pay the price of not toeing the line? No, surely not. Even if they did, surely brother-sister ties went deeper than that.

Then again, what did I know about brothers?

I'd had a brother who was four years older than me. Still did, if he was alive somewhere. When I was ten he'd hopped a freight to escape the cauldron of silent bitterness that was our mother, a brew whose stink permeated every room in the house. Even before that he hadn't had much to do with me, in part because he was seldom around. He roved with a pack of neighborhood boys. I could count on one hand the times he'd shown any brotherly interest in me. He had stepped in to drag me away so I wasn't beaten to a pulp by older girls when they'd made a snide comment about my mother and I'd thrown a punch.

More bothered than I wanted to be by my tangle of thoughts, I went to the windows and glared at the elevated railroad tracks running past them. I'd wasted enough time thinking about the past. It didn't matter whether or not some fancy lawyer cared about helping Rachel. I did. I wasn't going to sit around on my thumbs doing nothing.

***

Before taking action that seemed smart to me, however, I needed to do the other thing Rachel had asked me to do — burn the envelope I'd retrieved from her office. That wasn't as easy to pull off this time of year as it might have been in January. Chances of finding a fire burning merrily on a hearth during the day and in weather this nice were slim. One or two possibilities sprang to mind, but they were in public places. I couldn't toss something into the flames without somebody noticing.

After thinking about it awhile, I drove to the two-story white house where I rented a room and let the tulips and daffodils blooming along its front give their best shot at lifting my spirits. What had begun as a pretty spring day had lost its enchantment with Pearlie's first words about Rachel.

Jolene, a cute blonde who worked as a cigarette girl and was home in the day, bounced down the stairs as I entered.

"Has the mail come yet?"

"Got a mushy note you're eager to get to somebody?" I teased eyeing the envelope in her hand.

She waved it grandly.

"Applying for war work. I'd kind of been thinking I'd go home and help on the farm when my brother got called up, but Daddy said Mother can drive a tractor almost as well as I can even if she doesn't know a wrench from a bolt when it comes to fixing them, and Jenny's old enough to take over part of Mother's kitchen chores and Lois had to learn to milk and show the pigs who's boss sooner or later..."

From the day we met, Jolene's ability to talk for what seemed minutes at a time without pausing for breath had fascinated me.

"He says there's lots of other needs and I'm right here where I could volunteer at something, but I got to thinking they're wanting war workers, and that's a lot more important than working in a nightclub. Plus I'm already used to working funny hours, so I filled this out and if the place doesn't want me—"

"If they don't want you, they're not very smart. I need to see Mrs. Z about something. I'll keep my fingers crossed for you, Jolene."

Waving happily, she raised the lid on the mailbox.

Our landlady lived in a cozy downstairs apartment and was an absolute peach except for one thing: She owned a nasty yellow tomcat whose greatest delight was to shoot out past her feet and sink his front teeth into the first female leg he encountered. I knocked on her door and held the manila envelope down to deflect him.

Mrs. Z opened the door with her pussycat overflowing her cradling arm. He hissed at me.

"Oh, Margaret. Come in."

"Thanks, but I just want to know if it's okay if I burn what's in the trash barrel. I've been cleaning out some old files and had a couple of things I'd like to toss in. I'll stay and watch till it burns out."

"Of course, dear. As long as you watch it. Uncoil the hose in case you need it, if you don't mind."

I went out through the kitchen, which we girls got to use on Saturday mornings, and held Rachel's envelope over the metal drum next to the garbage can. Every backyard I'd ever been in had a can like it, or maybe a wire basket. When it filled up with discarded mail, paper that had wrapped meat and debris from the sweeper, you set it on fire so the contents burned down and kept things tidy.

I stirred the contents with a stick to fluff things up, then dropped in a kitchen match. I held the envelope over the flames.

Its weight told me it must contain quite a few sheets of paper. It wasn't sealed. The metal tab that held it closed had been bent and straightened numerous times. Either its contents had been added to bit by bit or someone had been a frequent visitor to whatever it held.

Nothing to do with this, Rachel had said.

Then why destroy it?

It wasn't up to me to question. Before I could change my mind, I dropped it into the flames. Then I sat on the back steps and watched it burn, savoring the forgotten pleasure of being alone in your own backyard, smelling the earth and listening to bird sounds, as I felt a sharp, sharp longing for my girlhood.

***

One thing I was curious about was how the cops had known where to find Rachel. I'd always supposed she lived with her parents. Something about the way she'd mentioned the "place" — apartment, presumably — where she'd been arrested made me suspect her family didn't know it existed. Who did know about it? I added that to the list of things that didn't add up for me, like the tip from the dog walker.

After a quick lunch at a diner I liked, I looked at the particulars on Rachel's arrest. The police logbook was open to the public, though members of the press, and probably lawyers and law clerks, were ordinarily the only ones to peruse it. The only new information it gave me was the exact time of her arrest, the names of the officers who'd gone to her apartment, and what I'd come for, the location. Without any idea what I expected to learn, or do, I decided to have a look.

Rachel's private little nest was in a brown brick building overlooking the river. It had five stories and a hint of Spanish or Moorish style thanks to a crenelated top and tile roof. Even with those touches it wasn't the sort of place that would attract a second look. It was small, two or four apartments on each floor, depending on size; respectable and quiet.

The police car I had an eye out for was parked discreetly in the alley beside it. Uniforms, or even detectives, were going over the place hunting evidence. There was no point trying to get in with them still there. I went back to the office where all I managed to do for the rest of the afternoon was wait for phone calls that never came while simmering in growing frustration.

Surely Rachel was out by now. If she was going to get out. She'd asked for my help, and for all the good I was doing I might as well be stuffed in a closet with my hands tied and a bag on my head.

I stuck around half an hour past my usual quitting time on the off chance Joel Minsky might call after his staff had gone home, or that Pearlie would call, or that Rachel herself would come strolling in. All I got for my optimism was thirsty.

SIX

The regulars at Finn's pub, and Rose and Finn who owned it, were the closest I came to having a family. A childhood friend had taken me there the day of my dad's funeral and I'd been finding my way through the door ever since. Framed photos of Irish scenes decorated its walls. The chairs at the tables were mismatched. Cops were plentiful among its clientele.

Somehow I'd managed to miss my childhood friend, whose teasing always raised my spirits. When Rose had pulled me a perfect Guinness, I made for a table where a cop with brindled hair sat alone with his legs stretched comfortably out. He was wearing civvies.

His name was Mick Connelly and for the better part of three years I'd been frustrated by his patient pursuit of me no matter how many times I told him I had no interest in kids and marriage. Somehow Pearl Harbor had changed things between us. I still didn't want any part of an ivy-covered cottage but I no longer tried to deny the connection between us. What we did about the physical attraction simmering below the surface, I didn't know, but life seemed better when we saw each other. I sat down.

"Off night shift, are you?"

"'Til next time, and glad enough of it."

Shortly after the attack on Pearl Harbor, Dayton's police

had adopted a schedule that left no question they were part of the war effort. Street cops like Connelly worked in what they called platoons, one week the day platoon, then evening platoon, then overnight, after which the rotation repeated. Their "week" had become seven days working followed by a day off. After six such weeks they got two days in a row off. Then the seven-one schedule started again.

"Seamus is on evenings now, though, so I've no one to keep me out of mischief." As he spoke, he reached across the table and turned my hand over, turning my insides to liquid with the circles his index finger traced in my palm. "That part falls to you for a bit. Think you're up to it?"

The lines fanning out from his steel blue eyes were deeper than usual.

"Tired as you look, you're not up to mischief. And no, I'm not equal to keeping you out of it right now." I caught his disturbing finger. "I'm working on something."

"Ah." Leaning back he drank some Guinness. "You look a bit angry, too. Don't think it's at me. It must have to do with whatever you're working on."

"It's not about you, so don't get a swelled head. My friend Rachel's been arrested for murder."

"Jaysus!" Connelly sat upright. "That Jewish woman?"

For reasons I couldn't identify, the words stung like a slap.

"Yes. My friend who happens to be a Jew. Is that the only way you think of her?"

"Maggie—"

"Not even 'the voluptuous one'? Or 'the one whose upstairs puts Mae West to shame'? She has her own

35

business — her own company! She's smart. She's pretty. That time we ran into her on the street and she mentioned reading Padraig Pearse, you nearly fell over. But that's what she is in your mind? 'That Jewish woman'?"

"Maggie—"

"Tell Seamus he's too old to be working evenings or nights either one. He was fixing to put in for retirement until the war came along."

Downing the remnants of my stout in two gulps, I stalked out. I wasn't sure if I was angry at Connelly's words or that Seamus, who'd been part of my life since I could remember, was working a schedule that was hard enough on younger men. Maybe it was something else altogether.

**

I got a bite to eat with one of the other women who roomed at Mrs. Z's. When we got back I curled up on my bed and tried to read, but I couldn't concentrate. I went downstairs and called the number Pearlie had given me to see if he'd heard anything about Rachel. The voice that answered said there was nobody there by that name and hung up in my ear.

Frustrated, and too restless to do anything else, I got in my car and drove to Rachel's apartment. The cop car was gone, but just inside the entry a rotund little man sat importantly behind an elevated desk signing visitors in and out and barring non-residents. No, he told me, Miss Minsky wasn't in. The way his otherwise pleasant expression grew mildly evasive when I asked for her suggested he knew about the police activity and was troubled by it.

Rachel and I were similar in several ways. When I'd had the pins knocked out from under me, or when I needed familiarity and a sense of control, I sought refuge in my office. I wondered whether it might be the same with Rachel. If her brother had managed to get her out on bail, that might be where she headed.

It was almost eleven o'clock now. Back in the DeSoto I cranked down the window to let in the night air, which had grown cooler. Its spring scents were pleasant, but my real motivation was that the open window let me hear things I couldn't see. A year ago the streets where I drove would have been better lighted. Now, even though there was no official blackout yet, lights had been doused.

War had been good for putting people without jobs during the Depression back to work. I drove east past factories that were running three shifts. The rutted street where Rachel's business was located was as silent as a graveyard by comparison.

A few feet shy of the turn-in to Minsky Construction, I parked at the curb with dwindling hope. There was no sign of Rachel's big Buick. There was no car of any kind parked at her building. The only vehicle visible anywhere was a pickup truck pulled close to a pile of coal that dwarfed it in the coal yard across the way, probably a casualty of overloading whose tire had blown or worse. Everything around me was dark shapes save for glints here and there where starlight bounced off facets in the coal.

My hand was on the gearshift preparing to abandon my fruitless mission when a flicker of something caught the edge of my eye. I turned my head toward Rachel's building. Had I seen a light?

No, everything was... There. A pinprick. Moving. At the rear of the building. On the side where Rachel's office was.

If anyone had been watching, my headlights had announced my arrival as effectively as a brass band. But then whoever it was would have doused their light too. I turned off the ignition. Easing my Smith & Wesson from its holster, I opened the car door wide enough to slide out. I closed it without latching it.

As I neared the building, I saw that a gate stood open into the fenced area given over to building supplies and unused construction equipment. I cut through. Huge metal dinosaurs with jaws and blades poised to crush and devour loomed over me. Belatedly I realized it made a swell place to lie in ambush for someone. Nobody was expecting me, though. And whoever had come this way wasn't Rachel. She owned the place. She would have walked in the front door.

The graders and diggers that could hide an enemy also provided good cover for me. As quickly as stealth allowed, I moved from the shelter of one to the next, fighting the notion one of them might start to roll. I expected another gate at the back side of the equipment pen. Instead, that side was unfenced.

Was there rear access to Minsky Construction from an alley or street? I couldn't see, but I could make out the back door to the building now and there weren't any cars.

As I ducked under the window to Rachel's office I spotted a jiggle or two of light. Someone inside was using a flashlight. No windows decorated the utilitarian back of the building. Keeping flush to the wall I got to the door. My eyes had adjusted to darkness enough now for me to make out a matchbook wedged in the door to keep it from closing.

Still sticking to the wall like paint, I moved to a spot where the opening door would hide me and reached for the door with my free hand. As my fingertips brushed the knob, the door itself opened. I dropped to a crouch as a man came out. He spotted the movement.

"Raise your hands."

I brought the .38 up to persuade him. He aimed a kick at it. Jerking the gun out of harm's way threw me briefly off balance. In the seconds required to keep my footing, he took off running toward the equipment yard. I plunged after him.

I heard a snap and ducked as close as I could to the side of the building. The sound repeated. He was shooting at me. When I returned the favor, the nonsense stopped.

Ahead of me, toward the front of the building, a man's voice shouted. It wasn't the shout of a man in pain from a bullet wound, though. Had someone happened by and heard the ruckus? Did the intruder have a pal who'd been waiting for him?

Moving cautiously, I stepped from the sheltering shadows next to the building far enough to have a look. A man was headed across the street at a run, making for the coal yard across the way. Headed toward the pickup truck I'd blithely dismissed as inoperable, I thought bitterly. I couldn't catch him, but I might get a look at the license plate on the truck. I started to run again.

An engine sputtered to life. All at once I became aware of a massive shape plummeting toward my head. Jumping awkwardly, I fell to the side and rolled on my hip.

The shape was at ground level now, coming at me full tilt. It was some sort of metal bucket with jaws, part of one of the big machines.

Pulling my legs up I managed a faster somersault than I'd ever done as a kid. Pain jolted up me as the bucket clipped my bottom, spinning me ninety degrees. Getting hit full force would hurt a lot worse. Through the darkness I could just make out the shape of those lethal metal jaws swinging back to have another go at me. Heart pounding, I dragged myself back on my elbows. Ducking bullets I understood. Trading punches I understood. This mindless chunk of metal was a different kind of adversary.

Another shout sounded. Sharp. Giving orders. I hadn't managed to scoot far enough. Searing pain swept the skin on my shins, and a second later flared again. I heard a cry and realized it was me.

The metal jaws were receding again. I hitched myself backward another few inches. This time as they launched another attack, they didn't come quite as close. As they retreated with the indifferent precision of a pendulum, I began to suspect that was exactly what they had become — a pendulum whose arc was decreasing. Whoever had been at their controls had taken off. Pushing up, with one eye on the swinging metal, I staggered to my feet and went a few steps forward. Slightly dizzy and hard pressed to make out more than shapes in the unlighted surroundings, I saw a car shoot from behind the coal across the way. Seconds later, the pickup I'd supposed inoperable took off in the opposite direction.

Limping a few steps more, I caught my breath and looked down at my legs. Blood oozed down them. The swinging bucket had scraped off some skin. Considering that it could have broken my bones or crushed my skull, I'd gotten off lucky. Still, as I hobbled toward my car, I wondered what the man I'd just tangled with had been after in Rachel's office, and what she'd gotten me into.

SEVEN

"Those trousers look nice on you," Izzy said as she slid my morning oatmeal in front of me at McCrory's lunch counter.

The skinny little waitress was off delivering toast and eggs to another customer before I could thank her.

For my birthday, the girls at Mrs. Z's had gone together and bought me a pair of tailored trousers like some stylish women and movie stars now were wearing. I hadn't worn them for work before because they didn't look as professional as a suit. Today, thanks to my encounter with the construction equipment, I'd decided they beat showing off my scraped shins. Izzy's verdict reassured me that what with a good blouse and tweed bolero, which had a few dots of color that went with the trousers, I looked reasonably smart.

I folded the morning paper I'd been reading and concentrated on my oatmeal. There'd been no mention of Rachel in yesterday's late edition of the *Daily News*, or in the *Journal* that lay beside me. If the *News* still didn't have anything when it hit the streets today, either the charges against Rachel had been dropped or her brother had done some serious string pulling to keep her name out of print. I wished I knew which.

Four things bothered me about the pickle Rachel was in.

First was how the police had known to go to her apartment rather than her parents' house. Second, who was the dog walker and what was he doing at the construction site? Third was how little blood I'd seen where the body was found, although Freeze might be right in what he theorized. Finally, what was the intruder doing — or hunting — in Rachel's office last night?

"Mr. Minsky's in court," his secretary said when I called and asked to speak to him. No point in asking her for information. She probably didn't know, and wouldn't tell me if she did.

I didn't know the name of Rachel's father. The phone book carried a listing for eight Minskys, all but one at good addresses. If all else failed, I could call my way through all of them and turn on my charm.

Right now, a faster way to learn whatever there was to learn might be to have a chat with Cecilia, so I drove out to Minsky Construction.

A car I didn't recognize was parked at the door. It was the make the cops used for their unmarked units. Two men, one roughly dressed, the other in a cheap suit, conferred behind the fence protecting the construction equipment. The gate to the enclosure now had a closed padlock.

"Maggie! Am I ever glad to see you!"

Cecilia sprang up and hurried to the counter as I went in.

"Is anything wrong?"

Her blonde head shook.

"No. Well, yes, but it's over now. Someone broke into Rachel's office last night."

"Broke in! Did they take anything?"

43

"I'm not exactly sure. They went though her desk and her file cabinet, even the blueprint cupboard. The police are here now."

"How did the intruder get in?"

"Drilled the lock or something like that. I heard one tell the other. Once I showed them back and answered some questions about things being out of place and was anything missing, they told me to stay out here and go about business as usual."

The business about the lock being drilled, plus the plain car out front, suggested it was the Robbery-Burglary boys who were here. I wasn't surprised.

"Had things been torn up?" I asked.

"Torn up?"

"Furniture broken, upholstery ripped, that kind of thing. Like whoever got in was angry."

"No. The only thing upholstered is Rachel's chair. That was over it the corner and one of the wheels had come off like somebody shoved it aside. Other than that, nothing was damaged."

The breath I'd been half holding eased out. If the burglar had been after the envelope I'd burned yesterday, it didn't appear they'd stumbled across its former hiding place.

"Rachel's not going to be in for a few days, by the way. She called."

My attention snapped back to Cecilia.

"She said things had come up that she had to deal with."

"Did she say where she was?"

"No, and she wouldn't give me a number. She said she'd check in now and then." Cecilia's forehead creased with worry. "Maggie, do you have any idea what's going on?"

Cecilia didn't deserve to be kept in the dark. Not when she was as loyal an ally as Rachel could have. Not when she was the one who had to deal with calls and people coming in. I took a breath.

"I'd just as soon you didn't tell anyone else who works here, but Rachel got picked up by the police. It's all a mistake. I'm trying to help her. But I don't know where she is either, or how to reach her."

"Picked up... for what? The police have been acting awfully pushy."

"Suspicion of murder."

She sagged against the counter, her hand to her throat. "Rachel would never kill anyone. Not unless it was self defense or-or something like that."

"Do you have her number at home?"

"No. She checks in first thing every morning. Calls, I mean. I think her family's, well, funny about outsiders. Sort of like some of the Greeks and Italians. I could be wrong, but from little things she's said, I got the impression they were pretty religious and strict and that."

While she'd been talking, another aspect of my visit here yesterday had occurred to me.

"Do you make a note of every visitor and every call that comes in, the way you did at the last place you worked?"

"Yes..."

"I need to let the police know I was here yesterday."

"They're likely to throw you out," she warned as I came through the gate in the counter and went past her.

"That's okay. I bounce." The bounce I'd been forced to take dodging construction equipment last night had left my hip sore, though it came in second to my scraped shins.

The door to Rachel's office stood wide open. I rapped on it to announce my presence to the two men working inside.

"You can't be back here right now," the one bent over the desk began, raising his head. "Oh, it's the Sullivan kid."

"Hiya, sarge." I couldn't recall his name.

"That applies to you too. You got no business here."

"I thought you might want to know, in case the fingerprint boys get involved, they'll find plenty of mine on that desk."

He straightened. I had his attention now.

"Why is that?"

"I stopped in to pick up a book Miss Minsky had borrowed. We ran into each other a couple of days ago on the street. She said she was sorry she'd taken so long to return the book. I wasn't in a hurry to have it. I said I'd stop by. She told me if she wasn't around, it was in her desk. She didn't say exactly where, though, so I had to look."

If he asked where we'd met on the street, I knew where she had her hair done. If he asked what the book was, I had a title ready. I needed to talk to Rachel, though. I needed to reach her.

"You and Miss Minsky know each other, do you?" Sarge asked instead.

"Yeah, for a couple of years."

I hadn't mentioned it to Freeze because he hadn't asked me. The question now told me the police had tumbled to a possible connection between the break-in here and the murder of Gabriel Foster. Unfortunately Rachel was the common link.

"The secretary says they came in through the back," I

said. "It took somebody mighty nimble to climb over that wire fence."

"They didn't come over the fence. The gate was wide open." He clamped his mouth shut; vexed he'd shared the information. "Thanks for telling us about the fingerprints. Scram now."

I scrammed.

***

One fib has a nasty way of leading to others. In my eagerness to explain my fingerprints in Rachel's office, it hadn't occurred to me I now needed an explanation for my presence today.

Cecilia was back at her desk. I planted my unbruised hip on the edge and leaned down so we wouldn't be heard.

"I told the police I'd been here yesterday in case they look for fingerprints. If they ask why I was here today, tell them I wanted to know if you'd found a silk flower that fell off the hat I was wearing. If you don't mind," I added as her eyes widened.

"I don't."

I hesitated. Not far away the two male clerks were in their chairs bent over whatever kind of work they did.

"Have you heard how whoever broke in got the gate open so they could get to the back?" I asked.

"Not really. The three of us were just arriving. The phone was ringing when I came in. It was a message for Rachel, so I went back to her office to spindle it. That's when I saw someone had—" She swallowed, reliving the moment. "— broken in. I... tore out in a panic. All I could think of was what if the person who'd done it was still in the building?

"But right then Rob and Terry came bursting in the front way shouting about who the Sam Hill had come in early and tried to start the bucket loader, didn't they know it was broken?"

"Somebody had opened the gate with a key? They hadn't cut the padlock?"

"I think so. It sounded like the men were upset that someone had started to take equipment out without logging it with one of them the way they're supposed to. Only I started yelling about a burglary then, and everything turned into an uproar."

Her eyes slid uncertainly toward the two men.

"I could ask if you like. They're a bit clubby, but—"

"That's okay. I'd rather you just kept your ears open. If you hear anything, give me a jingle."

"It's important then? About the lock?"

"It could be."

If a key had been used to gain access, it suggested at least one of last night's intruders had worked for Rachel, or come here often enough to nick a key.

What it didn't tell me was what they'd been hunting.

EIGHT

Unlike ordinary street cops who worked at the utilitarian building where I'd gone to see Rachel, Lt. Freeze and the denizens of the detective division worked out of Market House, which was smack downtown. The narrow white three-story building had enough decoration on it to shame a wedding cake. I climbed the stairs and made my way to Freeze's area.

His desk was vacant. Boike was there, using two fingers to peck away at a typewriter. Two men on the opposite side were the room's only other occupants.

"Freeze out having wisdom teeth pulled, I hope?"

Boike gave me a half-hearted glare. He didn't like it when I disparaged his boss.

"He's in a meeting. Anything I can handle?"

I hitched up the wooden folding chair in front of his desk and made myself comfortable.

"Yeah. Did you find any people with dogs who might have been walking their dogs Sunday night?"

"I can't say."

"Can't because you don't know or because you don't think it's my business?"

He stared at a point beyond my shoulder.

"Come on, Boike. You heard the pep talk I gave Freeze. I want to get to the bottom of this as much as you do."

"Except you're working for the opposite team."

"The opposite—" I was taken aback. "Boike. I want to know who did this same as you."

"You've got a different agenda, though. You want to prove our number one suspect's innocent."

"And you think I'd do something dishonest to get her off?"

The solid, stolid detective tugged his ear, avoiding my eyes.

"I think it might cloud your judgment."

I sat back, hearing the chair squeak behind me. His assessment hurt. I liked Boike. He kept his head down and his mouth shut and did better work, I suspected, than he got credit for. He looked uncomfortable now. A voice behind me broke the tension.

"What are you doing here?"

It was Freeze.

"I'm trying to learn whether your men ever found the mysterious dog walker, or even any neighbors with dogs who might qualify. Boike here seems to think it would compromise your investigation even to tell me yes or no."

Collapsing into his desk chair, Freeze scraped a match to life.

"Boike's smart enough not to give out information without my say so." He got his Old Gold going as he spoke. "But no. One guy with a lisp you could take a shower in has a dog, but the man who called it in didn't lisp. Other than him and the old lady Boike mentioned yesterday, there was a dizzy dame who never lets her Sweetums out of the yard. She'd fall apart if she went outside after dark, let alone saw a body."

He squinted at me through the smoke curling up in front of his face. He looked tired.

"So you could have been right. About the call being phoney. There's still plenty indicating she's the guilty party, starting with that earring we found."

"Which she could have lost any time before the body turned up. She pays almost daily visits to her construction sites."

Freeze propped his feet on his desk. His eyes had narrowed.

"You know her that well, do you?"

"I know her, yes. That's the other reason I'm here. I stopped by her office this morning and heard about the break-in there. I already told the robbery boys who were there, but I wanted to let you know too. I was out there yesterday to pick up a book I'd lent her."

"What kind of book?"

"Padraig Pearse."

"Never heard of it."

"I went back today hoping they'd found a flower that fell off my hat. A good silk one. Pink. You didn't happen to find it after I chatted with you at the crime scene, did you?"

Freeze ignored the question. Boike had gone back to typing, but I felt sure he was listening.

"Seeing as how the two of you are pals, I don't suppose you know where to find the torpedo who drives her around?"

"'Torpedo'? I thought that term went out with Stutz Bearcats."

"He used to work for the mob in Cleveland. A leopard doesn't change its spots."

A chill crawled halfway up my spine before I pushed it back. Whatever he'd been, or done, Pearlie wouldn't shoot someone and let Rachel take blame for it.

"I can tell you he goes by Pearlie. And that he plays the piano."

"Piano?"

"Yeah. That's all I know. As far Miss Minsky and I being pals, I didn't know she had an apartment. I thought she lived at home. How'd you find her so fast?"

Freeze had sagged back in his chair like a balloon that was losing its air. He gestured impatiently.

"Old lady across from the lot where they're building had gotten into some scraps with the suspect's workmen. Suspect came out to smooth things over and gave the old biddy a card. She wrote another number on the back and said it was for after hours. Now scram. I need forty winks."

I got up.

"One more thing."

"Thirty-nine. I'll get unpleasant if you keep spoiling my beauty sleep."

"Besides the earring, was there anything else of interest around Foster's body?"

"Yeah, two casings. Different caliber than the ones at her business."

As I closed the door behind me, I heard a soft snore.

Walking the few blocks to my office afforded me time to rid my ears of hearing Rachel referred to in impartial, scarcely human cop lingo. *The suspect.* Taking one deep breath after another, I forced my thoughts to other things.

Dollars to donuts Freeze wouldn't have told me about the shell casings if he hadn't been half asleep when he said it. It might not even be significant. The person who killed Foster could well be the same man who had shot at me outside Rachel's office. Some people owned more than one gun, and using a .22 to kill Foster might be another attempt to frame Rachel.

I wanted to talk to the neighbor to whom *The Suspect* had given her card. I wanted to find out more about the nature and seriousness of the quarrel the neighbor had with Rachel's workmen. Most of all, I wanted to know if the neighbor had seen or heard anything the night Foster's body was found.

If I spent a lot of time walking in the course of a workday, it wasn't unusual for my legs to draw one or two wolf whistles. Today my legs weren't even showing, yet by the time I reached the block with my office, I'd already had three. Maybe trousers weren't so bad.

"Hey, sis! Wait up," a voice called behind me.

A tow-headed kid with a newsboy's bag slung over his shoulder trotted up. He was probably thirteen now. I'd paid him to keep an eye out for something now and again, because he was smart as a whip. He had no family and slept in doorways most of the time, but his expression was one of perpetual optimism.

"Shouldn't you be peddling papers, Heebs?"

His grin was contagious.

"Already sold 'em all so's I'd have time to come see you. I got a business proposal."

"Oh, yeah?" Other than pestering me for an ongoing job, he'd never shown interest in any sort of business scheme.

Given the way his mind worked, it was likely to be a doozie. "Fire away."

"There's all kinds of jobs opening up because of the draft. I know I couldn't get factory work, but I figure that's what all kinds of fellows who aren't in the draft are doing, going where pay's better. The way I see it, that means their old jobs are vacant. So I've been looking at want ads, and calling some of the places. One said I could come talk to them this afternoon, but I'd have to take the bus, see, and I don't have fare.

"So here's my offer: You lend me a quarter and I'll pay you back thirty cents from my first wages. What do you say?"

"What kind of work?"

"Bellhop, real respectable."

"Okay then. Here."

Wondering whether he had a snowball's chance in his ragged clothes and poorly trimmed hair, I wished him luck and watched him hustle back toward the corner where he sold papers. When I entered my building, I found another kid a few years older than Heebs looking around uncertainly. His attire was considerably different, a spiffy tie and vest with a starched white shirt. He too carried a bag, but his was the sort used by downtown bicycle messengers.

"If you're hunting a directory, there isn't one. Could I help you?"

"Yes, m'am. What floor for Maggie Sullivan Investigations?"

"Third, but I'll save you a trip. I'm Maggie Sullivan."

"Message for you from Minsky & Feldman." He flourished an envelope and extended a clipboard. "Sign for it there, on that line. I'm to wait and take back an answer."

NINE

The envelope the messenger gave me was heavy, not because of its contents but because the paper itself was thick white linen. The Minsky and Feldman name was engraved, prominent but tasteful. I opened it and took out a single, folded, piece of paper. The message on it was handwritten.

My sister would like to see you at 5:15.

Joel Minsky had signed it.

There was an address.

A small envelope with a blank sheet that fit inside had been included. Using the pencil I carried, I wrote that I'd be there. I sealed the envelope, tipped the messenger a dime, wondering whether it was enough, and watched him leave. Relief lightened my feet as I climbed the stairs.

At least I knew that Rachel was out of jail now. The address where I was to meet her was in the area of the ones I'd seen in the phone book. As soon as I'd hung up my hat, I sat at my desk and took the directory out again to check. Abe Minsky was listed at the address in the message. I was betting he was Rachel's father.

I called the number Pearlie had given me.

"I need to talk to Pearlie."

"Never heard of him," the voice on the other end told me, as it had on the last occasion.

"Yeah? Well, if you should happen to make his acquaintance, tell him our friend's out."

I waited in case he said anything. All I got for my efforts was the sound of the connection breaking.

***

I drove to Rachel's construction site to see what was happening. That turned out to be worth watching. A trim gray-haired guy in neat workman's garb was muscling a man in a suit off the site as I drove up. The older man was exerting such vigor that the man in his grip had trouble keeping his footing.

"You come around trying to poach my men again and you'll get a broken jaw, not a warning." Shoving the interloper toward a late model car, the gray-haired man, who had to be the foreman here, stood watching until the car departed. It came just short of squealing its tires.

I sat for several minutes to give the man I took for the foreman a chance to cool down. Then I moseyed over to the sketchy hint of a building going up there. The interlude gave me a chance to look things over. The police were gone, but it looked as though work had come to a standstill. Half a dozen men sat talking and smoking. There was usually twice that many, maybe more, hard at work. They didn't look happy. Finally I walked over.

"I take it you're the foreman?"

He stood with his back against one of the uprights now, smoking. He tossed his cigarette to the ground, grinding it out as he straightened.

"If you're a reporter, I've got nothing to say to you."

I gave him a business card.

"I'm a friend of Miss Minsky's. She wants me to see if I can find out anything more about why that body turned up here."

"Maybe she should stop by and ask herself," one hulk of a man said sullenly. "Sure sticks her nose in any other time."

The foreman held up a hand. He looked from the card to me.

"Yeah, I remember you now. You've come to other sites I was on a time or two with Miss Minsky. We quit at noon on Saturday. He wasn't here then. None of us knew him."

Some of the men who now stared at me sat with their arms crossed. One nudged his neighbor, giving a nod at my slacks. Their prevailing mood, however, seemed sour. I didn't think it had much, if anything, to do with my arrival. If there was something to learn here, I might be better off to go after it in a roundabout way.

"I guess the police must have put a stop to construction? Last time I saw one of Miss Minsky's projects, all you fellows were busy as beavers. There were more of you, too."

I caught angry grunts.

"We can't do anything else until they pour concrete," the foreman said. "That was supposed to happen yesterday. The cops said forget it because of finding the body. They were crawling around the place like ants, so I had to send the men home.

"The concrete company was mad as hops when I called and cancelled. They'll probably bill Miss Minsky anyway, and now we've got to get back on their schedule."

"While we sit drawing half-pay until they pour," someone grumbled.

"Be glad you're getting any pay," the foreman said sharply. "Boss didn't have to do that."

"She's doing it because she needs us." The hulk crossed arms the size of hams. "Every builder in town is crying for workers. It's her pocketbook she's worried about, not ours."

A man with a square chin and droopy eye spoke with a twang.

"Some man you are, talking about her like that after she gave you a second chance."

The hulk was off the stack of boards where he sat in an instant. He caught the front of the other man's shirt, yanking him to his feet.

"Either of you throws a punch and you're both fired." The foreman inserted himself between them. He held a lead pipe in one hand.

The hulk had drawn his fist back to deliver what would have been a bruising blow. Three or four seconds passed before he lowered it. The foreman, a trim little guy, continued to stand between them with arms outstretched. He nudged the larger man's chest with the length of pipe.

"Hawkins, go home. Cool off before you come in tomorrow."

The other men watched Hawkins stalk away in silence. Some of them shuffled their feet. At least one of Rachel's employees seemed to be nursing a grievance against her. The man with the droopy eye smoothed his neatly ironed work shirt and gave me a nod. Maybe it was meant as apology.

"I know Miss Minsky appreciates your loyalty," I said. At least she would if she knew what was happening. It appeared these men had no idea she was being looked at as a murder suspect.

"Did anything out of the ordinary happen these last few weeks?"

Heads shook.

"Think a minute," urged the foreman.

This time a good minute passed. Frowns emerged here and there as the men searched their memories. Some ducked inquisitive looks at their pals. Something flared in the face of the fellow who'd nearly gotten into the fistfight. He darted a look at me. The foreman's forehead had wrinkled in thought.

"The rest of you might as well go home too," he said with a sigh. "Concrete's not likely to come today, late as it's getting, and not without somebody from Minsky coming to tell us. Come in usual time tomorrow."

Relaxing enough to talk now, with most of them picking up lunch buckets, they filed toward the street. The foreman watched for a minute, then lighted a cigarette and leaned back against the joist he'd leaned against earlier.

"I'll stick around the rest of the day," he said by way of explanation. "In case the police come back, or anyone drives out with any sort of instruction." He slanted his work cap back and looked at the sky. "If the weather turns and we get rain like we did up until last week, that means we can't have concrete poured either. Put us even farther behind."

He offered me the pack of cigarettes.

"No thanks." I took a seat vacated by one of the

workmen. "Those two who were fixing to duke it out, do they have some kind of bad blood between them?"

He nodded.

"Over what?"

"You'd have to ask them. Hawkins is a royal pain in the backside, but with those muscles of his, he does the work of two. And what he said's true, the supply of men for construction work keeps shrinking because of the draft, and isn't likely to get bigger anytime soon."

I stretched my legs out, thinking I could possibly start to like slacks. The sun directly overhead was making me squint a little.

"You looked as though something might have occurred to you right before you sent the others home."

He frowned and took his cigarette out to study it.

"It probably doesn't amount to a hill of beans, but when I'm in charge of a project, I drive by on Sundays, late afternoon usually. Just to make sure everything's okay.

"I was running late day before yesterday, almost suppertime. When I drove up, a car was parked on the opposite side. Right before that side street comes in."

"Parked facing the way you were coming."

He nodded.

"I hadn't really noticed it, but when I started to pull to the curb like I always do, so I can creep along and make sure nothing's been bothered, the car took off. It didn't exactly whiz around the corner, but it went too fast for a Sunday afternoon, if you know what I'm getting at."

"I think I do."

Instinct had told him something wasn't right about the situation. It was the sort of gut reaction I'd learned to listen to when I felt it.

Streets didn't run in a tidy grid where we were. To the north, a vacant lot abutted Rachel's building site. Across from the site, coming toward the two lots, was the street into which the departing car had turned. From the foreman's description, the place where the car had been parked before it took off would have been a dandy spot to sit and study the area. In particular, it offered a close look at the spot where the body had been found and how hidden it was from passersby. It also, as the foreman had noticed, afforded a quick getaway.

"Did you mention that to the police?"

He took a quick draw on his cigarette.

"I told them I'd come by to check things. I didn't want to say anything about the car. It could just have been some fellow out snuggling with his girlfriend."

"There were two people in the car then?"

He considered.

"I think so. Yeah, I'm sure I saw two heads right before it turned. Except..." He started to frown. "Now that I think about it, I saw two hats, too. Men's hats. Or at least I think so." He waggled a finger at mine. "Harder lines than yours. Like fedoras. Men's brims."

He hadn't noticed the make of the car, or the plate numbers. It hadn't been colorful. It was black, or dark blue. In other words, there was nothing to go on. It was one more thing assuring me Rachel was being framed for a murder she hadn't committed.

"The police said they were able to reach Miss Minsky because she'd left a business card with one of the neighbors around here. That she'd written her home phone number on the back."

"I can't say about the phone number, but yes. She gave a

card to the old bat across the street, trying to get her to simmer down."

I looked at the gray house with white trim he indicated. Everything about it proclaimed tender care, from the two chairs on its small front porch to its neatly tended flowerbeds and freshly painted picket fence in front.

"Simmer down from what?"

"A truck with a load of lumber swung around too fast and some of the boards slid off. Broke a couple of boards in her fence and wrecked some rose bushes or something. That chucklehead Hawkins was driving, so instead of apologizing when the old lady came out yelling, he probably smarted off. I was up on a scaffold, and before I could get to the ground, she went in her house and came out waving a rifle.

"Not sure what would have happened if Miss Minsky hadn't happened along just then, coming to check on something. She was out of her car and bustled across the street like a banty hen. She lit into Hawkins — you could hear parts clear over here — and smoothed things over with the old woman. When she got over here, she told me to treat the woman with kid gloves, that she'd see to new rose bushes and had given the woman a card and told her to call if she had any more complaints."

"Has she?"

The foreman shrugged.

"None that I know of. I've heard she had run-ins two, three years ago with the outfit that built that place." His head tipped toward the neighboring office building. "Waved her rifle at them at least once. You're not thinking of talking to her, are you?"

I smiled. "Why, as a matter of fact, I am."

TEN

The old lady with the rifle wasn't home. As I came back down the porch steps, I waved to the foreman who stood at the opposite curb, ready to dash gallantly across and save me. It had taken some talking to persuade him not to accompany me.

"I'll check in tomorrow," I called as I got into my car. My statement included the woman in the gray house as well, if she wasn't around when I swung past later today.

I had some lunch in the Arcade, looking up at its glass dome and enjoying the ham on white I'd gotten at one of the stalls. I watched a woman buy three jars of preserves and a younger one buy fresh-made noodles. The noodles would probably make an appearance in whatever she served for dinner tonight: soup, or chicken and noodles, or goulash. The place was always filled with bustle, all sorts of people swirling through. The streets outside were more orderly, and less colorful. The Arcade pulsed with life.

So far, I had one employee who apparently nursed a grudge or two toward Rachel, and a neighbor who sounded hostile toward her project, if not toward her. I also had a suspicious car with two men in it not too many hours before Gabriel Foster was dumped there or killed there. And two men who'd broken into Rachel's place of business last night, hunting something. Were they the same two men?

Possibly. But just as possibly not. All four could be mixed up in this but with different chores. Or even working different angles. I'd had a case last year where men who worked for a rackets kingpin and men who worked for an amateur turned out to be trampling each other's feet.

Balling up the brown paper from my sandwich, I tossed it into a wastebasket and headed back to my office to try calling Pearlie again.

I'd picked up my pencil to dial when the phone rang under my hand.

"I got something for you," said the voice I'd been waiting to hear. "I'll be here the next forty minutes or so. It's a restaurant."

He hung up before I finished writing the address.

From anyone other than Pearlie, I would have been miffed. As it was, I felt relief that he'd saved me some time and dug up information. I was also considerably curious about the sort of place he frequented when not with Rachel.

**

The restaurant was a hole in the wall deeper than it was wide. Its shape, and the lowered lights I encountered inside, kicked my wariness to the maximum. As soon as my eyes adjusted, I saw it wasn't at all like the narrow little café of which I had unpleasant memories. Three women sat laughing and talking at one table. There were plenty of couples.

A man with a white linen towel wrapped around him like an apron led me to one of the tall wooden booths at the back.

"What'll you have?" asked Pearlie as I slid in across from him.

"Just coffee, thanks. I already ate."

The restaurant looked like it might be Italian. People were eating things with spaghetti. A half finished steak sat before Pearlie.

"Bring her one of those tiara things. That'll go good with coffee."

He cut into his steak. Only a faint line of pink showed. Maybe Pearlie didn't like seeing blood.

"So did you get my message that Rachel is out?"

"Yeah. Kinda surprised she didn't get in touch, to tell you the truth."

There was something besides surprise in his words. Hurt feelings that he'd mattered so little.

"I haven't talked to her since the jail. Her brother sent a messenger over."

"The lawyer."

"Yes.

"He sent a note saying Rachel wanted to see me tonight. I'll let you know what I learn."

The waiter returned with my coffee and a fancy dessert that was layers of dark crumbs and white I couldn't identify.

"How about Foster? What did you find on him?"

Pearlie patted his lips with the checkered napkin.

"He's in the same game Rachel is."

"Construction?"

"Yeah." He reached into his pocket. "There's where his office is. There's where he's got his current job going up. There's where he lives — wife and three kids. That last one's his girlfriend. Name's Gloria."

65

His finger moved down the list of addresses in squarish print on the paper he slid me.

"You've been busy."

"Needed to get it done. I'm going somewhere else for awhile."

For the first time since I'd known him, Pearlie seemed uncomfortable. Wary, even. I recognized now that he'd been that way since I walked in. What was going on? Why was he leaving town right when Rachel needed him, for moral support if nothing else?

"Nice work digging up a girlfriend," I managed to say.

He nodded.

"Thought it might save time if I looked for places he wasn't a Boy Scout. From what I could find out, he started going out with her about three years back. Year, year and a half ago she moved from a room on Washington to an apartment on Booher."

"He paying the rent?"

"Don't know on that."

One thing was certain, Gloria had moved up in the world. Booher was a small street squeezed in between First and Second but parallel to them. The number wasn't enough to tell me the apartment's exact location, but I didn't think it was far from the Hulman Building or Dayton's swankiest hotel, the Miami.

"Any other places where Foster wasn't a Boy Scout?"

"None I found. Doesn't gamble, doesn't owe money to people who might take exception."

"What about his business? It in any kind of trouble? In the red or facing lawsuits?"

"Don't know how to find out about business things."

Pearlie looked at his watch.

"Gotta go. Check's taken care of. Look after yourself, okay?"

***

The old woman purported to wave a rifle still wasn't home when I drove over. Across the way, the Minsky Construction site with its scraped up earth and skeletal structure sat deserted. Since I had the place to myself, I got out and walked to where Freeze and the others had been working yesterday. Then I surveyed the spot where, according to what I'd been told, the body had been. In neither case did anything catch my attention or the idea of something to look at creep into mind.

The dead man had been in the same line of business as Rachel. Rachel hadn't liked him. Why?

I turned my face up to the cloudless blue sky, but I didn't see any answers there either. All I saw when I brought my gaze back to earth was the pink froth of a pair of redbud trees in the yard of the gray house across the way.

I could understand why the woman had been upset about the changes taking place on this side of the street. Before an office building went up next to where I was standing and this lot was cleared, she'd probably looked across at redbud trees and daffodils, followed by lilacs and mums. She'd looked and seen little houses like her own, a neighborhood where people knew each other.

Sharp as an icepick I felt longing for the house I'd grown up in, a modest house like the ones across the way. I'd had no choice but to sell it to pay off my father's medical bills.

I'd been eighteen. There'd been a plum tree in the backyard, and flowering quince. On long, lazy summer days I'd taken a quilt out and lain on it reading, or curled up petting one of my cats.

Shaking free of the past, I returned to my car and drove around having a look at the addresses Pearlie had given me, and wondering what each could tell me about the recently departed Gabriel Foster. The project he'd had going up was twice the size of Rachel's, its outer walls nearly completed. It looked as if work had come to a halt there. No men were in sight.

Next I drove past his office. It was fancier than hers, with a sidewalk leading up to the entrance and patches of grass at either side of the steps. At his two-story brick house the driveway was filled with cars, leading me to suspect a wake or other comforting of his widow might be in progress. The building where his girlfriend lived was four stories of tan brick with a small awning over the entry. Most of the windows facing the street had draperies as well as shades.

The afternoon was almost gone. I went home to peel the bulkier bandages off my shins so I could put on heavy cotton stockings and a suit before presenting myself at the home of Rachel's parents.

All the time I found myself thinking of Pearlie and the oddness of his manner and why he'd be leaving town when the woman I'd thought he was devoted to was in a pickle.

ELEVEN

The address in Joel Minsky's note turned out to be a substantial two-story brick house with an attached garage a few blocks off Salem Avenue. It was a neighborhood of quiet prosperity marked by deep front yards and mature trees.

Two other cars sat in the driveway, a Buick like Rachel's and a mid-sized navy blue Packard. I decided my DeSoto might feel more comfortable on the street.

I'd washed my face and fluffed and primped and was wearing my dove gray suit and best silk blouse when I rang the doorbell. Enough time passed for me to notice symbols I thought were Hebrew writing running down the trim on each side of the door. When the slab of carved wood finally opened, I found myself face-to-face with Joel Minsky.

"You're prompt."

"I try to cultivate a virtue or two."

He didn't seem to notice my wit, or he wasn't the sort to appreciate it.

"Come in," he said, turning. "Rachel's in here."

I followed him halfway down a hall softly lighted by ceiling fixtures with tulip shades and a Tiffany lamp on a small console. He led the way into a parlor, which from its size wasn't the main one. A log flickered in a fireplace faced with pink granite that showed no trace of soot. Rachel sat on one end of a sofa upholstered in deep rose. She was smoking, her familiar gold cigarette holder between her fingers.

"Good to see you," she said.

"Better to see you, here."

She looked tired, bereft of her usual bounce. She made no move to get up. Joel observed us.

"Sit." She indicated the other end of the sofa. "Since you were going to be here, I brought down that book I told you about. I thought you might enjoy it while you're cooling your heels before your appointment tomorrow."

Her eyes caught mine and she passed me the book in her lap. I didn't know what she was talking about. What I suspected was that I'd find some kind of message tucked in the book.

Joel moved toward the door.

"I'll be in the hall. Don't take too long, Rache. Mama's not happy about this."

Rachel gave a pale smile and squeezed his hand as he passed. The door closed firmly. I put a finger to my lips and started to rise. Rachel realized I meant to tiptoe to the door and shook her head.

"He won't listen." She drew a breath as if it were the first she'd had in a while. "I expect Pearlie's disappointed I haven't gotten in touch."

"A little. He's left town."

"He said he might." Hurt flitted through her eyes. "I didn't get a chance to call him. Joel had to pull strings to the breaking point to get me out on bail. It's contingent on my being in his custody, which was stretched to letting me live here. I've had a nest of eagle eyes watching my every move.

"My mother sleeps late, or I wouldn't even have managed to call the office this morning. Cecilia told me about the break-in."

"I'd already taken care of the matter you asked me to before it happened."

"Thanks."

"What are chances that's what the burglars were after?"

To my surprise, she tipped back her head and chuckled, a rich, throaty sound. "Less than zero."

"Any idea what they were after then?"

"No."

"Money?"

"We don't keep any, to speak of. Just what Cecilia needs for stamps and such. Nothing out front was touched, just my office. And it looked like whoever it was tried to steal a broken loader, which is totally nutso. He wouldn't have gotten two blocks driving a piece of equipment like that down the street at night. That's one of the reasons I've never had a watchman. I couldn't see a need."

"If you mean the big thing with the jaws, they weren't trying to steal it. They were trying to put me out of action hitting me with the bucket."

Her midnight eyes flared. Bending slowly she rubbed her half-smoked cigarette out in an ashtray by her feet. When she sat back up, the ends of the gold holder were gripped tightly between both fists. Her voice shook slightly.

"I asked you to help me. I didn't expect you to put your life on the line for me, nor do I want it."

"You've done it for me."

She was silent.

"Like it or not, Rachel, I intend to get to the bottom of this."

In as few words as possible, I filled her in on the fibs I told about going to pick up the Padraig Pearse book and losing the flower. It gave her time to get past the blow my encounter with the big machine had produced, and was something she needed to know in case of questions. I wanted to ask if any part of her office had been torn apart more than the rest. I wanted to ask about the set-to with Hawkins she'd broken up at her construction site. I wanted to ask a lot of things, but I wasn't sure how soon her brother would pop back in, so I got to what I deemed crucial.

"I can buy the cops tracking you down in your hidey hole through the card you'd left with that neighbor—"

"Hidey-hole. Nice description. Do you know where it is, by the way?"

"Yeah. I looked up your arrest report."

She grimaced.

"Good. You might need to go there sometime."

Again her gaze caught mine and held, conveying something unspoken. Did she trust her brother not to listen as much as she'd let on?

"What I don't understand is why they jumped to the idea you were Foster's killer so fast."

She took a cigarette from her tortoiseshell case and started the rigmarole that led to lighting it.

"They woke me in the wee hours, you may recall. Two o'clock, two-thirty, something like that. I'm not at my best when I wake up. They asked if I knew a man named Gabriel Foster. I said something like 'regrettably, yes.' Then one of them said, 'Mind telling us what he was doing at your construction site?' I more or less hit the roof, wondering what he'd done there. I said, 'Trespassing, the s.o.b.' Except I wasn't awake enough to abbreviate."

"You hadn't realized he was dead?"

"Not until I whirled to get into some clothes and go over there only to have a cop stick his arm out and start asking me where I'd been all evening. About then another cop went in the bedroom and came marching poor Morrie out in his undershorts."

"Morrie. Your alibi."

She nodded.

"A sweet, funny man who didn't deserve to get caught in this nightmare. Fortunately, people at Beerman's confirmed he's a drapery salesman who probably wouldn't know which end of a gun is which, and he had connections with enough clout back in Chicago that they've let him go."

Jutting her chin to the side to direct smoke away from me, she exhaled.

"Someone's trying to pin this on me. They found an earring of mine, Joel says. One that went missing months ago."

"Could anyone confirm that?"

"Oh, I'm sure I ranted about it. Whether anyone remembers..." Her mouth gave a twist. "I rant a lot. And if someone did remember... my mother, Cecilia... who's going to believe them?"

"Who hates you enough to want you in jail?" *Or in the electric chair.*

Rachel snorted. "Do you have that pad you carry around for making lists? The thing is..." She stood and paced, her free hand cupping the opposite elbow. "We'd had words, Foster and I. Quite heated ones. In front of witnesses."

The opening door interrupted us.

"Rachel. Go be a good daughter. I'll show Miss Sullivan out. Tell Mama I'll be along in a few minutes."

She drew in breath. Her shoulders straightened imperceptibly.

"Thanks for coming, Maggie."

***

Joel Minsky accompanied me to the front door in silence. Watching us from a vantage point farther along the hall was a stern looking man with a short steel gray beard. I nodded to him. He didn't nod back.

"If I was abrupt when you came to my office, I apologize," Joel said when we reached the door.

"No harm done." I could be as cool as he was. "I expect you found it hard to believe what I was telling you, and you didn't know me from Adam. Or at least from Eve."

His face lost some of its rigidity. He almost smiled.

"Rachel's done plenty of things I deemed unwise, but that was the first time she'd gotten herself in anything like this. I knew what a murder charge meant. I'm not sure she's grasped it yet."

"Oh, I think she has a fair idea." My words came out sharper than I intended. "I saw her in jail, remember? In the cell. Your sister has nerves of steel. I've seen them. She was trying to hide it at Ford Street, but she was scared."

Opening the front door, he gestured and followed me out.

"Look. Sometimes Rachel and I are able to talk, even disagree, and get along fine. She thinks about things and

74

she's not as insular as Marv and Sam and the rest of the family. But when she's got her mind set on something and I try to reason with her, we fight like two cats in a bag."

Twilight was descending. A faint humidity settled on my face. Joel paused with his hand on the half open door as if choosing his words.

"I'm afraid this may be one of those times when we're cats. My sister may not always see that I'm trying to help her. When I try to find out things I need to defend her, she's likely to see it as sticking my nose in. If I rub her the wrong way, she'll explode and turn stubborn."

A grin escaped me.

"Rachel does have a temper."

"She's very insistent that she wants you helping on this. I apologize for being dismissive when you offered earlier. People I know assure me you rank with the best in your line of work. I suspect Rachel will be more cooperative with you than with our firm's usual investigator."

He removed a check from his pocket.

"If you're still willing, and your present workload allows you to work on this full time, or close to it, I want to hire you. Please. I suspect you know Rachel better than anyone else. Certainly better than I do."

I took the check without looking at it.

"I'm not sure anyone knows Rachel."

TWELVE

It was a quarter of nine when I rang the bell at the gray house across from Rachel's construction site. Since I hadn't had luck catching the woman who lived there at home the previous day, I wanted to try before she headed out in case she went somewhere on a regular basis. She'd been home in the daytime during the run-in with Hawkins that Rachel broke up, but people of all ages were signing up for Civilian Defense jobs. Even though it was unpaid work, some of the positions demanded regular hours.

The door flew open. The fragrance of freshly cooked bacon poured over me. A lean woman on the tall side with her pepper gray hair done up in a short braid stared out at me.

"Yes?" She had nails where her eyes should be.

I gave her a nice smile.

"Are you the woman who lives here?"

"That's right. Willa Lee Cottle. Who are you?"

"My name's Maggie Sullivan."

Still smiling, I gave her a card. Her sharp eyes made quick work of it.

"A detective. Huh. Well, you'd better step in."

Her cozy living room wasn't anything like her. China doodads lined the mantel and crocheted doilies covered the backs of the chairs. A wedding couple, one of whom was

Willa Lee Cottle at a much younger age, held pride of place in a silver frame.

"The woman whose company is putting up that building across the way hired me," I said as she pointed me to a chair.

"About that body they found over there, I guess. I already told the police everything I know."

"Sometimes I listen better than the police."

Her grunt suggested she might be receptive to that.

"Miss Minsky, the woman whose men are working over there, had given you a card with her home number on it."

"That's right. She seemed like a nice enough lady. I can't say the same for some of the fellows working for her. One big lummox ruined the rosebushes William had planted. Tore them up all the way down to the roots. When I raced out shouting for him to stop and to look what he'd done, did he apologize? He did not. Turned all snotty and told me to simmer down, I could plant new ones.

"But my William planted those. With his own hands. Part of him was *in* them."

The grief in her voice made it easy to guess.

"Is your husband dead?" I asked softly.

Looking away, she cleared her throat.

"Two years now. Some days I still wake up thinking he's there right beside me."

"I'm sorry." I looked toward the photo. "He was very handsome."

Willa Lee shrugged, but a pleased smile tugged at her mouth.

"Had you had problems since then with the workmen over there? It seems like you found Miss Minsky's information awfully fast when the police woke you up asking — what? How to reach someone from the construction site?"

"I never could understand folks letting things get disorganized. I keep a list in one of the drawers in the kitchen. Neighbors in case I fall or something, my doctor. I put her card right with that list as soon as I got it." She made a face.

"'Course I might not have understood what they wanted as fast if I hadn't been up an hour or so earlier. I hadn't dropped back off yet, so I wasn't quite as fuzzy as I could have been."

"Why were you up earlier?" I held my breath. If she'd been answering a call of nature, the question might make her indignant enough to throw me out.

She blinked. "Why, the ruckus across the way."

Somewhere in the house a faucet dripped. Its slow beats ticked off several seconds. If Willa Lee had been up and about an hour before the cops turned up on her doorstep, the disturbance she was talking about must have occurred around the time Gabriel Foster was killed, or dumped, across the way.

"I bet you anything it had to do with that body they found over there, too," Willa Lee volunteered. "I thought at the time it might have been shots, but they were little bitty pops, and I decided it must be kids with firecrackers. That's bad enough, mind, boys out running around in the middle of the night. Once I decided it was just kids — and the scream made me think that too — well, once I decided that's all it was, I went back to bed."

The scent of information that could prove useful

crowded out the smell of bacon in this orderly little house.

"Would you mind telling me more about it? If you have time?" I crossed my fingers that her prolonged absence yesterday was a fluke, and that she'd be flattered I thought she might have a busy schedule.

"I roll bandages three days a week, but not til afternoon, and not today." She got comfortable in her chair. "There's not much more to tell. The police didn't make much of it, and you may not either."

"You have a very logical mind. I'd like to hear anything more you can tell me. And your ideas about it, too."

"Well, then." She frowned, organizing her thoughts. "Like I said, I was up. That happens more as you get older, I guess. Afterward, I came into the kitchen to get a drink. Water tastes better after it sits, so I keep a jar in the Frigidaire. It's warm enough now that the window over the sink was open a few inches. Guess that's how I heard the pops."

The kitchen would be at the back, behind where we sat now. She must have good ears, especially for someone her age.

"How many?" I asked.

"One, then a good time in between, then another one."

"Two pops."

"Right. But not one after another like you were shooting at something. That's part what made me think of firecrackers.

"I know what guns sound like. My daddy ran a good-sized still in the holler where I grew up. It's how we made ends meet, that and rabbits and squirrels for meat and the garden. The sheriff and his deputies, now, they were kind of partial to their pistols. That's a littler sound. What I heard over there was even littler. And there was that time in between."

"But with firecrackers, you light one and throw it." I summoned forgotten details of summer nights. "Then you have to strike a match and get a new one lighted before you can throw it."

"That's it. The other thing is, you don't expect to hear gunshots around here where people live, either. It's not like we've got honky-tonk houses and such along here."

It was shaky, maybe, but it also made sense.

"Did you tell the police all this?"

The old woman flicked her hands in disgust.

"I tried to. They weren't interested. Asked where I was standing and could it have been the house creaking. I know every sound of this house! Lived in it over thirty years."

I listened to the faucet drip. Something else in her account had caught my attention.

"You mentioned a scream."

Willa Lee nodded. "Right when I was turning to go back to bed."

"Not during that pause between shots?"

"No. It was after. I wondered if maybe they'd started to light another firecracker and something had gone wrong and gave them a scare. Like dropping it, or the match burning one of their fingers. Something like that."

It hadn't been Foster screaming in fear before they finished him off then. I wondered if Willa Lee with her logic had reached the same conclusion.

"Could it have been the man they killed, do you think?"

Her head was shaking before I finished.

"No, because it was after the shots. Since I'd decided there was nothing going on to worry about, I put the stopper back in the water and set the jar back in the Frigidaire. Then I went back to close the window over the sink. That's when I heard that part. The scream and then a voice — another one — like a squabble.

"It made me mad, all that noise when people were trying to sleep, so I started out to give whoever it was a piece of my mind. By the time I opened the door, though, all I heard was running, that slapping kind like when kids go pell-mell, jostling each other. But it already must have been half a block away by then."

THIRTEEN

I needed time to digest what Willa Lee Cottle had told me. While I did, I still had most of the morning to put to good use if I'd interpreted the finger-sized note I'd finally found in the book from Rachel correctly. It had taken me four passes before I saw it deep in the crack between pages.

1:30 "Expected"

I hoped that meant her apartment. If so, my next stop would give me a swell chance to compare real estate.

The green awning fluttered over the entry to Gloria the girlfriend's building as I went in. With a smidgen of regret that I was going to miss what was shaping up to be another nice day, I turned my attention to the rows of mailboxes in the lobby. They were set in the wall and had brass doors that opened with keys. Each had a slot at the top large enough for letters and folded up magazines to be inserted. Brackets below the boxes gave the owner's last name.

Gloria Overbrook lived one floor up, three doors down on the left. Like the outside, the interior of the building was nice without being flashy. The carpet runner in the hall was free of worn spots. The management kept the place in tip-top shape. I knocked on Gloria's door and waited.

No sounds of movement reached me from inside. No

radio played. I knocked again. That's when my nostrils caught the smell of something sour. Not the smell of a body. It was more like the stink of a damp shirt left too long before ironing or milk gone bad. Frowning, I stepped back. As I did, something thumped against the other side of the door.

The yowl of an unhappy cat split the silence. From the volume and the frequency with which he repeated it, he had a serious grievance. The racket he was making drew my eyes down to where I could hear him scratching frantically at the door between us. I saw the source of the sour smell. Something white had oozed out beneath the door and congealed in a thin line that was sticky to my touch.

I stood a minute trying to think while the cat wailed. It had been quite a while since my girlhood kitchen where things were put in and out of the icebox and milk got spilled. Spills that were noticed got wiped up right away, but now and then a glass with milk residue got overlooked, or some of the contents dribbled down the side and left a ring. When that happened it took more than a couple of hours for milk to turn sticky.

My eyes slid toward the lock on the door. I'd had considerable experience plying the crochet hook in my purse to open a locked door. In most cases, if I thought I might find something useful on the other side, I wouldn't hesitate. This time another instinct kicked in. I needed to make sure everything I did here was completely aboveboard and couldn't possibly be construed otherwise. Failure to do so might prove detrimental to Rachel's legal defense.

Going back downstairs, I knocked on the door marked MANAGER. A woman answered.

"I just went up to see Miss Overbrook," I said. "Her cat's kicking up an awful fuss and there's milk seeping under the door and spoiling your floor. The milk smells like it's several days old. I'm worried something's happened to her, that she might be sick or something."

"Oh, dear! Let me get my husband."

I could hear her repeating almost verbatim what I'd told her. A man in an olive green cardigan hurried back with her. He was past middle age.

"Milk spilled, you say? I'd better get my keys."

His wife hadn't asked me in. From the hallway I watched him set the pipe he'd been carrying in an ashtray. He opened a cabinet and took out a key ring. When he headed upstairs, I tagged along.

"Like I told your wife, I was worried when I saw the milk. Something like that's hard to clean once it sets."

He grunted and knocked on the door.

"Miss Overbrook? Miss Overbrook, it's the superintendent. I'm coming in."

A cat shot past us as soon as he opened the door. It was down the stairs before I could blink.

"Miss Overbrook? Well, what on earth...?" The super stood shaking his head at the broken milk bottle that lay at his feet.

Just inside the door, a spindly console table for visitors to set a hat or handbag on held an empty tumbler. Since the broken bottle lay between it and the door, I suspected the bottle had been on the table too. A quick stoop showed me the paper tab was gone from the bottle. The milk had been opened. It looked to me like Foster's girlfriend had been about to pour herself a glass of milk when someone knocked. She'd set the glass and bottle down to open the door ... and then what?

"I, uh, I suppose I ought to have a look in the bedroom. See if she's too sick to call out, or-or...." The superintendent swallowed. He glanced toward me now as if glad for my presence.

The place had an empty feel. Only the sound of the Frigidaire kicking on in the kitchenette broke the silence. The bedroom was empty, its bed neatly made. I tucked my hands under my arms so I wouldn't touch anything.

A pretty little vanity table held an overturned lipstick tube and two perfume atomizers. Not a lot of primping supplies for someone with a sugar daddy. The louvered closet doors to the closet stood open. Enough clothes to make me faintly jealous hung there, but there were empty hangers as well, half of them on the floor. Gloria was untidy.

"You'd better check the bathroom," I suggested. "In case she fell and hit her head."

As soon as he stepped out, I used my hanky to open the drawers in the vanity table for a quick peek. One showed signs of spilled powder. Another held a couple of scarves. No stockings there, or in the chest of drawers, whose contents were jumbled. No comb or hairbrush either.

I met the super as he was coming out of the bathroom.

"Well, it looks like she must have set that milk down and forgotten about it, and the cat got hungry and knocked it over while she was away. I guess it's nothing to worry about, except she'll have to pay for it if that floor outside her door needs refinishing. And I think I better tell her to get rid of..."

He stopped, his gaze following mine as I stepped in for a

closer look at a smudge I'd spotted on the hallway wall. It was just above eye level, a faint rust-colored smear that looked as if someone had made an attempt to wipe it away. I stepped back and stooped, and saw spots here and there on the carpeting.

"We need to go down to your place and call the police," I said. "This is blood."

FOURTEEN

"Tell me again how you came to know Foster had a girlfriend?" said Freeze.

"Possibly because I'm a first-rate detective?"

I gave him a breezy smile. Thanks to two-way radios the city's entire fleet of police cruisers had gotten two years earlier, dispatch had been able to reach him while he was out elsewhere and give him the message that brought him to Gloria's address.

"I've got a few sources, Freeze, just like you've got yours. When I'm sniffing at suspects, trying to find out if they should move up or down on my list, I start with things they might want to hide. Gambling and girlfriends are right up there. Which you probably know. It occurred to me the same thing might apply to a victim."

"If you were hunting someone to pin it on, because you didn't like the suspect we had."

"Which I don't."

He grunted.

"And the door wasn't conveniently unlocked when you got here? That's a first."

We were standing in Gloria Overbrook's living room. While waiting for the police to arrive, I'd worked up a couple of things that might persuade Freeze to let me stay. I hadn't needed any of them. He strolled around the corner and looked at the stain on the wall.

"That's blood alright. Dried. It's been there overnight anyway, same as the spilled milk." An unlighted cigarette dangled from the corner of his mouth. He took it out and jabbed it in my direction. "What would you make of it?"

His invitation to put my two cents in left me momentarily speechless. Judging by Boike's expression, it had startled him too. The landlord had no reaction. He was downstairs in his apartment, sitting on the couch with his head in his hands so he wouldn't faint.

"I think Gloria was about to pour herself a glass of milk when somebody knocked. She set the bottle down on that little slip of a table and answered the door. Then..." I took a breath. I wasn't sure a homicide cop would be willing to make the same leap I did.

"No telling when the milk got spilled, but I'd say the minute Gloria opened the door, somebody pushed his way in. He, or they, knocked her around pretty hard."

"Hard enough to leave blood on the wall."

"Right."

"Because?"

"Because she knew Foster? Because whoever hit her wanted information they thought she might have?"

"Or because they were looking for something?"

"Maybe..."

"Something they didn't find at Minsky Construction?"

These rapid-fire questions were a side of him I'd never seen. I stole a look at Boike, who was listening intently. Was this what Freeze was like to work with? It suggested a keener mind than I'd ever witnessed.

"There's no sign anyone went through things." I looked

around. "The pictures are straight on the wall. Her bed was made. All the drawers were closed."

"One of the sofa cushions is turned upside down so the patterns don't match. Broads are fussy about things like that."

A match flared to life in his hand. Looking pleased with himself, he started his cigarette. I nodded slowly.

"I missed that. But here's the thing, Freeze. Gloria could be dead, what with that blood on the wall and her gone. What I think's more likely is that she got scared and ran. I think she cleared out in a big hurry, even a panic."

Freeze crossed his arms and leaned one shoulder against the wall. "Go on."

"Her hairbrush is gone, and some of her clothes, and — trust me on this one — most of her makeup. I didn't poke around, but I peeked in her closet. I didn't see a suitcase anywhere. Did you?"

"Boike? You look under the bed?"

"Harris did. Nothing."

Freeze nodded slowly.

"You get good ideas sometimes. I've been starting to think there might be something to what you said about everything being too pat where we found Foster's body. The earring I might take as a lucky break I don't get enough of. But it plus the phone call about the body when no one around there looks like a candidate for the dog walker? Yeah. It's awfully convenient.

"Which doesn't mean I think the Minsky woman's innocent. I just think something's off."

Cupping a hand beneath the ash that was on the verge of falling from his cigarette, he looked around. With alacrity suggesting it wasn't the first time he'd seen his boss in such a fix in unfamiliar surroundings, Boike grabbed an ashtray from a table next to the sofa. Freeze took it without missing a beat.

"The suspect's office getting torn apart could fit a man she'd had differences with showing up dead on her property, but this business here, I don't see how."

Thank goodness for sofa cushions put back the wrong way.

A wee unfriendly voice in my brain told me Freeze could be buttering me up so I'd let my guard down. I decided to ignore the possibility. For the moment.

"There's something else that bothers me about all this," I ventured. "Those shots Mrs. Cottle, the woman who gave you the card with Miss Minsky's phone number, heard."

Our truce began to break down. Freeze snorted.

"Claims she heard. In the kitchen at the back of the house. A woman that age?"

"How many shots did she tell you she heard?"

"Two."

"That's what she told me, too."

"So?"

"So you found two spent casings, right?"

"Yeah."

"When you were first combing the scene I commented on the lack of blood. Besides the bullet that killed Foster being small caliber, you said it was also dead aim, one shot in the back of his head."

"Is there a point to this? I can look at Boike's notes if I want a summary."

"Yes, but will they ask you why, if it only took one well-placed shot to kill Foster, Willa Lee Cottle heard two shots? And why you found two casings?"

He hunted for an answer.

"There could have been some kind of struggle."

"In the course of which Foster's assailant managed to overpower him, then pop him neatly in the back of his head? And the moon could be made of green cheese, too, Freeze."

***

Since cops were currently questioning other residents of Gloria's building I couldn't do the same thing. In any case, I wanted to have another look at the area where Foster's body had been discovered. I headed there hoping they weren't pouring concrete yet.

The building site was all but deserted. A solitary figure straddled a crossbeam not very high off the ground. His back leaned comfortably against the upright behind him. His arms were crossed. He looked completely content.

As I drew closer, assuming it was the foreman, I saw it was the fellow with the droopy eye instead. He spotted me at the same moment and sat up, his legs still dangling.

"No concrete?"

"Tomorrow. One of the men from the office just drove out to give us the word. Foreman said we might as well all go home, and expect to work an extra hour every day until we make up lost time. I was just sitting enjoying this weather. Could I help you with something?"

"I want to take another look at where they found the body."

"There," he said pointing. "I guess you know that."

I nodded. "I didn't see it, though." A thought occurred to me. "Did you?"

"Not much." He hopped down. "The police were already here when we started arriving. As soon as they saw us, they took our sawhorses and put them up with cloth over them, to keep us from watching. Not long after that, the coroner's truck came and they took the body away. So all I can really tell you is the body was there." He pivoted to point again.

Shots that could have been firecrackers.

The possibility kids were out running around at an hour when kids shouldn't be.

Signs of a violent struggle at the apartment of a murder victim's girlfriend.

All I had to show for my morning's work was a jumble. Still, a jumble was better than Rachel as a clear-cut suspect. Remembering yesterday's confrontation between this man with an eyelid at half-mast and the hulk named Hawkins, I realized this was a perfect opportunity to learn what might lie behind Hawkins' seeming animosity toward Rachel.

"It might help me help Miss Minsky if I could find out more about the charming Mr. Hawkins," I said. "Any chance you'd be willing to forego whatever's in your lunch pail and let me buy you some lunch?"

The man in neatly pressed khakis had clear gray eyes with flecks of brown. The skin around them was crinkled from working in the sun. And from smiling, as he did now.

"I don't get many chances to have lunch with a good-looking woman. My name's Morris, by the way."

FIFTEEN

Morris didn't have a car, so I drove a few miles to a café that was near the trolley line he took. We were on the early side for lunch, but I wanted to be on time for my meeting with Rachel. I didn't think a man who worked construction would object, since they were usually pounding nails before offices opened.

"How did you get into this kind of work?" he asked as he looked at the card I'd given him. "If you don't mind my asking."

"My dad was a cop."

We both had coffee to help pass time til our plate lunches came — creamed chicken on biscuits for me, hot pork for him.

"Why didn't you do that? They have policewomen now, don't they?"

I didn't feel like telling how my brother had taken off when I was nine, and how my dad wrote letters to distant places and made calls trying to find him in scraps of time remaining between his workday and his efforts to placate my increasingly difficult mother. Nor did I want to talk about the young neighbor woman who had killed herself after her rat of a husband made a fool of her.

"Sometimes people need help the police aren't able to give." I moved my elbow as our food arrived. "And I'm not as good about following rules as he was."

He chuckled. "What was it you wanted to know about Hawkins?"

"He doesn't seem to like Miss Minsky much. Any idea why?"

"Just the fact that she's boss would be reason enough for him. Her being a woman doesn't help."

"It sounds like you're telling me he's got a chip on his shoulder."

"The size of a four-by-four."

"Any particular reason?"

He chewed thoughtfully. "Some men are just like that, I guess. With him and Miss Minsky, there was more to it. A year or so ago, on another project of hers, some of the men had items go missing out of their toolboxes."

"You all buy your own tools?"

"Hand tools, yes. Good quality ones. They're worth a good bit if you sell them. One of the fellows who had something turn up missing had seen Hawkins hanging around his toolbox the day before. He asked Hawkins if he'd picked it up by mistake, but Hawkins denied it and got all huffy. About a week later, I opened my box and saw my best hammer was gone. I didn't ask. I strolled over and opened Hawkins' box."

"And there it was."

He grinned.

"No, and he knocked me three ways to Sunday. I found it in a pawnshop not far from there, though, and the owner described the man who'd pawned as a big bruiser."

"That explains why there's bad blood between you two, but what does it have to do with what you said about him getting a second chance?"

He paused to pat his mouth with a paper napkin. Because of the war, some places had stopped putting holders of them on the table so you could help yourself. I wasn't sure whether the move was to save paper or because the machines that made them were needed to make something else.

"The foreman on the other project, the one where things disappeared, mentioned it to Miss Minsky. I don't think he even knew anyone was suspected, just that men were grumbling. Not long afterwards that Buick of hers pulled up and she came out of the backseat like she'd been shot from a canon. She told the foreman to get us all down to ground level, then stood there with her hands on her hips and lit in. She let us know in no uncertain terms that she wouldn't tolerate thieves on her crews. One or two might have snuck a look at Hawkins. Anyhow, she finished her piece up staring right at him."

His mouth curved at the memory.

"Then over here he pulled that stunt with the truck full of lumber. Swerving around too fast and ruining that lady's bushes. And I'll tell you why he was wasn't driving better. He was hung over. He ought to be kissing Miss Minsky's feet that he still has a job, not grousing about her."

On the surface, Hawkins sounded like nothing more than another perpetually disgruntled loudmouth. I couldn't see him having a motive to kill Foster. I could, maybe, see him helping someone cast suspicion on Rachel, either for money or because he resented her. He was at the construction site every day, and if Rachel herself hadn't dropped the earring, somebody had planted it.

* * *

"Miss Minsky is expecting me," I told the dumpy man sitting behind the desk that controlled visitors to Rachel's apartment building. If he recognized me from the previous day, he didn't show it. Happily, I'd interpreted Rachel's note correctly. Once I gave my name he told me the apartment number and I took the single elevator up.

Rachel opened the door before my knuckles had left it. In contrast to the drab and not-too-brightly lighted halls I'd come through, the living room I entered seemed awash in light. Pale pink walls made sophisticated by a faintly grayish tone formed a background for Eames chairs and a claret red sofa. By chance or design it created an exquisite setting for the dark-haired woman who had started pacing as soon as she closed the door.

"I lunched with Joel. He had a deposition to get to, and agreed to drop me at Rike's on provision I check the fit on a dress I was having altered and go directly home." She pointed me to a seat. "I've already asked them to deliver it day after tomorrow. I suggest you get right to the things you want to ask. We can risk about twenty minutes.

"Drink?"

I shook my head.

"First of all, tell me about the quarrel you had with Foster. Where it was, what it was about, what was said?"

"Outside the Stockyards Inn, three weeks ago. There's a builders group that meets for lunch every month."

Sinking into a chair, she surveyed her surroundings and made a soft growl of contentment deep in her throat.

"I didn't threaten to kill him, if that's what you're

wondering." Kicking her pumps off, she reached for her cigarettes. "I may have said something that could be interpreted that way, though."

"Which was...?"

She frowned in thought and blew out smoke. "As near as I can remember, I called him an underhanded s.o.b. and told him one of these days he was going to get what was coming to him."

Aware how it sounded, she shrugged irritably.

"Meaning?"

"Meaning that life, God, the things you do or whatever you want to call it has a way of catching up with you. I was pretty sure he'd been behind some vandalism to a piece of equipment a month or so back. To that bucket loader you tangled with, as a matter of fact. I was still fuming over how the repairs had delayed things. Part of it was frustration because I'd just given away one a few years older that I'd kept as a backup.

"That's one of the ways I've kept my costs down, having machinery so we can do our own horizontal work. Five years back or thereabouts, when businesses were still going under, I bought an extra loader and a grader dirt-cheap and kept them as spares. But projects are drying up because of the war. There was word that machines were in short supply for something they're doing at Patterson Field. I decided to do my bit rather than letting two machines we'd almost never needed sit and rust."

It took me a moment to absorb all she'd told me. I understood now why the equipment area at her office had looked emptier than usual.

"What made you think it was Foster behind the vandalism?"

"We'd had differences before. I'd all but accused him of cheating to get the contract for the project he had under way when he died. The rest of us were more or less clumped together in terms of our bids. His was enough lower that my jaw dropped. I wouldn't have said anything if he hadn't been so damn cocky, but the miserable gob of excrement smirked at me and said, 'Better luck next time, honey.'"

"The 'honey' part didn't sit well?"

Her eyes became fathomless pools. Their darkness chilled me.

"I might have managed to hold my tongue if he hadn't followed it up by telling me now I'd have more time to spend at the beauty shop. At which point I said he must be planning on cutting corners *and* underpaying his people to come in so much lower than the rest of us. He turned so red I was braced for him to take a swing at me."

"And there were witnesses to that too?"

"The other bidders were still around, and a few other people. I'm sure some of them heard. Win Lamont was looking daggers at him."

I noted the name on my pad.

"Am I to understand your bid came in second?"

"Yes." Rachel eyed me steadily. "I haven't made this easy for you, have I?"

"Did you know Foster had a girlfriend?"

My change in direction threw her as few things did.

"The point being, Rachel, there are other leads."

She sat silent a moment.

"Thanks."

"The other bidders you mentioned, who were they? I have Lamont."

"Phil Clark and... I'm not quite sure. Oscar Jones? Arnie Snow?" She shook her head. "Sorry. Are you saying this could have something to do with Foster rather than me? With his project?"

"I'm just saying there are other possibilities."

She glanced at her wristwatch, removed what remained of her cigarette from its holder, and rubbed it out. "What else?"

"Where's your gun?"

She frowned. "Why?"

"I need to know."

She jumped up.

"Wait. Show me. And don't touch it."

I held my breath, uncertain whether or not to pray there would be a gun. She led me down the hall to a bathroom where she pointed to the kind of closet that held towels and extra soap and such.

"In there. In the bottom of the toilet plunger."

Wondering if I'd heard her correctly, I picked the rubber plunger up by its long wooden handle. I tilted it and looked at the concave rubber part. All I saw were faint indentations under the lip.

SIXTEEN

Until we knew the whereabouts of the missing gun, we were waiting for the other shoe to drop. When I got back to the office, I opened the window halfway, then dialed the detective squad. Boike answered.

"Hey, Boike. I've got a couple of questions."

"No sweet talk first? No roses?"

"Freeze must be out."

"Shall I have him call you?"

"No need. I expect you know the answer. Did you find the gun that killed Foster?"

His breeziness disappeared.

"I'll have the lieutenant call you."

"Come on, Boike. Just this morning we were buddy-buddy, sharing ideas."

His sigh gusted down the phone line.

"Yeah, I know. And regardless of what I said a couple days back, I don't really think being friends with Miss Minsky would make you turn a blind eye to something. It's just..."

"You've got a job to do and you can't be a hundred percent certain."

"Well, yes." Cautious silence hung between us. "I guess it doesn't hurt anything telling you. No, we haven't found the gun. Why?"

I crossed my fingers.

"What about the one you found in her apartment?"

More silence.

"The fact it was a different caliber doesn't mean anything," he said at length.

"Yeah, sure, I know that." Of course I hadn't known they had it, let alone the part about different calibers. I wondered whether Joel Minsky did. "What I meant was where did you find it?"

"In the bottom of a toilet plunger. Even Freeze had never heard of hiding one there before."

"Had it been used?"

"The gun or the plunger?"

"The fine points of housework don't interest me, Boike."

"There wasn't any residue on the gun, if that's what you mean. It didn't smell recently cleaned, either, but—"

"She still could have killed Foster, using the one you haven't found. I get the picture. When you fine fellows searched her place, did you see any signs of anyone else having searched?"

He thought a minute.

"Like we did at the girlfriend's apartment, you mean?"

"Exactly. Or torn up like at Miss Minsky's office."

He thought.

"If the Minsky wo— if Miss Minsky's guilty, she wouldn't search her own apartment, but she might someone else's."

"She wouldn't tear her own office apart."

"It could be two different parties searching."

"You're a pain in the neck when you're logical, Boike."

He chuckled.

***

Walking to the window I opened it an inch to let the air in and stood staring out. Let's say my basic theory was right and the earring had turned up where Foster's body was found because someone wanted to frame Rachel. They would need to know her well enough to know she had the earrings. They would need to get their hands on one. They'd have to be a better pickpocket than Harry Blackstone, who had huge audiences laughing with that part of his magic show, to remove the earring while Rachel was wearing it. That suggested to me that whoever took it had access to her apartment and knew where she kept her jewelry.

What that person hadn't known was where she kept her gun. Or even that she had one, possibly.

I leaned on the windowsill and breathed in the scent of the city. Just as I felt myself hovering on the edge of progress, Dayton still hovered on the edge of spring without quite getting there. The produce market a few blocks away didn't yet have the berries and fruit whose fragrance sweetened the air in the afternoon sun. Its sounds were soothing though. The clatter of feet on cobblestones, voices, stall owners calling orders to assistants. Their words were too faint to make out, but the rise and fall made a kind of music.

Before I lost too much time to the pleasant world outside, I returned to my desk and added items to my list of things to do next. Rachel had indicated at least one of the other bidders might have nursed hard feelings toward Foster over the contract he won. I wanted to talk to them.

My pencil was moving methodically when my door popped open.

"Hey, Mags, I've got a favor to ask."

The man who planted himself in the chair in front of my desk had the physique of a praying mantis and a halo of reddish gold curls. Assorted camera gear hung from his neck. He was a shutterbug for the afternoon paper.

"A favor? Jenkins, as I recall, you owe me about a dozen before we're anywhere near even."

His cherubic face beamed at me with deceptive innocence. We'd been friends a long time.

"Ah, but this one's actually for Ione. I need you to hide her birthday gift."

"Um. Well, maybe then. As long as it's not some sort of animal. Or bird, or reptile, or fish..." I tried to list them all on my fingers. Jenkins loved to wiggle through technicalities as well as I did. Usually the favors we pretended to keep track of involved information, which sometimes we traded and other times guarded like crazy. At least once a month he and his wife Ione and I went out to listen to jazz together, or spent a long evening at their apartment talking and drinking.

"I wouldn't leave anything alive in your care." He looked pointedly at the plant whose brown remains had decorated a corner near the window for several years. "It's a sewing machine."

My jaw fell.

"Jenkins," I said when I could finally speak, "why on earth could you possibly think Ione would want a sewing machine?"

He preened, pleased at his own cleverness.

"Well, she may not want one, but she loves clothes. You know that. And unless this war ends a whole lot faster than anyone paying attention thinks it will, clothes are likely to be rationed here just like in Britain. I can't see Ione trading dresses with other women when she wants a new one, or rummaging through a used rack, can you? This way she can make her own."

I sat staring at the man who had a college degree and read half a dozen magazines, and wondering how he could possibly be so wrong about this. True, Ione was a clotheshorse. What was also true was that she bought most of those clothes in New York. She earned a pretty penny writing for magazines there and elsewhere, and several times a year she took the train to talk to editors there. Those trips also involved a healthy amount of shopping.

"Does Ione even know how to use a sewing machine?"

Jenkins waved his hand.

"If she doesn't, her mother or sister can teach her. And the thing is, Mags, the Singer store only has a few left, and won't have any more new ones until the war ends because making new ones takes metal." He paused. A serious note crept in. "Besides, if my draft number comes up, having something new to do might keep her from worrying while I'm gone."

I didn't agree with his last assessment, but it got to me.

"Every Tom, Dick and Harry and all their relatives can jimmy the lock on this door, and I think you'd be better off getting her perfume, but if you have your heart set on it, you can leave it here."

SEVENTEEN

"I need the names of a couple of companies run by people that Rachel knows." Betting myself that her secretary wouldn't even need to look it up, I settled my backside into my office chair the next morning.

"Which ones?" Cecilia's cheerful voice asked.

"Phil Clark and Win Lamont."

I won the bet. She rattled them off. Then she told me to hang on a second and gave me their phone numbers too.

"Anything else?"

"Does Rachel have any sort of list that shows who else bid on the same contracts she did?"

"Oh yes. It's not an official list unless it's a project that used public money, but I type one up for her on every project. She keeps track of who the contract was awarded to, and as near as she can the rank of the other bids."

"She doesn't actually know who bid how much?"

"Again, not unless it involves public money. Sometimes she hears things, though. From what she tells me when it's just the two of us, men can be as catty as they accuse women of being when a business deal doesn't go their way."

"Could you please see who, besides Clark and Lamont and Rachel herself, bid on the project Gabriel Foster was working on when he was killed?"

"It will take me five minutes or so. The contracts and lists were one of the things in that file cabinet in her office the burglars went through. I think I've got everything back where it should be, but there have been a lot of distractions. Shall I call you back?"

"Yes, please."

I hung up and swiveled my chair to help me think better.

Should I take a closer look than I'd initially intended at the people who'd been in the running on Foster's project? When I'd asked Cecilia for names, my only interest had been talking to people who witnessed her set-to with Foster. Now I began to remember what I'd been hearing about the war making such projects scarce.

Maybe I also ought to look at who had bid on Rachel's project. With Foster dead and Rachel charged with his murder, were two projects and the profits that went with them suddenly up in the air? Were they worth committing murder? Was there any link between the two projects? I wished I knew a lot more than I did about the construction business.

Cecilia called back with several minutes to spare.

"Oscar Jones was the only other bidder. His company's Jones Brothers, but there's no brother. He died about the time I started here."

"Thanks, Cecilia. I don't suppose you happen to know if any of the outfits who bid on that project bid on Rachel's."

"No, but I'm in her office and I have the folder lying right in front of me."

Cecilia was a paragon.

Only two other companies had submitted bids for the project Rachel was working on, though. Neither name was one I recognized. I glanced at the clock.

"If I have time later today, I may stop by to look through that file if that's okay."

"Of course. I'll be here."

***

Two of the witnesses to Rachel's quarrel with Foster couldn't see me until tomorrow. Phil Clark could manage this morning. I recognized him as soon as he rose to greet me. He was the man I'd seen all but physically evicted from Rachel's construction site for trying to poach her workers. He wasn't much taller than me, dark-haired, and more than a little good looking. Rachel had good taste there. I put his age somewhere in his late thirties.

"A private detective," he said when I'd introduced myself and given him a card. "You don't look nearly rough and tough enough for that kind of work."

He smiled.

I smiled.

His office was a far cry from Rachel's. Walls and floor were quality wood. They glowed with regular polishing. A desk lamp with a green shade matched the green leather of his desk blotter, and his walls held a generous assortment of minor awards and photographs taken at business events. On his desk a gold tone frame held a photo of some kind of spaniel. He indicated a chair in front of his desk.

"What occasions a visit like this?"

"I'm gathering information relevant to the death of Gabriel Foster."

Clark grimaced.

"Terrible business."

"An opportunity for someone like you, though."

He looked up sharply. "What do you mean?"

"A chance for you to pick up workers from two projects whose immediate futures look less than certain." I let the words dangle a second. "I saw you at the Minsky site two days ago as you were leaving. The foreman there didn't appear to appreciate your efforts."

"Ah. Yes." He managed a look of strained politeness. "The hard truth is that able bodied men are in short supply, and that the workers there need paychecks."

He wasn't a man who worked in his shirtsleeves. An unbuttoned suit jacket seemed to be his only concession to informality in his own office. He glanced at his wristwatch.

"Now. How can I help you?"

"I understand Rachel Minsky had fairly nasty quarrel with the dead man a few months back."

"More like eight months, but yes."

"You and some other people heard it?"

"Yes."

"This was at..." I pretended to check my notes.

"A building trades luncheon. Outside. By the entrance."

So far it matched what Rachel had told me. No reason why it shouldn't, but I wanted to check. Unimportant questions relaxed people, too.

"What did they quarrel about? What was said? In general or more specifically if you can remember."

"She was upset about a contract they'd both bid on. So had I as a matter of fact. She thought his bid had come in unrealistically low."

"And had it?"

He spread his hands.

"I've looked at a lot of numbers since then. All I can tell you is that it was the low bid, since he got the job."

"Isn't that part of the business you're in? Sometimes you submit the low bid, sometimes someone else does?"

"Yes."

"Then why was Miss Minsky upset?"

"Well... she's not the best of losers. She's quick to take offense."

"What did she say?"

"I can't recall."

"Mr. Clark—"

"Look, I don't intend to say anything pejorative about Miss Minsky. The fact is, we used to see each other."

"Dated, you mean?" It was one of the very few things for which I was unprepared. "When? For how long?"

"As for when it started, I can't exactly recall. About this time a year ago."

"And ended? Has it ended?"

"Yes. Last fall. October, maybe."

"Why?"

"No reason. These things just run their course."

"Then let's get back to her quarrel with Foster. Gallantry's all well and good, but telling me what was said could be to her benefit in the long run. Did she threaten him?"

"I suppose it could be interpreted that way."

"What did she say?"

"Something about him getting what he deserved. But I could be remembering wrong."

"Any chance the guy who edged you out in her affections

was one of the other people there that day?"

I had aimed for a nerve, and I hit my target. Clark's polite tone slipped.

"I wasn't edged out. I broke up with her."

"Why?"

"I told you. These things run their course." Snapping his wrist for another look at his watch, he rose. "Now if you'll excuse me, I have a meeting. I'll show you the way out."

Since his office door opened directly into the small reception area where his secretary worked, I was fairly confident I could have managed without a guide, but I didn't argue.

EIGHTEEN

They were pouring concrete at Rachel's construction site. The foreman wouldn't have time to talk. I returned to my office. A couple of bills had arrived, so I wrote out checks. Then I sat and thought about my talk with Clark, and what I'd learned so far that could help Rachel.

Not a lot was the answer. But maybe a little. If Clark and Rachel had dated over a space of months, he might have spent a night or two at her place. If so, he would have had an opportunity to filch her jewelry and plant it. On the off chance Rachel might be able to talk to me on the phone as reward for what she'd termed good behavior, I called her at home.

A woman answered and said she would see if Rachel was available. There followed an interlude so prolonged that I was wondering if I should hang up when Rachel came on.

"Cecilia called a while ago and said you'd asked about contracts," she said in greeting. "I told her to give you whatever you need. Have you learned anything?"

"That you and Phil Clark used to be an item. How long did you go together?"

"Six months. Thereabouts. Why?"

"Why'd he break things off with you?"

I heard her chuckle.

"I got a contract we were both bidding on. Apparently

his pride was wounded. Oh, he gave some cock-and-bull story about why he was calling it quits, but since he did it the same day the contract was let and nearly ruptured my eardrum banging the phone down, it didn't take Einstein to see the connection. That's hardly motive enough to frame someone for murder, is it? If that's what you're thinking."

"Well, you are a pretty hot tomato."

"I have to go." Her voice had gone flat. She hung up.

I blinked in disbelief at the receiver in my hand. Then I pushed the button to break the connection at my end and dialed her again.

"Minsky residence," she said with forced cheer.

"Don't hang up. I need to ask you one — no, two — more things. I'm sorry if I offended you."

Her single syllable chuckle was as weary as it was amused. I wondered if someone had been listening in, or passing. Since she didn't hang up, I continued.

"The project you're working on now, who's the money behind it? Who'll own the building?"

"Merlin Kellogg. Cecilia can get his particulars. It's on the contract. What's the second question?"

"Was Phil Clark one of the bidders? Is that the one that miffed him?"

"That makes three questions. 'No' to both."

I smiled and sat for a second even though I knew it was time to hang up.

"Good talking to you, Rachel."

"Same. And thanks, Maggie."

***

Kellogg's secretary told me he could see me that afternoon. I wasn't sure what I hoped to find, but often my job entailed the tedium of collecting pieces of lint. Collect enough lint and you got a wad you could roll together and twist into string. Then you looked for longer pieces of string that matched yours. Right now I was collecting specks of lint that had to do with the construction industry.

I sat at my desk and listed those specks:

– The commercial construction seemed to be inbred. Not every company bid on every project, but there was plenty of overlap.

– Some of those people, like Clark, could get jealous.

– Workmen were becoming scarce because of the war.

– Company owners weren't above trying to lure workmen from other companies.

I looked at the list. What was this about? Why had Foster been killed and why had he been dumped where he was? It had to have something to do with the line of work he and Rachel were in.

At noon, I waited outside the cleaning supply firm where Gloria had worked and asked to tag along with the girls who'd worked with her when they came out for lunch. The business cards I passed out produced an eagerness to chatter about a co-worker they hadn't liked.

"The only reason she even went to lunch with us was to brag about where she'd gone with her boyfriends," one said.

"Boyfriends?"

"Each one better off than the last to hear her tell it."

"This latest one even got her an apartment," a dishwater blonde told me.

They didn't remember any names though, hadn't bothered to since they didn't like Gloria. The man I knew as Gabriel Foster, she'd referred to only as Mugs.

"Something about him always wanting his coffee in a mug," one volunteered.

Needless to say, she hadn't been in touch with any of them. As far as they knew, she didn't have any relatives.

***

They were better company than the balding real estate developer who would own the finished building where Rachel's men were working. He had a nice office in a nice downtown building, and it soon became apparent that his only concern about Foster's murder and Rachel's trouble was that his profits would suffer.

"If Miss Minsky had to bow out of the project, because of legal problems or anything else, what would happen?" I asked when I'd gone through preliminaries to put him at ease.

"I would lose money. A lot of money," he said curtly.

"Because the bid that came in after hers would require you to pay more than what she's doing the project for?"

"Yes, my costs would go up. I will also lose income because of delays, if a shift becomes necessary. Worst of all I won't realize income from the building as soon as expected. I should think that was all quite apparent." His face was starting to redden.

"I'm afraid I don't know much about the construction business. I'm trying to get a feel for who might benefit from this kind of trouble and who might lose."

"Well, I lose, that's for damn certain. How would anyone benefit?"

"I don't know. Maybe I've assumed too much. Would the next lowest bidder pick up the contract? Or would you start the whole bidding process over again?"

"I don't know!"

Verging on explosion, he swept his hands over the sides of his nearly bald head. They curled into fists.

"I have no idea how this will work if the Minsky woman defaults on her contract. It's never happened before. All I know is that firms like the ones who'll lease space in the building that ought to be going up there are clamoring for offices. Outfits who do business with companies making doodads for airplanes, or Jeeps or all the other things factories are making now. Every day that building isn't completed means money out of my pocket."

***

The man bankrolling Rachel's project wasn't likely to get an award for patriotic fervor. His lack of interest in anyone's troubles but his convinced me he could be eliminated as a murder suspect.

When I got back downtown, I walked over to buy a paper from Heebs.

"Aw, sis, you just missed a chance to meet Marcie," he said.

"Who's Marcie?"

"My girlfriend. She's a peach."

He sounded so starry eyed that it worried me.

"Uh, swell. Did you get that job?"

His face fell, but just for a second.

"Soon as I walked in, they said they'd already filled it. Didn't even talk to me. Can you beat that? I'll pay you back, though."

"Don't worry about it. I'll take it out next time I need your help on something. So tell me about this girlfriend of yours."

It was a slow time of day for peddling papers. He flashed a grin that showed the tiny gap some people have between their two front teeth.

"Can't hardly take her eyes off me. And is she a looker!" He glanced around, preparatory to confiding something. "She's older than me. Says I'm mature for my age."

Glumly I reflected that Heebs, who had no one to rely on and give him advice except other newsboys, had probably reached an age to be frisky.

"Well, uh, make sure you don't do anything to get her in a family way."

"Aw, sis." He ducked his head bashfully. "It's not that way. She's a nice girl. Gets real lonely 'cause her mother works second shift and isn't around, so she comes by and talks, is all. You can tell she comes from a nice family, too, the way she dresses. Not fancy, except she makes anything she wears look fancy. And she's funny, and smart. Kind of reminds me of you."

I knew a losing cause when I saw one, so I tugged the bill of the flat cap he wore down over his eyes and went back to split my time fretting over him and the day's news. At a quarter til five, per appointment, I took a seat in the outer office of the developer financing Foster's project.

After I'd cooled my heels for half an hour, three unhappy looking men filed out. The man I was waiting to see ushered me into his office with weary apologies.

"Whiskey and water?"

He looked as though he needed one, so I said sure. His answers to my questions were much the same as those from the man financing Rachel's project. Replacing the contractor on the project would cost time and money, not to mention possible legal complications. The men I'd seen leaving were his co-investors.

"It's a roll of the dice, really, whether to see if one of the previous bidders has men available or would be willing to take over Foster's crew, or whether it's better putting out bids again," he said rubbing his face. "And demand for office space is soaring every day."

"Other than his turning up dead where her men were working, do you know of any connection between Miss Minsky and Mr. Foster?"

"Only the rumor, which I've only heard about secondhand."

"It's not exactly a rumor. Several people heard their argument."

"Oh yes, that. I thought you were fishing about... the other."

"What other?"

He stared at me for several seconds with his glass halfway to his lips.

"I assumed someone had told you. As I said, I've only heard second hand, but apparently Foster bragged to several of the other contractors that he and Miss Minsky had, ah..."

"Been intimate?"

"Yes. I didn't believe it. She didn't strike me as the type. Even if it was true, I don't think much of a man who'd tell.

It bothered me enough I almost dismissed his bid because of it, but in the end I'm ashamed to say I chose profits over principles. I regret that now."

NINETEEN

Rachel had two dandy motives for killing Foster, the quarrel and the rumor he had spread about her. Assuming it was a rumor. Why hadn't she told me about it?

On the other hand, new commercial buildings, and the contracts for constructing them, were prize commodities these days. Those made better motives, in my book, so Friday morning I decided to take a look at the site where Foster's men had been working at the time of his death. It didn't tell me much.

The building under construction by the murdered man's crew was half again the size of Rachel's. Maybe more. It was also further along. The walls were all up. I parked across the street and watched the activity.

The men didn't have much spring in their step, which wasn't surprising, given the uncertainty of their future. That set me to thinking about the attempts to lure Rachel's workers to other employment. I wondered if similar attempts had been made here. If so, was it only because workers were in short supply, or could there be more behind it? I couldn't answer the question, and I couldn't think of a tale tall enough to pry information out of the foreman here without the connection I'd had at Rachel's place, so I started the DeSoto and let the clutch out and moved on.

In contrast, the pace of work at Rachel's site seemed faster today. Partial scaffolding was in place and sounds of hammers driving nails home filled the air. Someone was whistling. The foreman was so busy giving directions that I was close enough to touch him before he noticed me.

"Looks like things are going well," I observed.

Removing his cap, he wiped a sleeve across his forehead and nodded.

"Concrete's poured. Pay packets are coming tomorrow. For now we're managing. Miss Minsky sent word through a fellow who works her front office. That helped morale, knowing she's keeping tabs on things."

"I see Hawkins hasn't left for greener pastures yet."

The sullen workman with the oversized muscles was sawing away at a board set on sawhorses. The foreman glanced over and made a face.

"Yeah, he's a pain in the neck, but I'm glad he hasn't."

"Any more trouble with other builders coming here and trying to recruit?"

"Nah." All at once he bellowed at someone beyond me. "Did you mark that? I don't want it touched til it's marked."

***

Foster.

Rachel.

Which was the target?

Was it possible both were?

I hoped a visit to Rachel's office could give me some answers. To my surprise, Cecilia met the request I made there with a frown.

"You want *all* her contracts? Going back *how* long?"

"Four years. Not just contracts, everything she's bid on, whether she got it or not. Don't you keep paperwork that long?"

"Well, yes." She bit her lip. "Couldn't you look at them here, though? You could use Rachel's office and spread out. I know you'd be careful, but that's going to be an armful of folders and things can slip out...." She brightened suddenly. "I don't have much to do with Rachel away. Could I go through them and type out what you want from each? Who the developer was, who bid, how much they bid if Rachel knew that? It might be easier to compare them all, if that's what you want to do."

Cecilia was sharp, no question about it. I could understand her reluctance to have materials from the files leave the building, and what she was suggesting made sense. It would be more efficient, too.

"Cecilia, if I had a fairy godmother, I wouldn't ask for a prince. I'd ask for a secretary like you," I said.

She laughed. "I'll call when they're ready."

I blew her a kiss and set off to keep my appointment with the builder who had been next in line for Foster's project after Foster and Rachel.

***

Oscar Jones, the bidder who'd come in third on Foster's project was a broken little man who moved a pencil aimlessly around on his desk and sighed a lot as we talked.

"I don't know what the world's coming to, with decent people getting their throats cut."

"His throat wasn't cut," I said.

"Well, no. I just meant well, dead. Killed." He shook his head. "First the Depression, and then just when things were turning around, this war... Oh. But you said you wanted to ask some questions about him, didn't you? Gabe Foster."

I smiled reassurance.

"Did you know him well?"

"Oh, saw him at business lunches, and a holiday party we do for the gals."

"Was he successful, would you say?"

"Oh, more successful than me, at least." He gave a weak laugh.

His telephone rang and he answered it. It gave me a chance to study his office. Like Rachel's, it had a honeycomb cabinet with rolled up blueprints sticking out and maps of the city and of outlying areas on the walls. Like Phil Clark's, the walls and floor were finished, though not as glossy.

"Do the best you can," he told whoever had called, and hung up. "Now where were we?"

"Gabriel Foster. Rachel Minsky made the second best bid for work on that project. With her out of the running until her name is cleared, it looks like you'd be next in line to take it over."

"I suppose I would." He preened for an instant, then deflated again.

"I can't though. Couldn't possibly. I don't have men enough for another project."

"What about using the men who are already there?"

"Using... Oh, now there's an idea. I don't know. I'd have to think about that one."

I started to wonder how he'd gotten as far as he had.

"Tell me about Mr. Foster and Miss Minsky. I understand there was bad blood between them."

"Well, yes." He chuckled uncomfortably. "I suppose there was. They had a set-to after a meeting. Over his bid. She all but accused him flat out of being crooked."

"And the other?"

He squirmed.

"A woman would have every right to be angry over something like that. A man telling other men she was... easy. He didn't tell me that, mind you. I don't pal around over drinks like some of them do, but I heard them snickering about it after. For several weeks.

"Gabriel Foster was a-a cad, if you ask me. Of course he wasn't a very pleasant man in general. A terrible needler. I suppose I have to go to the funeral, though."

TWENTY

I went back to my office and looked over all the notes I'd made in hopes something new would occur to me. It didn't. Restless, and increasingly vexed at my lack of progress, I bought a sandwich at the Arcade and walked a couple of blocks to eat on a bench overlooking the river.

The sun was bright. The Great Miami sparkled and twisted. It was running high just now as spring runoff from the Stillwater River to the north and the Mad River to the east fed into it. A stiff breeze sent strands of hair whipping across my mouth between bites of cold pork on dill bread. The day was perfect for flying kites, as my dad and I had come here to do on countless occasions.

Usually on a day like this, in the course of a sandwich, I'd get to watch at least one kid and father or grandfather tugging a kite string. Today there weren't any. I wondered if it was because dads were away now, and old men stepping up to fill vacancies or even work on assembly lines. Compared to places like London, we were lucky here. We hadn't dodged bombs yet. Still, in countless tiny ways, it seemed the war was silently nibbling bits of everyday joy.

Around two o'clock, after more wasted time at my desk, I went to buy a paper from Heebs. From half a block away I realized it was a bad idea, but he'd already spotted me. I couldn't retreat.

"Hey, sis!" he sang in greeting. "I've been hoping you'd come by. This here's Marcie I've been telling you about. Marcie, this is Maggie."

"Hiya," she said without interest. She picked at the ends of her hair. "You never told me she was so old," she said to Heebs.

He looked slightly abashed.

I smiled determinedly. The girl Heebs claimed reminded him of me was a pouty little blonde who on close inspection couldn't be more than fifteen but probably passed for older. Battleships would be hard pressed to match the way she thrust her modest prow before her.

"School let out early?" I asked.

"What's it to you?"

"Just making conversation."

Heebs was looking awkwardly at his shoes. As usual, they were starting to come apart on the sides from wear.

"Lend me a dime so I can go get a phosphate, Heebsie. That little bottle of Coca Cola you bought us wasn't near enough to get rid of my thirst."

"Nice meeting you," I said to her back.

She didn't respond.

"She's usually nicer," Heebs mumbled. "I think maybe she was nervous."

"Yeah," I said. "I have that effect on people."

***

Winfred Lamont, who had come in one slot from the bottom in the bidding that the murdered man had won, had an office farther to the east of downtown than the other two builders I'd talked to. Like Rachel's, it had fencing to one side where some supplies were stacked. Except for a large pickup truck whose bed could handle long boards and heavy loads, no equipment was parked inside the fence. It fit with what Rachel had told me about having an edge because she had machines capable of moving earth around.

Lamont, a compact man with carrot red hair and freckles, was polite as they came and nervous as a cat. He came to the front to meet me and led me back to an office with a host of framed photographs on the wall behind him. A fishing rod and two fish caught on taxidermy plaques decorated the wall he viewed when at his desk.

"Looks like you're a fisherman. Where do you go?" I'd never baited a hook in my life, but I'd heard men talk about such things.

"Oh, uh, locally, mostly. Michigan if I get lucky." He plopped into his seat and laced his fingers behind his head. "My girl said you had some sort of questions about Gabe Foster?"

"I'm talking to people who knew him. Trying to get a line on who might have had differences with him."

"Differences?" He paled. "Surely you don't think—" He swallowed. "I didn't. Have differences with him, that is. I didn't like him. A terrible braggart and a needler, to tell the truth."

Needler. Colorless little Oscar Jones had used the same term. It gave me a good idea the sort of man Foster had been.

"Good to his wife, though. Brought her to the Christmas party some of us go to every year."

And kept a girlfriend on the side.

"I always say you can tell a lot about a man by how he treats his family," Lamont babbled.

Lamont was clearly big on family. The photographs on the wall above his left shoulder included a formal one of an older couple and their freckled offspring, including the man I was talking to and a girl a bit younger. Others showed Lamont with a woman and two wee tots, no doubt his wife and kiddies. The picture where people appeared to be having the best time showed Lamont and his wife, the girl I presumed to be Lamont's sister, and a bug-eyed man with straw boater several sizes too small perched on his head like a clown's hat mashing his hair out. They all sat on a blanket laughing, enjoying a picnic.

"The only one I can think of who might have felt some animosity toward him was Miss Minsky," Lamont was saying. "The woman they've charged. But I guess you know that. She's the one you're working for. I guess you probably know about the argument they had, too."

While I hadn't specifically said I was working in Rachel's behalf, it didn't take a huge amount of logic to reach that conclusion. What itched my curiosity was how he'd known I was already aware of the argument between Foster and Rachel. Grapevine, probably. The murder of one of their own was bound to be a topic of conversation. Clark or Jones or one of the two developers might have alerted him, and since scheduling had put him last on my list of appointments, he'd had twenty-four hours to worry and stew.

Some people were naturally nervous when they were asked about crimes, even when they were innocent and had nothing to hide. I took Lamont for that kind.

M. Ruth Myers

"I understand she was upset about Foster's bid being so much lower than everyone else's, and that you seemed upset too."

"I don't... oh... possibly. Startled, more than upset." He gave a weak laugh.

"Why do you think it was so much lower?" I was struggling for patience.

"Oh, uh, just tugged at his belt like the rest of us, I imagine. Or—" He warmed to what he was saying. "—or he was willing to take a loss on that project because he thought it would pay off somewhere down the pike."

"How?"

"Oh, no idea," he said breezily, "but he was a clever one, Foster was. Always hunting an angle." Nodding, he leaned forward as if imparting a confidence. "I always suspected he might be a bit underhanded. Not that I know anything, or ever heard anything to justify that, mind you."

It was the most interesting thing I'd heard about Foster so far, and definitely worth pursuing, though not at the moment.

"What about the story he spread about Miss Minsky?"

His pale face pinked up nicely.

"I expect it was just his idea of a joke. One of those crude things men say when they've had too much to drink. I tried not to pay attention when I heard it mentioned, to tell you the truth."

The fact I'd had two confirmations now of another grudge Rachel must have had against Foster didn't cheer me any.

"Since Miss Minsky's out of the running, you'd be one of the ones in line to take over Foster's project if the owner

128

wants to go that route, wouldn't you?" I said to change direction.

The man across from me jumped as if I'd stuck a pin in his toe.

"Oh, I couldn't. Still have a ways to go on what we're working on now. I don't have manpower enough for another project."

"The men on Foster's crew will need jobs, won't they?"

"Well, I-I-I suppose. But I couldn't manage more men on payroll. I'd get myself in a pickle. I'm stretched thin as it is."

TWENTY-ONE

Getting derailed can give you a new perspective. You spot different things when you're upside down.

Monday morning I got derailed bright and early.

Most weekdays I got my paper from Heebs before I went to McCrory's for breakfast. Lost in thought about how long it might take Cecilia to compile the information I'd requested, and where to dig around in the interim, I crossed the street to the corner where Heebs hawked headlines. My steps slowed abruptly.

Heebs wasn't there.

In his place was an older kid, taller by at least three inches. He had a thin mouth and a rooster strut in every move.

"Where's Heebs?" I asked, my nickel in hand.

"Do you see him around?"

"Would I ask if I did?"

"Beats me, sweetheart. You dames are kinda dim sometimes. Paper, mister?"

His arm nearly smacked me across the breast as he swung it out. A man in a suit took the paper and paid, then went on his way. I fought an urge to scrub the smart aleck smirk off the newsie's face.

"Look. I just want to know why Heebs isn't around. Did he get hurt?"

"Guess he got tired of this spot, moved to another corner."

My mental lie detector spiked. Newsboys defended their corners fiercely, especially if they had a good one. I'd witnessed one incident where they came to blows. Heebs had been selling papers in this exact spot for five years, maybe longer. He hadn't grown tired of the place, and he wouldn't have moved to another spot without telling me.

The interloper was glaring now. Assuming he was concluding a sale with me, hurried customers were passing him by.

"You going to buy a paper or not, toots?"

"Not from you, I'm not."

I walked five blocks in hopes another boy Heebs had traded places with a time or two in order to help me with something still was yelling out headlines there. The kid was only ten or so and his voice didn't carry very far, but he was there.

"I'm a friend of Heebs," I said, buying a paper. I dropped the change back into his hand. "He's not where he usually is, and the kid who's there just smarted off when I asked where Heebs was. Do you know?"

The flow of foot traffic here was a trickle compared with Heebs' spot. I made sure to stand back out of the way so I didn't interfere with sales. The boy nodded, solemn eyed.

"Got beat up, is what I heard. Hurt bad."

My heart stuck in my throat. "By that punk that's in his spot today?"

"Nuh-uh, I don't think so."

He stopped to sell a paper, then twisted his toe back and forth.

"The way I heard it, there was a bunch of them. Well, two or three anyway, and they weren't newsies. They're just kids who go around making trouble. Jumped Heebs while he was sleeping. Guys were whispering about it when we got our papers this morning. Said after awhile this big white car that's been going around drove up, and a man jumped out and put Heebs into it."

He paused to sell another paper. I asked more questions, but he didn't have any answers. He'd told me all he knew.

I went to McCrory's and made a pretense of reading my paper and eating my oatmeal. Inside I felt numb. It wasn't as if I had any connection to Heebs. He was just a kid I'd watched grow up on the streets and happened to like; a smart kid who seldom ran short of optimism or fresh remarks. Now, suddenly, he'd been beaten up and shoved into a car. It didn't make sense. More than that, it worried me considerably.

***

I needed to focus on Rachel. That's what I ought to be thinking about. Instead I vacated my stool at the lunch counter with my bowl of oatmeal half finished. I went to the office. I didn't intend to be there long enough to remove my hat.

In the front of my phone book I kept a handwritten list of people I needed to contact from time to time. I dialed the one for Lulu Sollers, head of Dayton's Bureau of Policewomen. She and the women who worked with her were full-fledged sworn police officers. Their badges were scaled smaller than those worn by their larger male counterparts, but the women who wore them were street-smart. When a situation required it, they could be downright tough without throwing punches. They saw plenty and dealt with plenty: prostitutes, drunks, dancehall girls. And juvenile crime.

"Well, aren't you calling bright and early," Lulu said. "What's up?"

"Are you hearing anything about kids getting snatched from the streets? Older kids, twelve, fourteen."

I heard her indrawn breath.

"No, why?"

"A kid I know, a paperboy who beds down in doorways most of the time, got beaten pretty good last night. Some of the other newsies claim a white car came along and he got shoved into it."

On the other end, she murmured something that sounded like 'white.' I knew she was making notes about the car.

"Has this boy been in trouble?" Her question was brisk.

"Not as far as I know. I've trusted him with several things to do with my work and he's never let me down."

"Could the white car they were talking about have been the ambulance?"

I considered. "I don't think so. These are street kids. They know what the ambulance looks like. Although as often as Sally's in the garage for repairs they may only have seen Black Mariah."

She laughed. The newer and fancier of the city's two ambulances was notorious for being out of service. Mostly it was the back-up ambulance, a converted paddy wagon that arrived when called. Critical injuries often were rushed to the hospital in the back of a police cruiser.

"Could you ask around?" I asked. "See if anyone's heard anything?"

"Not now. Have to get to a meeting."

"I'll check back this afternoon."

"This afternoon I'll be trying to locate a hound who deserted his toddler and pregnant wife."

"Sandwich when you get off work then? We've both got to eat."

"That'll do it. Does this kid who got hustled into a car have a name?"

"Heebs. That's the only thing I've heard him called. Heebs."

***

I was locking my office door when I heard the phone I'd hung up not two minutes before start to ring. It was Cecilia.

"I have the information you wanted typed up," she said. "If you decide later you want something more, I'll do an addendum."

"I'll be right over."

Usually the two men who worked with Cecilia stayed fairly busy ordering supplies, coordinating deliveries, and otherwise meeting the needs of the building crews. When I got there, one was leaning a hip on the other man's desk and they were talking lazily.

"Not much to do just now, with only one job site and Rachel out," Cecilia whispered. Inviting me behind the long counter, she spread out the sheets she'd typed so we could both look at them in case I had questions.

There were eight of them, two for each year. Within each year, the projects Rachel had submitted bids on were listed chronologically. Next to the project, she'd noted square footage and number of stories. Beneath each project, indented, she'd listed the company or individual inviting bids on the project, followed by the names of contractors who had submitted bids. Each name was on a separate line. The dollar amount of Rachel's bid followed her name. Sometimes numbers followed other names as well, often followed by a question mark.

"I've put an asterisk next to the name of the contractor who won each bid." Cecilia pointed with the tip of her pencil. "It's usually the lowest bid, but there were two that weren't, and it just seemed easier for you to keep track of things."

I nodded gratitude. As it was, I saw a mammoth task staring back at me.

"Why would someone other than the lowest bidder get a project?"

"Well, on this one, I think it was something about not meeting the deadlines on a couple of projects they'd done before." Her pencil tapped. "And this one..." She frowned. "Something to do with their estimate on materials? Sorry, it was when I'd just started here. I think I heard something, but I can't recall."

TWENTY-TWO

For three solid hours I pored over the neatly typed pages supplied by Cecilia. It took only the first five minutes for me to realize I would have drowned if I'd stuck to my original idea of going through the files themselves to extract information. Even with the secretary simplifying my task, what I learned came down to three things:

1) Neither of the builders who'd been passed over despite having low bids was anyone I'd talked to or even heard of so far.

2) Rachel had come in second to Foster one other time with no casualties.

3) Every contractor who had bid on the project Foster was heading at the time of his death, or on Rachel's, also had competed on others in the four years covered. So had plenty of people whose names weren't familiar to me.

I needed to spend some time in more familiar territory. Digging into people's backgrounds. Following them. Sitting in my DeSoto while my backside developed calluses as I waited for someone interesting to turn up on their doorstep. Punching someone in the nose, or getting my own punched, also qualified as familiar territory, but I wasn't quite desperate enough to go hunting either of those.

One thing I'd learned since I hung out my shingle was

that money was often the lever that started someone rolling toward trouble. They took some, then did desperate things to cover their tracks. In other instances, they borrowed money from people who put a bullet in them when milder tactics didn't motivate repayment.

Pearlie had told me Foster didn't fall in the owing money to dangerous people category. His unexplained absence in the midst of this gnawed at me. Should I maybe double-check what he'd said?

Unfortunately, I'd burned my bridges with a man who knew all about loan sharking in the city because he controlled it. Lacking access to a crime boss who might be willing to chat, I called Freeze. He was out. So was Boike.

While I sat contemplating a trip out to engage with a tuna fish sandwich, Jenkins staggered in lugging a box that edged out his camera for space on his chest.

"The elevator doesn't work," he gasped setting it on the floor in front of my dead philodendron.

"And may not until after the war if they can't get the parts they need. I take it that's the sewing machine?"

Too winded to speak, he blotted his face with his handkerchief and nodded.

"Brought a piece of cloth to cover it with so it's not an eyesore." He flipped a square of green velveteen over the box and set the plant on top.

"Ione may not be thrilled at having to lift it onto the table to use it," he admitted rubbing his back.

I'd put money on Ione using it as a doorstop, which would solve that problem.

***

Hoping against hope that Heebs' replacement had vanished, I walked up Jefferson to take a peek. He hadn't. Since it was only three blocks more to pop in on Freeze, I took a chance on finding him.

He and Boike were both at their desks. Freeze was folding a piece of waxed paper as I came in. He wiped his lips with the resulting rectangle.

"Let me guess. You're here after information."

"You win the kewpie doll, lieutenant. Maybe you should give up detecting and become a swami."

"You ever do any of your own work?"

"You mean like finding out Foster had a girlfriend? You mean finding where she lived? You mean recognizing she'd taken off in a hurry — breathing or otherwise?"

"Yeah, yeah. None of that has paid off."

"Keep hurting my feelings and I may start to cry."

I planted myself in his visitor's chair and swung my leg. Was it possible he was starting to like my sass? Unlikely. I'd caught him when he happened to be well fed. Maybe he'd decided I was useful, too.

"Foster's financial records, have you gone over them?"

"Boike spent most of Friday morning looking at them. Didn't find anything interesting."

"No sign that he owed anyone money?"

"Nope."

"Business wasn't in trouble?"

"Didn't look to be."

"I don't suppose his bank account was heading toward the cellar either?"

"If anything, it was going the opposite way," Boike volunteered.

"Any idea why?"

"Business getting back to normal after the Depression? Watching his pennies more. All I can tell you is there was more in it the last eighteen months or so."

"Why the interest?" Freeze narrowed his gaze on me.

"Just trying to find something I can take hold of. I'm floundering." I put up my hand. "That's the God's honest truth. I'm not trying to put one over on you."

So much for my needing-money-is-the-reason-people-get-in-trouble theory.

"Maybe he was getting bigger projects," Freeze suggested. Or more of them. Or he'd paid something off or found a way to trim costs in his operation."

"Yeah, maybe." The neatly typed sheets in my office would tell me the size of the dead man's projects. They wouldn't tell me how many he'd had, since he might have bid on things Rachel hadn't.

"The thing is, paying his girlfriend's rent took money," I said.

Freeze was lighting a cigarette. He let some smoke out.

"You're thinking that's hard to square with more money in his bank account."

He and Boike seemed to agree. We kicked it around. None of us had any answers, though, so I left.

***

The lists Cecilia had typed weren't any friendlier about showing me a pattern than they had been the first time through. I looked at them seated. I looked at them standing. Alternating with those exercises in futility, I cast baleful glances at the clock, where the minutes until I found out whether Lulu had learned anything about Heebs crawled through glue.

The hour hand had managed to make its way to three and I was standing with fists planted on hips, when a soft knock sounded at my door. At my invitation, which was marginally pleasant enough for prospective clients, Mick Connelly came a few steps inside, and with him the clean, simple smell of soap that never failed to stir my senses.

"Truce?" he asked. His mouth gave the hint of a rueful smile.

"I'm the one who ought to be asking for one. I was upset and spoiling to bite someone's head off when you said what you did."

I came around and sat on the edge of my desk. He closed the distance between us. A single curl had escaped his neatly combed red-brown hair. His uniform collar was buttoned. He was ready to check in for his evening shift.

"Are you feeling contrite enough for dinner and dancing tomorrow? I've a day off."

"I might be persuaded."

"If things are going okay with your friend."

"Thanks for understanding, Mick."

"Guess I ought to remember that you working's part of you." He came to lean on the desk beside me. "It's just that we never see each other these days."

"No, and it seems to me like I don't see much of anyone else either. I'd even settle for hearing Billy scold."

He chuckled. It felt good, his shoulder and mine against each other.

"Does it make sense, these constantly rotating schedules?"

"Smarter men than me claim they do. Fortunately, I have lesser decisions to make. Like where to take you for dinner dancing. Hotel Miami sound okay?"

"Are you on the take, Connelly? That sounds pretty extravagant on a cop's salary."

He laughed.

"I'm not getting many chances to spend it at Finn's, and I can't send it home, what with Nazi U-boats thick as lice between here and Ireland."

"Hotel Miami sounds grand."

Sliding from the desk, he pressed a kiss into my palm and folded my fingers around it.

"Quarter til six, then? And if something comes up so you have to cancel, give me a call, will you?"

"Promise."

"Absent a gun to your head."

"Absent that."

He walked out whistling.

The good mood he'd engendered lasted through another two hours of looking at the sheets from Cecilia. This time around, I hunted reasons Foster might have been reaping more profits than in previous years. My inexpert eye couldn't spot anything. To someone familiar with commercial construction, it might leap off the page.

Someone like Rachel.

I called brother Joel. His secretary said he'd just come in and would call back. Five minutes later he did.

"Have you found something?"

"Not yet, but I may have found a new place to check. I need Rachel to explain some construction things to me, though."

"I need something definite. The judge is pushing to set a preliminary hearing."

"What about Foster's girlfriend? Can't you argue that we need to find her, find out what happened?"

"He's running out of patience."

"Then it's even more important that I talk to Rachel. I need to talk to your family, too, about anything unusual any of them may have spotted." I took a breath. "And see if any of them might have an enemy."

"An en—"

"Who might be framing Rachel to get even."

"*I* am the only one remotely likely to have that kind of enemy." A chill had crept into his voice. "I assure you I've considered that possibility. The investigator we usually use looked into people released from prison, people in or out who might blame me for something. He's come up empty."

"Which makes input from your family more important than ever. One of them may have noticed something, had something happen that wasn't quite right."

"I'll ask if they have."

"No. I need to do the asking. Look, you know how to question people in court. I know how to tease things out."

"They'll clam up with you. Besides, we start holidays Thursday."

I held the receiver away from my ear and stared at it. Surely I'd misheard.

"You're going on *vacation*?"

"Not vacation. A religious observance."

"Does that mean you're not going to be working?"

"Of course I'll be working," he snapped. "But even if I thought you were right about this, which I don't, Pesach complicates things."

"Rachel's life is on the line. Uncomplicate them."

TWENTY-THREE

I was five minutes late for my rendezvous with Lulu Sollers. As I was locking up, a woman had appeared at my elbow asking if I could locate her missing Persian, and how much I charged. A tactful turndown takes time.

"Sorry. Somebody came in at the last minute." I slid into the booth where Lulu sat.

Her hand lifted dismissively.

"It gave me time to get some coffee, which I sorely needed. How have you been?"

"Fine, thanks."

We traded some pleasantries. Lulu was tallish, with bobbed gray hair and eyes as shrewd as they were friendly behind her wire-rimmed glasses. I'd seen pictures of her from shortly after she was put in charge of the Bureau of Policewomen back in 1915 or thereabouts. She'd been a looker and she still had a sparkle that made her seem younger. Her small police badge gleamed on her bodice.

When our plate dinners came, she addressed the question of Heebs along with her food.

"I don't believe the boy you asked about was the victim of foul play. The getting beaten up part was, I'm afraid, the result of a new problem that's cropped up for the city. One that's growing by leaps and bounds and likely to get worse unless we make provisions."

"Does the problem have a name?"

"Oh, yes." She gave a somber nod. "The war."

She paused to extract a hanky trimmed with lavender cutwork iris in one corner and dab at her nose.

"Factories are begging for workers, running three shifts to make weapons, munitions, goodness knows what. I'm sure you know that. You're probably also aware that women are starting to take such jobs.

"For some it's a matter of patriotism. Helping the war effort. For others, it's more a necessity. Their husbands have been called up. Instead of his paycheck from working in one of those factories, or at something else substantial, the wife now is faced with feeding a family and paying the bills on serviceman's pay, which I'm told at least for enlisted men is not substantial. And I suspect for some women, it's the lure of a chance to..." She shrugged. "Spread their wings, I suppose."

"Forgive me, but I don't see what this has to do with Heebs' disappearance."

Lulu smiled.

"Some of those women are working at night. Children, boys mostly, go out even though they've been given strict orders not to. Before all this, living on the streets wasn't especially dangerous for those who had no other choice like your young friend Hobbs."

"Heebs."

"Of course. Heebs. You told me he's a newsboy, I believe?"

"Yes."

She sipped some water.

"What I mean to say is that while their existence was

hard, it wasn't violent. The newsboys got into scrapes sometimes, over territory. They might trade a few punches. One might get a black eye. That was the extent of it. Governor Cox wouldn't stand for his employees on the street acting like ruffians any more than he would the ones in his newsroom."

James Cox wasn't governor now, but he had been for two terms. He'd also been the unsuccessful Democratic candidate for President in 1920 with a young FDR as his running mate. Cox owned the *Dayton Daily News* and a lot of other papers, in Ohio and other states.

"Conditions have changed with this new contingent of young people. Ten days ago another boy was beaten. Rather badly, I'm afraid. He was also a newsboy."

"Why?"

"Because they can." She shook her head sadly. "Mostly these truants — I'll call them that since they're certainly not where their mothers meant them to be — mostly they stick to petty vandalism. Drawing Kilroy on a shop window with soap. Getting rowdy on trolleys. Tipping over a trashcan or, in one case, setting it on fire.

"But the streets are new to them. They're not as brave as they like to pretend. They do their roving in groups of three or four or six. When you have children that age together, unsupervised, they tend to egg each other on." She sighed. "In a few cases lately, they've made a sport of isolating a street boy and roughing him up. Possibly he's refused to give ground when they tried to bully him. Possibly they have tendencies which, if not nipped early, will one day turn them into real troublemakers."

In my mind I could see Heebs refusing to give ground,

especially to boys whose better clothes suggested they weren't as tough as he was. The cocky kid wouldn't think twice about being outnumbered.

Suddenly another thought leapt at me. Kids out at night. Willa Lee Cottle had insisted she heard kids at the construction site the night Foster's body made its debut there. Freeze had dismissed it outright, and I'd been skeptical. Now I set the matter aside for further consideration and focused on the subject at hand.

"But Heebs' friend told me two men pulled Heebs into a car—"

Lulu had taken a bite. She held up a finger. I waited.

"A white car. Yes. I think he's in good hands." She swallowed and blotted her lips. "Perhaps not willingly. Boys like him often resist help even when it's in their best interest." Her eyes twinkled.

From a pocket she produced a slip of paper with four phone numbers on it and slid it toward me.

"I suspect you may locate him through one of these, though not knowing his real name makes it somewhat difficult."

I glanced at the numbers and then at Lulu. She seemed completely unruffled.

"What are these places?"

"Church groups. More accurately, a handful of volunteers at several churches. They've noticed the problem of juveniles roaming at night and grown concerned. They've begun to organize meetings with other churches. I've spoken at them a time or two. They're trying to build support for a curfew. I believe it might be in the city's best interest.

"Until they have a better solution, some of the volunteers drive around and pick up children they find out on their own after ten o'clock. One of our patrolwomen says she's certain one of the volunteers drives a white car."

***

As soon as Lulu and I said our goodbyes, I stopped at a pay phone and tried the four numbers she'd given me. None of them answered. If anyone other than Lulu had given them to me, I might have wondered if they'd even checked to make sure the numbers belonged to the people she claimed they did.

According to her, the do-gooders picking up unaccompanied kids would take the ones with homes back where they belonged, then notify their mothers the following day. Ones like Heebs, with nowhere to go, they would keep overnight. The next day they would try to find a spot for those unfortunates in a children's home or with foster parents. It all sounded well-meant, but a kid like Heebs who had managed on his own for so long would hate being stuck somewhere against his will, and I wasn't far behind.

It wasn't late, but no one I knew very well was around when I got to Finn's. I sat at the bar and had a Guinness and yakked with Rose when she wasn't serving other customers. Then I went home and waited to use the telephone in the downstairs hall. A girl who had moved in the previous week cooed and whispered to her boyfriend for a good ten minutes, at which point I started whistling. That did the trick.

Managing not to wilt under the glare she gave me, I tried the four numbers again. There still was no answer at three of them. A female voice at the one remaining told me shyly to call back in the morning, that everyone was gone except her.

Feeling uncommonly defeated, I dragged upstairs and waited my turn for a bath, which didn't come until half-past eleven. I shampooed my hair so I'd look my best for dancing with Connelly tomorrow. By the time I'd toweled my hair dry enough to make pin curls, my eyelids were drooping. When sleep claimed me, though, it was interrupted by images of a tow-headed newsboy running from shadowy figures, and wondering why Pearlie had left town and what had been in the envelope I burned for Rachel.

***

While my conscience yelled in my ear that I was irresponsible, and that in an entire week what I'd found to help Rachel could fit in a thimble, the first thing I did the following morning was try to find Heebs.

"Yes, we do have a boy who was beaten up, and yes, he gives his name as Heebs," said a cautious voice where I'd spoken to the young woman the previous night.

"What's your address? I'll be right over."

"Are you a relative?"

She'd already told me the address before she asked her question. Pretending not to hear it, I hung up.

The address went with a modest white frame house of medium size on a quiet street. A neatly painted sign in front said HELPING HANDS. A slip of a girl not old enough to vote yet let me in and showed me into a cramped room that served as an office for a hatchet-faced woman.

"I'm Maggie Sullivan," I said. "I'm here to get Heebs. Lulu Sollers said you were probably the ones who had him, and told me about the swell job you're doing looking out for kids."

I gave my brightest smile. Hatchets don't soften easily.

"Lulu Sollers," she repeated. "The police matron?"

"She's not a matron." My smile began to wither. "She's a sworn officer."

"Well, you can't just waltz in and take him. If you'd stayed on the phone a minute, I would have told you that. We've already made arrangements for him to move to Miller Children's Home this afternoon. They'll house him and feed him and teach him a trade."

"Then I'm saving them a bed, which I've always heard are in short supply at such places."

"I can't just turn him over to you on your say-so."

"Do I look like a white slaver?"

The sound of glass shattering on the closed door to an adjoining room interrupted what was shaping up to be a fine set-to.

"Hey, sis!" yelled Heebs. "Maggie! I'm in here!"

Hatchet Face stormed to the closed oak door.

"And you're going to stay in there until you settle down, young man. This door is locked, as is the one in the hall. You might as well save yourself further pain and stay in bed."

"The Bible comes next, lady."

Hatchet Face paled.

"Stay put," I shouted from my spot at her elbow. "And don't throw anything else! She's going to unlock it."

I whirled. The woman beside me retreated a step.

"What do you mean about pain? What kind of pain is he in?"

She threw up her hands as if fearful I might hit her.

"He'd been beaten up. By other boys, he said." With amazing alacrity she fished a ring with a couple of keys from her pocket. Her hand shook so she could scarcely fit it into the lock. "We had a doctor look at him. We thought his ankle might be broken, but the doctor said it was just a sprain. He recommended bed rest for a day, but the boy won't cooperate. I have other chores. I couldn't sit here keeping an eye on him every minute, so - so I locked him in."

The door swung open. Heebs sat propped up in a bed with pillows behind him. One of his eyes was black and purple and swollen completely shut. The other had a bandage beneath it suggesting a cut. One cheek was scraped and his mouth was swollen.

"Holy smokes," I managed when I trusted my voice. "You trying to copy me?"

In spite of his thick lips he gave a lopsided grin.

"Hey, sis, am I ever glad to see you."

"You *said* you didn't have relatives." Behind me, Hatchet Face was recovering enough to be indignant.

"Aw, I was sore at her. She keeps making up rules."

I sighed dramatically. "Well, *you've* seen what he's like," I said to the woman. "You'll have to mend your ways, Heebs, if you want to come home with me."

The woman scooped pieces of the crockery mug Heebs

had broken onto a folded newspaper. She smacked it into a wastebasket in irritation.

"You are a family member then? If so, then I can release him into your care."

Heebs' one good eye sought mine in mute appeal. I took a breath.

"Do second cousins count?" I asked carefully.

"Second..."

"Or maybe twice removed. Those cousin things get so confusing." If you started with Adam and Eve, didn't we all qualify as cousins?

"Well, I suppose... If you're going to be responsible for him..."

Heebs stuck one leg out from under the covers. The ankle was heavily bandaged. "I'll behave, sis. Honest. So if you two ladies will step outside and let me put on my trousers—"

"Hang on just a minute, Heebs."

Reality was hitting me. I hadn't thought this through. I hadn't expected to find him in this bad shape, either. An ice bag and a glass with milk residue sat on a small table next to him. Heebs was being well cared for here and it looked like the people running the place had good intentions, even if I couldn't say much for their techniques.

Letting the kid get sent to an orphanage was out of the question, though. It might be the best thing for him, but I couldn't stomach the thought. Trouble was, I couldn't think of an alternative.

"I need to make some arrangements for him," I said. "Can I leave him here until four o'clock?"

TWENTY-FOUR

Not having the least idea what to do about Heebs, I concentrated on work. After talking to Lulu last night, I wanted to see if Willa Lee could tell me anything more, any little detail, about hearing kids at the construction site, or in the vicinity, on the night Foster's body was found.

Things appeared to be humming along on Rachel's project. I parked the DeSoto half a block away in case Hawkins came backing out and swung around too fast the way he had when he mashed the rose bushes. Crossing my fingers that Willa Lee wasn't away every Tuesday morning, I rang her doorbell. She didn't answer. It was a beautiful day, and she was a woman who took a lot of interest in her yard. I went around the side of the house thinking I might find her in the back yard. And hoping she didn't have her rifle if she was.

"Oh, it's you," she said looking up from where she knelt in a good-sized garden plot. "I wondered who was ringing the bell."

If I'd shared any of Freeze's skepticism about her hearing, I didn't now.

"Nice garden." I looked at rows where shoots of green were just coming up, some with slender poles at the end of the rows and some with no indication that something was in them except their furrows. "Spinach, peas and... turnips?" I guessed.

Willa Lee gave the end of a row a smack with her trowel and sat back on her haunches. A broad-brimmed straw hat with an unfinished edge shaded her gray head. She was wearing overalls.

"Salsify. Don't care for turnips much. But you're not here to talk gardening. What do you want?"

"I'd like to ask a few more questions about those kids you heard, if you have time."

"Have to get my planting finished this morning. Have places to go come noontime."

"Could we talk while you work?"

"I've been planting beans all my life, just about. Reckon I could plant 'em in my sleep." Picking the trowel up, she used it to point at the back stoop. "You can sit if you don't mind getting your skirt dirty. Fire away."

Tucking my skirt beneath me, I sat on the steps. For several moments I sat just enjoying the feel of the sun on my face and the sound of the birds. It was partly for Willa Lee's benefit. She was watching me from the edge of her eye.

"What kids around here have been in trouble before? Or maybe just aren't supervised as well as they should be?"

"None that could be the same ones I heard over there, if that's what you're thinking."

It brought me up short.

"Why not?"

"Not old enough." She began dribbling seeds so small I couldn't see them into the furrow she'd just drawn. "Houses around here, half the people in them are old as me, or older. Those where people have died or moved out, young families live there now. Their children are still little.

Joanie Beck and her sister Nancy are the oldest around for at least eight blocks every direction. Well, just two directions really now. It's all businesses there and there." She pointed. "Anyway, those Beck girls are what, nine and ten now? Still in the elementary school. Those ones I heard running that night the feller got killed, they were teenagers."

I managed to recover my voice.

"You saw them?"

"Nope." She hesitated. "I may have caught a glimpse. Just of shapes, though. I thought I saw a couple of heads bobbing. But it was just for a blink, and that was all. Could have been shadows. How I know it was teenagers was the sound of the running. The way the feet slapped."

I must have looked blank. She sat back on her haunches again.

"Don't have children, do you?"

"Uh, no."

"No younger brothers or sisters?"

"No."

"We had a boy," she said softly. "Died when he was thirteen and a half. That's how I know how they sound, listening to him and his friends as they grew up.

"Little ones, now, they've got little bitty feet. When they run they go pitty-pat. But come around eleven or twelve, those feet of theirs grow. My law, how those feet slap when they run."

She smiled at memories. Her face was almost pretty. Recalling herself she drew the trowel along to make another furrow with neat precision.

"Anyway, that and who's in the neighborhood is how I know they were older."

I had wrapped my arms around my knees, fascinated by what she said. It wasn't the sort of thing Freeze would give much weight to, or Joel Minsky either. As logical as she seemed to be, I was inclined to believe her, not only that there'd been kids around, but her assessment of their ages. Was it possible there had been witnesses to Foster's murder?

***

The foreman at Rachel's project stopped to watch as I crossed the street.

"You've been at that old lady's this whole time and she didn't run you off?" he asked in disbelief. "I saw you heading over there."

"She's interesting, but then I haven't seen her with a rifle yet."

He chuckled.

"Do you have time for me to ask you a couple of things?"

"I do. Could use a break anyway. We've been at it since half past seven, trying to make up some time."

He gestured to a stack of boards and we seated ourselves.

"You've had kids poking around here, somebody told me."

"Just a couple of times. It happens once the weather turns nice and they start cooking up things to do Sunday afternoons, or after supper when it gets light enough. Take a board and put it over a sawhorse to make a seesaw, sometimes. Never realize they could get hurt if they started the stack they got it from falling."

"They don't take anything?"

"Naw. Well, a box of screws a few weeks back. Wasn't worth ten cents."

A few weeks back. It more than fit the timeframe of the problem Lulu Sollers had described to me. It was also close enough to the night of Foster's demise to catch my interest.

"You're sure they've never been around at night."

"Kids? Naw. Although..."

He frowned. My eyebrows urged him on.

"The morning that body turned up and all the police were here, I did notice the tarp we put over that big pile of lumber yonder was flipped up and kind of crooked. I wouldn't have seen this side from the street when I drove by Sunday, though. And they could have come around after supper, like I say."

"But you're sure that was kids?"

"Yeah." He dragged it out in the mildly indulgent way some men use to dismiss harmless foolishness in the young. Same bunch, too."

"How do you know?"

He chuckled. "Candy wrappers. One of the kids must like Whiz bars. Left two wrappers both times. He doesn't just crumple them up and throw them down, though. He folds them flat and twists them in the center like bow ties before he drops them."

It sounded to me more like something a grownup would do.

"How do you know it's not one of your own men?"

"First of all, I'd wring their necks for throwing trash down. And men don't go around eating candy bars out where people can see them."

"What?"

"Oh, I like one now and again. My wife brings home a couple of Milky Ways in case I want one in the evening, or on Saturday when I'm mowing the grass and that. But I've never brought one to work, and I've never seen one of the men working with me take one out of his lunch pail."

It didn't persuade me quite as much as Willa Lee Cottle's footstep analysis, but I nodded. He stood up and stretched.

"Better get back."

"One more quick question. Once when I stopped by last week, you were helping a man who wasn't too pleased about it to his car. He'd come by trying to hire men from this crew."

His voice hardened. "I remember."

"You said there'd been someone else who tried earlier. Who?"

He shook his head. "Nobody I'd ever seen before. Can't give you a name."

"I know who he was."

Morris, the man with the droopy eye, had come up. His khaki shirt showed patches of sweat, and he was breathing as if he'd loped over.

"There's a problem at that corner," he said to the foreman.

Forgetting me entirely, the foreman took off. Morris lifted his carpenter's cap and wiped his face with a bandana.

"His name's Lamont. I was part of the crew on a project of his back before I got on regular with Miss Minsky."

Lamont. A man who had professed to be stretched too thin to hire more workers.

TWENTY-FIVE

Freeze wasn't interested in Willa Lee's information about kids running when I called to share it. I turned my attention to Heebs. When I still hadn't figured out quite what to do with him after half an hour of nonproductive doodling on the tablet in front of me, I called a woman I knew. She ran a second-hand shop aimed at helping people, and knew just about every resource there was in the city for people who were down on their luck. Twenty minutes after that, she called back with an address for me, and information enough to answer the questions she knew I'd have.

Gasoline had shot up in price. It was fifteen cents now. I filled up and drove by the place that now might figure, in my plans for Heebs. The ugly little brick building was squeezed in between two equally drab but decently maintained commercial buildings. The name above the door said Weldon House and it was a shelter. It wasn't like a gospel mission where you got a cot and a meal in return for sitting through prayer meetings. It charged a fee that was slightly more than you'd pay at a flophouse, for which you got, I was assured, considerably better facilities.

Directly across the street was a small café. I parked and got out and checked to see if the café served breakfast through supper. It looked okay. I crossed the street and went into Weldon House. It looked okay too, so I made some arrangements.

With that off my mind, I had a fresh look at what I'd learned from Willa Lee in our two conversations:

– She'd heard two shots.

– A short time later, she'd heard a scream.

– After that she'd heard kids running.

The part about kids being present fit with candy wrappers turning up at the site across the way. So did the dislodged tarpaulin the foreman had noticed. Suppose some kids had been nosing around the site and they'd heard or seen a car pull up. Ducking under the tarp would have seemed like a smart move to them. At least it would have to Wee Willie and me when we were that age. Which meant those kids had seen, or heard, whatever happened to Gabriel Foster.

That scream Willa Lee had heard... According to her, there had been a lag between shots and scream. The running came after the scream.

I bounced my index finger up and down between my teeth to create a woodpecker sound.

What I had was plenty of theory without much evidence to back it up, but it wasn't the first time I'd wandered into that territory. Wasn't that how theories were supposed to work? You had an idea and looked for evidence that proved or disproved it.

As much as I liked the theory, I wasn't about to focus my efforts on finding some kids who might or might not know something worthwhile. Especially when all I had to go on was that one of them liked Whiz bars and folded the wrappers funny when he discarded them. It was worth giving Lulu Sollers a call, though, which I did, leaving a message with the particulars.

Taking care of routine business matters like paying bills

and making a couple of calls for the background checks that provided my bread and butter ate up the morning. It left the early hours of the afternoon for thinking about the other fact I'd unearthed that morning — that Lamont, who pleaded hard times, had been attempting to hire away Rachel's workers. The day I talked to him, I'd written off his nervousness as just part of his nature. Now I wondered if there could be more to it.

Lamont had been quick to insist he didn't have the means to take on the project left rudderless by Gabe Foster's death. Had it been because he saw that saying otherwise might be construed as a motive for Foster's murder? If he was simply a worrywart, he might have seen that possibility even though innocent. Or, he might have pleaded lack of resources because of a guilty conscience, not because he'd killed Foster, but over something else.

Whatever the case, it was worth having another chat with him. Right now it was almost time to pick up Heebs.

***

"Least I got a new pair of shoes from this place," Heebs said as we inched our way from the place that had kept him overnight to my car.

"Yeah, I noticed. Shirt and pants too, looks like."

"Inside out." His swollen face approximated a grin.

"Sure you don't want to hang onto my arm?" Having had a couple of beatings myself, I knew walking must be causing him discomfort, if not outright pain.

"Nah. I'm okay."

"Suit yourself. I don't offer many fellas a chance like that, though."

"Hadn't thought of that."

He took my arm.

"What're you going to do with me?" he asked when I'd settled him in the car and pulled away from the curb.

"That's your decision. I'll tell you about it when we get to my office."

To my amazement, the elevator in the building was going up when we entered the lobby. I grinned, thinking Jenkins should have waited a day to bring up the sewing machine. Heebs hadn't said half a dozen words on the way over. He didn't utter a one on the way up. The unease coming from him was palpable. The longer we'd known each other, the more he'd come to trust me. Now I might give him reason not to. When I'd turned on the lights in my office, I swung a chair around for him and sat across from him.

"Here's the deal, Heebs. There's a move afoot to get kids off the street at night. Right now it's volunteers like the people who picked you up, but the city's looking to take action too. That means if I let you go back out there the same way you have been — which I'll do if you want — you're likely to get picked up again. If that happens, you'll get sent to one of those homes like they were fixing to send you to this time, and I can't run around looking for you again. I've got work to do, Heebs."

He swallowed.

"Now I've got a business proposition for you. Just for a week or so, while your face is so banged up no one's going to buy a paper from you anyway. I need somebody to answer my phone. I'm out a lot, and I can't afford to miss any calls right now. I've paid a week's rent for you at a place with rooms. If you're interested, you can work it off answering my phone and maybe doing another thing or two around here. I won't pay you anything more except enough for meals and maybe a magazine now and then. What do you say?"

His mouth was opening to accept without even thinking when the phone rang. I grabbed it before Heebs could take it into his head to show off his skills.

"Maggie Sullivan."

A woman cleared her throat.

"Miss Sullivan, this is Miriam Minsky. Rachel's mother. I... One of my daughters believes if you met our family, it might make it easier for you to help Rachel."

It took a second to find my voice.

"It might. Yes."

"Could you come for coffee with my daughters and me tomorrow? I know it's short notice, but—"

"It would help me considerably, and I know you have some sort of, ah, religious days about to start. What time?"

"Half-past three? If you have things you'd like to discuss with Rachel afterward..."

"I'll be there. And thank you, Mrs. Minsky. Thank you very much."

The nature of the invitation, as well as its unexpectedness, made me forget Heebs' presence until he spoke.

"Did you just break a case, sis?"

"Umm? No. Something that may help, though. Let's get going."

"It's early."

"Not much, and I have a date tonight. I want to primp."

TWENTY-SIX

"Based on my impartial survey, you're the second prettiest girl in the room," Connelly murmured in my ear as we moved to the hypnotic strains of "Dancing in the Dark" at Hotel Miami.

Leaning back a few inches to see his face, I lifted an eyebrow.

"And number one is...?"

"The girl selling cigarettes. I've a weakness for redheads."

The cigarette seller was middle-aged and the red so obviously out of a bottle a blind man could see it. I laughed.

On rare occasions I felt pretty, but never beautiful. I almost did tonight. On Ione Jenkins' last trip to New York, I'd given her money to buy me something swanky at a discount place she'd told me about. I was wearing her selection, a steel blue jersey number with a darker appliqué edged in sequins on one shoulder. Or maybe it was Connelly's arm around me that made the difference.

The music brought us to the end of the dance floor and we turned. I missed a step.

"Maggie? Anything wrong?"

"That man coming in. He works at Rachel's site."

It was Hawkins, dressed in a suit with his hair slicked, looking out of his element and all the more belligerent for it as he glared at the maitre d'. The head of the girl with him came to his shoulder. She was looking around in awe.

"Big bruiser," Connelly observed.

"Yeah, and I'm wondering where he got the money to turn up here."

"Shall I go and inquire?"

I pretended to consider. "He might take exception."

The music stopped. We returned to our table. Hawkins wasn't satisfied with the first one he was shown to, and the waiter led the way to a second. As soon as he sat down, Hawkins looked around. His eyes came to rest on me and he gave an unpleasant smile. Surely he wasn't following me. I would have noticed him, and he'd have to go home and put on a suit and find a date, assuming he wasn't married. I resolved not to let Hawkins' presence spoil my evening.

Our second cocktails of the evening arrived.

"I took my physical today," Connelly said casually. "Selective Service."

I looked up in dismay.

"You needn't worry," he said with a wry smile. "They wouldn't have me. Some nonsense about rheumatic fever might have weakened my heart."

"You never said anything about getting a draft notice."

"I didn't. I meant to enlist. Water under the bridge now."

"The chief will be glad not to lose you."

"And you?"

The tip of his finger touched mine on the table.

"Yeah. I'm not going to pretend I'm not."

Uncomfortably I recognized that it made a difference when the vague abstraction of men going off to war changed to the concrete image of someone you cared about. Now I understood why a woman down the hall from my office had fought tooth and nail in behalf of isolationism. She couldn't bear the thought of her only son going.

Connelly smiled at me.

"Let's dance some more."

What he'd told me made me gladder than ever to be in Connelly's arms. Twice more in the course of the evening I caught Hawkins staring at me. Whatever his reason for being here, I wasn't going to waste thought on it until tomorrow.

"Since it looks like you're going to be underfoot," I said over dinner, "what have you heard about kids on the streets at night? Or seen when you're working that shift?"

"Kids?"

I told him about Heebs, and my conversation with Lulu. He hadn't noticed anything out of the ordinary.

When the hour grew late and we left the restaurant, Hawkins made no move to follow. He noticed our departure though, and favored me with another malicious smile.

Connelly usually drove when we went out together. He'd started to talk about getting a car of his own, but the war had put an end to that as production of new cars stopped and prices for used ones rose. At the widow's house where he rented an attic room, he came around and opened the passenger door for me to get out.

"Thanks, Mick. It was the loveliest night I've had in years. Maybe ever."

"Me too. Aren't you going to walk me to my door and say a proper goodnight?"

I laughed. "Sure, why not?"

The springtime weather was holding. Somewhere close at hand a flowering bush filled the night with light, sweet scent. At the foot of the wooden stairs leading up to his outside entrance, he slid an arm around me and gathered me to him. We kissed lightly, and then more deeply, exploring each other as we never had. My hands slid under his jacket. He cupped me against him more tightly than we'd been on the dance floor. The kisses grew deeper. Our breathing quickened.

Abruptly his mouth left mine.

"Come up with me, Maggie."

***

In the upstairs hall at Mrs. Z's the next morning, I leaned against the wall with a towel on my shoulders, waiting with some of the other girls for my turn in the bathroom. By unspoken agreement, no one took a bath in the morning. You washed your face, brushed your teeth and did your business. No dilly-dallying.

While I waited, my thoughts floated aimlessly between extremely pleasant memories of Connelly's arms around me when we were dancing, and regret about saying no to him at the end of the evening. It hadn't been from fear of losing my virginity. I'd given that up to curiosity when I was in high school. The experience had been disappointing. I had a feeling with Connelly it would be anything but.

When I was with Connelly I didn't feel alone; I felt safe; I felt part of something I wanted to grab and hold forever. And I feared that I might lose myself if I did. So instead, I'd caught his face in my hands and given him a quick kiss, and walked to my car.

The bathroom door opened. Familiar smells of toothpaste and Palmolive soap puffed out. It was my turn.

When I got to my office, Heebs was sitting on the floor outside my door. Hampered by his sprained ankle, he got awkwardly to his feet.

"Say, that place I'm staying is okay. There's a bed and a chair and space enough to turn around without hitting your elbow if you don't do it fast. There's even a room downstairs where you can read or play cards.

"I was in by eight like you said. Good thing, too. I could hardly keep my eyes open long enough to wash my face. I probably ought to have another pair of drawers, sis, since I'm working for you. So I can wash the other pair out every night."

"Sure. Okay."

I'd laid down some ground rules before dropping him at the place he was going to stay yesterday. In addition to being in by eight every night, he wasn't to have any words with the braggart who'd taken over his corner. The kid would give it back when the time came, I assured Heebs, without adding that I intended to see to that personally. Most important of all, he wasn't to do anything if he spotted any of the boys who had beaten him. He was to let me know where and when he'd spotted them, if he did. I hinted that the police were interested in them and didn't want them scared off. It seemed like a smart fib.

Since more than a dozen hours had passed, and Heebs hadn't been in the best of shape when I dispensed them, I had him repeat the rules back while I fished out money for underwear.

While he did, letter perfect, I went to the oak file cabinet to get him a tablet. I didn't want the messages he took to get mixed in with the jottings and lists I had on mine, or worse, a page of mine to get ripped out. When I opened the drawer of the oak file cabinet, a pencil rolled off the top. Oblivious to some question Heebs was asking, I bent to retrieve it.

Pencils came in handy at a file cabinet. They were better than a finger for sorting through files. You could stick one in to mark where you'd removed a folder. But I'd learned a long time ago not to leave one on top because as soon as I opened a drawer it would roll to the floor. If the women who cleaned found a stray, they put it in the pencil holder on my desk. Between the time Heebs and I left together yesterday and when we came in this morning, someone had been in my office.

**

Being an early bird did pay off in worms. Winfred Lamont, the nervous one among the other bidders on Foster's project, was in when I called. He didn't seem thrilled at the prospect of renewing our acquaintance, but said if I could get there in the next half hour, he would spare me a few minutes.

I took just long enough to give Heebs some basics. I showed him the list of most used numbers in the front of my phone book, and the temporary list I'd attached to it.

"With anybody named Minsky, get all the information you can and tell them I'll call as soon as I get back. That shouldn't be more than an hour, hour and a half. If Joel

Minsky calls, or someone from his office, tell him where I was headed in case he wants to try and reach me there. This goes for the whole time you're working here, by the way."

He scribbled furiously on his pad. Reassured that the kid would manage, although possibly in a less-than-conventional way, I took off.

Two men in workmen's clothes were leaving the nuts-and-bolts side of Lamont's construction office when I arrived. One backed a pickup truck around to the side of the building while his pal ambled after him. I parked and went in the door to the fancier part.

"Mr. Lamont said to bring you right through," his Girl Friday said, jumping up to comply. No sooner had we stepped through the archway into the short hallway leading to his office than we could hear him on the phone.

"Don't think for a minute I'm going to— You told me I didn't need to— What if I can't, huh? What if I can't?"

His secretary rapped discreetly on the door and cleared her throat.

"Mr. Lamont? Miss Sullivan's here."

"Someone's here," he snapped. A minute later, he opened the door.

"Come in." Despite his attempt at a smile, he looked furious. Red flushed his cheeks.

"Bad start to the day?" I asked mildly.

"Oh, er, family squabble. You know how that can be, I expect. Some days it sounds tempting to be an orphan." His chuckle was forced. "Sit down. What was it you wanted to ask?"

"When we talked last week, you said that even if an overture were made to you to take over Gabe Foster's project, you didn't have the wherewithal to hire more men.

169

Shortage of funds, I believe you said."

"That's right. I'm not proud to admit it, but there you are."

"That makes me wonder why you tried to hire workers away from Rachel Minsky's site a day after she was arrested."

"I... Wherever did you get that idea?"

"From the men on the site."

"They - they misunderstood." His eyes flicked nervously to the family photographs on the wall behind him, avoiding my gaze. "I wasn't... That is, I just thought one or two of them might be interested in guaranteed work since - since there was no telling what would happen on that project. I've lost one man to the draft and one to factory work. Anybody will tell you that's happening."

I waited. He shifted irritably.

"I suppose I might have hired a third if I could. Just in case."

"In that case, I hope the foreman didn't hustle you off by the arm the way he did Phil Clark when he tried to poach workers there."

"Clark?" If possible, he was redder now than when I'd come in.

"You didn't know he went there?"

"No. No, of course not. Why would I? He's a-a rival."

"Scuttlebutt? You fellows in the construction business seem fond of that. Which makes me wonder why you didn't tell me about the story Foster spread about Miss Minsky."

He colored, as I'd known he would.

"I don't believe in spreading gossip. It would demean me as much as the person who started it."

TWENTY-SEVEN

Heebs had fielded three phone calls in my absence. One wanted to sell me insurance, one was a wrong number, and one was a woman wanting me to find her missing cat.

"I took down her name and her number and told her you'd call back to set up a time to come in," he said proudly, handing me the slip he'd written.

"You did great, Heebs, only I forgot to tell you I don't look for dogs or kitties."

"She says it's real valuable, sis. I could do it, I bet. I've helped you out three or four times now. I know how—"

"You need a license, Heebs, for which you first need experience, either as a policeman or guard or store security.

"Now listen. Are you in good enough shape to go across the street and get a sandwich when you get hungry? Here's some money. I want to take a gander at something at Market House and I'm not sure when I'll be back. Maybe before noon and maybe after."

Or maybe in the next fifteen minutes if Freeze threw me out on my ear.

***

"You want to look at Foster's financial records?" he repeated staring at me. He had his hat on and was standing

171

behind his desk, but I wasn't sure if he was coming or going. Boike was on the phone.

"I know it's a lot to ask, Freeze."

"Yeah. It is."

Taking a cigarette from his mouth, he contemplated it for a moment.

"What is it you think you'll find?"

"I don't know. Honestly." I considered it some myself. "I want to get an idea how much a contract like the one for that project he was working on is worth. What the expenses are. Whether his bank account was getting fatter because he'd been getting bigger contracts, or even a different sort of contracts. Does that make sense?"

"Yeah. Maybe."

"I have data on some other construction projects around here. Maybe if I get a picture of Foster's doings and compare it with those, something will pop out."

Freeze scraped his teeth across his lower lip while wrinkling his nose. He was thinking.

"If I let you look through them, you'll share anything you do come across with me?"

"Cross my heart."

He did the business with his teeth and nose again.

"Not sure I should do it, but it's coming at it from a different angle, not what Boike and I look at. And like you said a while ago, we're short on help. I've got to lend a hand to the auto theft boys, and Boike's off to have another go at Foster's widow. Those three boxes there." He pointed. "Nobody's using the desk they're on. Don't take them out of the building."

***

As soon as I undid the lid of the first box, I had a feeling I'd bitten off more than I wanted to chew, never mind my ability. Invoices. Payments. Receipts. For nails. For lumber. For permits and inspection fees; for moving piles of dirt around; electricians, plumbers, taxes and wages. You name it. His cancelled checks on personal and business accounts were just the tip of a very large iceberg.

From time to time one of the other detectives sharing the room with Freeze or Boike came in or left. They talked on the phone. One pecked at a typewriter. Most looked at notes they'd made on pads like the one Boike carried. Two left and returned shortly carrying mugs of coffee, confirming the rumor that they kept a hotplate somewhere in the building. The one at the desk nearest me was working his way doggedly through a pleated file. Occasionally he held one of the sheets it contained in front of his desk lamp and squinted.

My eyeballs felt as though they'd been scoured by the time Boike returned. Two hours had passed.

"Learn anything?" he asked.

"Yeah. That I'm glad I'm a one-person operation and the only supplies required to do my job are pencils and brains."

"And bullets. You use some of those."

"What about you?"

"I decided I don't blame Foster for having a girlfriend."

"Why? Is the wife a shrew?"

"She cries."

"You'd be suspicious if a newly widowed woman didn't cry, wouldn't you?"

"I don't mean she just cries about the deceased — how wonderful he was, and she doesn't know how she'll stand it sitting down at the table without him. She cried about how she'd ordered a new sofa and he won't get to see it. She cried about how his secretary and the poor clerk who's struggling to keep his office stumbling along keep calling her for decisions. I don't think it's even crossed her mind to be grateful to them. The woman can't get two sentences out without turning on the waterworks."

"Or giggling." Freeze came through the door and tossed his hat on his desk. "When she's not crying, she does that. Get anything, Boike?"

"Not that we didn't get last time. Just asking if Foster had gotten any strange phone calls or had differences with anyone made her dissolve."

I'd never heard them talk so openly about someone on the periphery of one of their cases, let alone with such disgust.

"Are you sure Mrs. Foster's not just a good actress?" I asked.

Freeze snorted.

"The dame's too dizzy to think about anything but clothes and wallpaper. Nothing sticks in her head long enough to even come up with the idea of killing her husband, let alone hire someone."

I wasn't so sure. A dainty little vision of an adoring wife had almost killed me once.

"You finding anything?" Freeze asked me, indicating the boxes.

"Not yet."

He tilted his head at Boike. "Let's go eat."

***

Around two o'clock that afternoon, I found what I'd been looking for.

At any rate I came across a crumb that drew my attention enough to make me pause. Near the top of the third box, among other checks, was one Foster hadn't cashed. It was stapled to a blank sheet of paper and made out for the not insubstantial sum of fifty dollars. It was from Win Lamont.

Leaning back in my chair, I blinked my eyes to try and summon moisture back into them. I wanted to make sure I was seeing correctly.

The check had been drawn on Lamont's personal account, not the one for his business. It was made out to Foster personally as well. Whatever the check had been for, it didn't appear to be a business transaction. Yet Lamont had explicitly told me his only connection with Foster was through business and that they didn't socialize.

Most likely there was an innocent explanation for the payment, but I couldn't think of one. A hefty contribution for some charity? If the check were made out by Rachel, or even Phil Clark or Oscar Jones, I might buy that explanation, but Lamont didn't seem like the type. Especially the way he'd grumbled about hard times the last few years. The overriding question, however, was why it hadn't been cashed.

Fifty dollars wasn't chicken feed. Given that the minimum wage was thirty cents an hour, it would cover a month's rent on a nice apartment like Gloria's with money left over.

I'd been working my way back through the financial

documents. Now, quickly, I went through the ones for the previous two months. It was new territory. Nothing further jumped out at me there.

I looked at the date on the check and noted it on my notepad. Using it as the pivot point, I went forward again. Roughly five weeks after the check had been written was when Foster had signed the lease on his love nest for Gloria. It was also around the time his bank account began to have more money in it.

Had Foster needed a loan for some kind of investment? For some undertaking on the side, maybe? If so, it didn't seem logical that he'd ask for one of that size from someone he didn't know outside of business. Why not just go to a bank? And again, if he'd needed money, why had the check remained uncashed?

I went back for a more orderly plod through the two months prior to the check. No invoices hinted at unexpected expenses. No fifty dollar expense was evident in Foster's business or personal accounts. The only thing I could see that had changed was that right about the time Lamont wrote the check to Foster, Foster's fortunes had taken a turn for the better. Right up until he got a bullet in his head.

TWENTY-EIGHT

Standing on the doorstep of the Minsky house that afternoon, I had a new understanding of what young men must experience as they faced initial inspection by the family of a girl they wanted to court. I'd put on my good suit and silk blouse and the strand of pearls my dad had given me for high school graduation. Rachel greeted me with a hug and a peck on the cheek, something we didn't usually do, or ever do for that matter.

A woman with a firm chin and steel gray hair done in an impeccable French twist stepped forward and offered her hand.

"Miss Sullivan, I'm Miriam Minsky, Rachel's mother."

"Maggie, please. How nice to meet you."

She led the way into a parlor considerably larger than the one where Rachel and I had talked on my previous visit. She introduced me to the three women arrayed there. One had wavy red hair and wore too much jewelry. One was determinedly plain with her victory roll, shapeless navy dress and absence of makeup. The third, who wore a smart sailor dress and had a gleaming cap of black hair, was called Mo. They were Rachel's sisters-in-law.

Silence thundered around us. They studied me with polite but uncertain curiosity.

"Rachel says you used to work for the Rikes. In their

store," said the one called Mo after several awkward seconds had passed. "That must have been interesting."

"We generally shop at Beerman's," the redhead noted.

"How do you manage to watch what's going on in such a large area?" Mo asked.

I appreciated their attempts at conversation, stilted as they were. I tried to hold up my end with my responses. Rachel sat clasping her hands together as tightly as they'd gripped the bars of her jail cell. Her eyes whipped from speaker to speaker, and occasionally darted a glance at her mother.

Meanwhile Mrs. Minsky poured coffee from a silver pot that would have challenged the muscles of some of the men at Rachel's site. She was taller than Rachel, and well preserved for her age, but the flesh around her mouth was taut with worry. When she'd passed around a plate of coconut macaroons she cleared her throat, bringing conversation that had become more relaxed to an end.

"I'm afraid we're a bit short on time today," she apologized. "We're preparing for a religious observance. We understand you think talking to us might somehow help you prove Rachel's innocence? Perhaps we should start."

"Joel said we might think some of your questions insulting." The one without makeup spoke softly. Her voice was lovely. I had the impression she was Joel's wife.

"I'm not going to ask if any of you are hiding a past as a gun moll, if that's what you're thinking."

The redhead giggled. She smothered it at a look from her mother-in-law. Mrs. Minsky nodded at me.

"Ask whatever you need to."

"We want to help Rachel. All of us," Mo said.

Joel Minsky underestimated the womenfolk in his family, I thought. I set my coffee cup aside.

"What I'm hoping is that one of you may remember something out of the ordinary these last three months or so. Even the smallest thing. A phone call where someone hangs up when you answer. Someone you met who asked a lot of questions related to Rachel. Perhaps one of your husbands mentioned someone angry over a business matter. Things like that."

Rachel's mother fingered a double strand of gray pearls circling her neck. If they were real, as I suspected, they were impressively large.

"You think this might be because of someone else in our family rather than Rachel?"

I shook my head. "I don't think anything. I'm looking for what I might not have considered. There are things — a lot of things — about this that don't add up."

The women looked at one another. No one averted her gaze. No one appeared uneasy.

"My husband makes a lot of enemies, I'm sure. Because of his work," his wife said softly. "He's never mentioned anything, but..."

"We've already talked about it. He had a man in his firm look into it."

They sat thinking. Mrs. Minsky stirred, preparing to rise.

"If anything does occur to us—"

"Wait." Mo held up a hand. "It's a small thing, but it *was* odd." She looked at her mother-in-law. "That night I was over here so you could help me undo the mess I'd made with my cross-stitch. The phone call. Remember?"

The older woman frowned. "Faintly. Something about the philharmonic?"

"Philharmonic?" echoed Rachel.

"I teased you about it next day, about who was your mystery man." Mo addressed me now. "Mama had her big glasses on and strands of yard twisted around her fingers from the stitches she was picking out. The phone rang and I said I'd answer it. A man asked if Rachel had left for the philharmonic yet, that he was supposed to meet her there, but she hadn't shown up.

"I said she'd already gone and offered to take a message. But he said, 'Oh, here she is,' and hung up the phone."

Rachel had started to nod.

"When you kidded me, I told you the only person I was supposed to meet that night was Cassie Kline."

The others seemed to know who that was.

"When was this?" I asked.

She thought for a minute.

"Not this last time. It must have been the time before, so a couple of months."

Mo tried, but couldn't remember any more details. At an undetectable signal from Mrs. Minsky, the three younger women said goodby and returned to the kitchen. I heard excited murmuring as they compared notes.

Mrs. Minsky, smiling slightly, watched until they were gone. Then she turned to me. "Good women, all of them, but so is my Rachel. Rachel is my treasure."

Her daughter shot a startled look in her direction.

***

"Who would have thought my own mother could amaze me?" Rachel flounced onto the rose colored sofa in the small parlor across from the one we'd been in. She extracted a pack of cigarettes wedged between cushion and arm.

"They care about you, Rachel. All of them do." In the beginning I'd wondered about it. Now I didn't.

"Yeah, I know. I want to think the worst of them because they treat me like a prisoner, even though I know they have to. I resent the fact I'm in this mess, and I turn it on them."

"I could lend you a rosary if you want to keep confessing sins. I'm pretty sure I still have one somewhere."

She gave me a hard look, then grinned. Taking a drag or two on her cigarette had improved her mood.

"That phone call Mo mentioned, did that come before or after your earring went missing?"

"Don't know. I'm not exactly sure when I noticed about the earring. I went to put them on one day and one wasn't there."

"When you started to put them on."

"Yes."

"Not when you went to put them away?"

"No. Why...? Ah." She sat up, shrewd and alert like the old Rachel. "You're thinking that means it didn't fall out of my ear?"

"Exactly. Somebody took one out of your jewelry box, or wherever you keep them. If someone established that you were tucked away at a concert for a couple of hours, they'd have plenty of time. If they could get in."

She made a sound of annoyance. "Which they probably could. The cleaning people open the window at the end of the hall to air things out while they're cleaning there. They forget to lock it again more often than not. I've heard the supervisor chewing them out about it a time or two. The window opens onto the fire escape."

I digested that. "They'd still need a key to get into your apartment. Did anyone else have a key?"

Her head shook insistently. "No."

"But you have a spare?"

"Yes."

"And keep it where?"

"In a dish on the kitchenette table. The police took it though. Joel said."

Up until which time anyone could have taken it, had a copy made, and returned it.

"Joel said you had some lists or something you wanted me to explain."

"Just look at mostly, to see if anything useful pops out.

"Did Winfred Lamont have any kind of business arrangement with Foster that you know about?"

"No, why?"

"Can you think of any other reason Lamont would have written Foster a check for fifty dollars?"

"Fifty dollars! When?"

I told her what I'd learned and showed her the lists I'd worked up on Foster's finances.

"So about the time he got that check, his bank account began to look rosier." She frowned in thought at my handwritten pages.

"Did he start any sort of sideline that you know of? Sell off something Lamont might have wanted?"

She shook her head slowly.

"Not that I've heard of, but men get together sometimes, for drinks or golf and such. Needless to say, I'm not invited. Still, if Foster had launched some new venture, I think I would have picked up at least a hint. As to selling something to Lamont, I don't know what it would be. Foster didn't have any sort of equipment; he sub-contracted. A used truck possibly. Or a bribe?"

"It wouldn't be very smart writing a check for a bribe." Then again, crooks weren't always smart.

"If Foster was starting some sort of sideline, I suppose it could be earnest money he required from Lamont for a buy in," Rachel said slowly. "Good faith money put up with the understanding Foster wouldn't cash the check until whatever the sideline was began to pay out."

Something had begun to pay out to Foster, but not, by all appearances, to Lamont. Putting aside that line of exploration with some reluctance, I handed Rachel the lists from Cecilia. She studied them, muttering occasionally, but saw nothing of interest there. When she handed them back I gathered myself for what had to come next.

Rachel exhaled a stream of smoke, watching me.

"I'm guessing there's something more you want to ask."

"Why didn't you tell me Foster had started a rumor about you?"

Her dark head gave an insolent toss.

"Figured I'd see how good a detective you are."

"Dammit, Rachel—"

"Yes, dammit! Do you suppose I *like* this? Do you suppose I like having my private life pawed at and picked at for the whole city to see? Do you think I like knowing that if you can't pull a rabbit out of some hat, my backside's going to sizzle in the electric chair, and that if you do—" Her voice cracked. "—if you do, there'll still be such a cloud over my name that I'll probably never get a chance to so much as bid on another contract?

"Oh, and just for the record — before he started the rumor, Foster propositioned me and I turned him down."

TWENTY-NINE

The more I thought about it, the less outlandish it seemed that the check from Lamont might represent some kind of bribe. He hadn't gotten much in return if he was telling the truth about the precarious state of his finances. Bribing Foster would, however, go a long way toward explaining his nervousness.

Before I wasted time on a theory that might be inaccurate, I needed to put out some feelers. The men-only gossip circuit which Rachel had mentioned, and which I knew existed in business and just every other aspect of life, seemed like the place to start.

"I regret to say I've got a pretty full schedule all day today," Phil Clark apologized when I reached him Thursday morning.

"Tomorrow?"

"I'm driving down to Middletown, and I can't say precisely when I'll be back. I take it this additional information you mentioned isn't something you want to discuss over the phone."

"I'd rather not."

He was silent a moment.

"Look, I'll tell you what. Your place of business is downtown as I recall?"

"Between Patterson and St. Clair, yes."

"I often duck home at midday and take my dog for a run. I could do that along the river in front of the Engineers Club if you wanted to talk with me while we walked."

"I'd be glad to, and thanks."

Oscar Jones, the sad sack builder who'd also been an unsuccessful bidder for Foster's project, had never heard of Foster having any sort of sideline project when I talked to him.

"But why would he and Win Lamont do something together? They were both doing very well by themselves," he asked in bewilderment.

I hadn't told him about the check, just that I'd come across something suggesting they'd had private dealings. He nodded and looked as blank as if I'd been speaking Romanian.

On my way back, I detoured to stop by Gloria's building and see whether any mail had come for her in her absence. Just some magazines she subscribed to, the super told me. His missus had looked at them and then thrown them out.

"If I don't hear from her by next week, I'm going to box up what's left of her things and advertise her apartment."

"Didn't she have a lease on the place?"

"When the rent comes due, if it's not paid, the lease is up as far as I'm concerned. I had to pull up three boards and replace them because of that milk soaking into them, not to mention repainting that wall that got blood on it. I'm not going to be out any more money because of her. I was nice to her, looked the other way about a gentleman paying the rent because, well, a girl on her own's got it hard, doesn't she?"

His wife, who was on her hands and knees scrubbing baseboards, looked up and gave him a glare.

***

Late morning was a slow time for peddling newspapers. In my book that made it a dandy time for having a follow-up chat with the disagreeable young wiseguy who'd helped himself to Heebs's corner.

"Hi," I said with a big smile. "Remember me? The first of the week I asked you where Heebs was. You said you didn't know."

"So?"

I snatched a folded paper from the bag slung across his chest and gave his shoulder a smack with it.

"Hey!"

I shoved the paper back at him so forcefully he had to backpedal in order to take it.

"So either you're the dumbest newsboy in the city or you're such a sneak the others don't have anything to do with you. Every other newsie in the city knew Heebs had been beaten up. In fact he was in the hospital, but he's out now, and when he's ready to sell papers again, you're going to let him have this corner back. Period."

"Life's hard, lady. Your little pal can take his knocks like anyone else. I'm here now."

"Perhaps I didn't make myself clear. When Heebs shows up, you relocate."

"Or what?"

I held up the small leather folder that displayed my badge and folded up license.

"Or I make your life extremely unpleasant."

Two newsboys who worked farther along the block had edged closer to listen. Mr. Tough Guy was torn between falling back a couple steps more and playing to them. He compromised by leaning away from me some.

"You can't do anything to me. I'm not breaking the law."

I leaned in and pretended to flick a crumb from his front.

"The police don't have time to waste time on would-be punks like you. I do. I will. I know people in Governor Cox's merry little news emporium too, and if I put a word in the right ears, you won't get papers to sell anywhere in this city. Understand?"

"Yeah, I got it." His eyes swung left and right. He was worried the other newsies would see him backing down from a woman, and even more worried I'd prove as tough as I sounded if he got smart.

"When Heebs shows up, you won't even make him ask. You'll tell him you're glad he's better. Then you'll turn and walk away."

"Yeah. Okay."

***

The swath of lush green embankment where I was to meet Phil Clark stretched for a couple of blocks between Monument Avenue and the Great Miami. When I got there, I saw two shapely young women cooing over a man with a dog. More accurately, it was the pooch who was getting attention as they bent, petting his ears. I wouldn't have bet much on whether man or dog was the real object of their interest, though. When they straightened, one twisted back and forth like a schoolgirl and light, giggling laughter reached my ears.

Catching sight of me, Clark waved a hand in greeting.

The girls looked in my direction, exchanged a few more words with Clark, and with backward glances took their leave. Clark came to meet me. No doubt about it, he was a good-looking man.

"Do you always attract a crowd?" I asked in greeting.

He laughed.

"Cupid does have that effect on people."

"Cupid because he attracts women?" I nodded toward the departing duo.

"He's a she, and the somewhat embarrassing name is because the first time she looked at me, it put an arrow right through my heart. Say hello to Miss Sullivan, girl."

The dog obediently put up a paw, which I bent to shake. She was knee-high with a white and butterscotch coat that curled where it covered her long ears.

"She looks like a tall cocker spaniel."

"English cocker." With murmured praise and pats of affection, he unsnapped her leash. She took off running, flopping happily along. "If you don't mind, let's walk closer to the water so I can call her back if she gets too excited. I usually take her out across the way, at Deeds Point there, or in a park by my house. When I bring her here she goes nuts because of the novelty."

"But she'll come back if you call?"

"Oh, yes. She's very well trained."

We'd fallen into step. He gave me a sideways glance.

"I admit I'm curious at what you've turned up that you didn't want to ask about over the phone."

The dog circled left and raced back toward us, displaying prowess or maybe just joy, then veered to race off again.

"I was wondering if you knew of any financial connection

between Foster and Winfred Lamont."

"Connection? What kind of connection?"

"Any sort."

"Not that I'm aware of."

"No loan? No venture they went into together?"

"None I've ever heard about, though a loan would be something they kept close to their vests, wouldn't it? Why?"

"There's indication Lamont gave Foster a significant amount of money."

The dog began to make its way down to the water. Clark whistled it back. Rewarded with an ear scratch, it took off for more loops.

"How do you define 'significant amount'?"

My head shake told him not to expect an answer. "Lamont talks as if he's hard-pressed. I wondered if he'd borrowed money from Foster and then paid it back."

"Oh, that's just Lamont, the eternal worrier. I've never heard any hint of his having trouble. Monday's the latest installment of those builders' luncheons like the one where Rachel had words with Foster. I could sound out a few people, quietly, see if anyone heard anything about some sort of deal, if you like."

"I'd appreciate it." If Lamont got wind of questions being asked and it made him nervous, all the better. Nervous people made mistakes.

The dog came bounding up, and this time seemed content to slow her pace and amble just a few steps ahead, intent on sniffing now.

"How's Rachel holding up?

"Feeling a lot of strain. You're the first to ask."

"She doesn't deserve this. She's an exceptional woman."

"Did that story Foster told about her have anything to do with things ending between you?"

"I always supposed it was sour grapes on his part, that he'd made some kind of pass and she'd turned him down. It was long before we started dating. The reason we broke up..." He looked thoughtful. "A man wants a woman who supports him.

"I grew up dirt poor, Miss Sullivan. Lots of days I didn't have even a chunk of bread to eat because my father was the neighborhood drunk. When my mother did manage to get a nickel or two and sent me to the store, I risked other kids beating me up for it if my cousin a few years older, with considerably more muscles than I had, didn't tag along.

"He earned pocket change now and then pulling nails out of boards at a construction site so they could be reused, but he smarted off and got fired. I begged the man in charge to let me have the job. I kept it and got big enough to swing a hammer and climb scaffolding with the best of them. Eventually I got to where I am today.

"Rachel understood that. Not the being poor part, but the fighting tooth and nail to make something of yourself, because she'd done it too."

"Yet you didn't want her to compete with you? Or was it just her winning that you didn't like?"

He whistled the dog back and bent to fasten the leash to her collar.

"Both, perhaps. I thought she should have stepped aside instead of bidding against me. A man needs success. It's how he measures himself."

As much as it hurt, I managed to bite my tongue.

THIRTY

"Hey, sis, you just missed a call from Lulu Sollers." Heebs' unswollen eye looked ready to pop from his head as I walked in the office. "She said she may have found something for you — a bus driver you ought to talk to. Something to do with a candy wrapper."

He shoved a piece of paper into my hand.

"There's his name, and the route, and his bus number."

I was already dialing. But Lulu was known for keeping a brisk pace. She was gone. The girl who had answered her phone said I might be able to catch her at the end of the day.

Heebs was still goggle-eyed when I hung up.

"She's that policewoman, ain't— isn't she? The real tough old bird."

"You get points for knowing she's a cop, not a matron. If she's tough, it's because she has to be to face off with some man who's beating his wife or a dance hall girl swinging a knife."

And to put up with guff from half the male cops when she's proved herself a hundred times over.

I waved the slip of paper.

"You did a first-rate job taking down information, Heebs."

On my way in that morning, I'd stopped by a secondhand shop I knew and bought him a vest. With that on over his shirt, he looked older if anyone stopped in, and more businesslike. He could pass for a young clerk from the mailroom in a modest sized business. A clerk with one eye still swollen half closed, and some of his bruises turning from purple to yellow now.

"You came in before I finished writing the last part," he said. "Miz Sollers said the driver's shift starts at eight p.m. I asked her if I'd heard that right, and she said yes, at night."

I copied the information to a folded sheet of paper I kept in my purse. Heebs moved to his own chair and I sat down to make notes on my meeting with Clark. Then I suspended a pencil between my index fingers and thought.

Since three of Lamont's competitors knew nothing about any possible link between him and Foster, or weren't willing to admit it if they did, I wondered what might come out of the horse's mouth itself. After twice catching him in a lie, I saw no reason to be optimistic I'd get the truth from him about the check. Guilty or innocent, he'd realize its discovery raised suspicions. Better to let him stew for a few days while I nosed around some more.

For the first time, I wondered whether that check, buried deep in Foster's financial records, could be what someone was hunting at Rachel's office and Gloria's apartment. But no. It might be what they were after at Gloria's place, but why look for it at Rachel's?

I sent Heebs out for sandwiches for us. While he was gone, I continued to mull over Win Lamont and what he was guilty of, and whether that guilt had led to murder. What if he was guilty of something, but not of murder?

I sat up, blinking at a new idea.

"What if I've been approaching this from the wrong end?" I said aloud.

Heebs opened the door as I said it.

"What was that, sis?"

I got up and paced.

"A man wrote an unexplained check to a man who was killed."

"Who? Killed... you mean murdered?"

"I've been assuming the check writer wanted something from the dead man. That it was a bribe, or he wanted in on a deal. But what if it was the dead man — yeah, he was murdered — what if he was after something from the one who wrote the check? What if he had demanded money?"

"You mean blackmail?"

"That's usually more than once," I said absently.

But not always.

Maybe Lamont had believed a one-time payment would buy Foster's silence on something. Maybe it hadn't. Foster's steadily more robust bank account from the time of the check onward could be the result of blackmail rather than a business investment. One check wasn't enough to prove something like that, or even to build a fire under Freeze.

It would, however, be a dandy motive for murder.

**

Heebs peppered me with questions while we ate our sandwiches. Without giving names, I answered some of them. Talking through things that were puzzling me while he tried to follow made me wish I could do the same thing with Connelly. He was a good sounding board when I was stuck on a case.

My thoughts began to drift to the last time we'd been together ... the interlude at his door. I jerked them back.

"I need you to hold the fort for a couple of hours," I said jumping up and grabbing my hat. "I'm going back to Market House."

Somewhere along the way while talking with Heebs, I'd had the merest germ of an idea. It might not lead anywhere, but it was better than sitting, so I trotted over to Main and climbed the stairs to Freeze's office.

He was out. So was Boike. The cartons containing Foster's financial records still sat on the vacant desk where I'd looked at them yesterday.

"Mind if I have another look at these?" I asked a detective at a nearby desk.

Covering the mouthpiece of the phone cradled on his shoulder, he shrugged.

"Freeze was okay with it yesterday. I don't see why not."

My eyes began to cross at the mere prospect of being forced back to the mountain of documents. I looked around in hopes of spotting an adding machine. I didn't. Since I didn't know how to use one, it was no more disappointing than not seeing a magic wand.

I set up the equipment I'd brought, a tablet and a freshly sharpened pencil. Then I dug into the box with the check from Lamont and as quickly as possible put things in neat stacks.

This time around, I was only interested in the total of Foster's bank deposits each month, one for his business account and one for the personal one. That made things easier. I drew a vertical line down my tablet and entered the monthly totals for both accounts, starting six months before the check from Lamont. Then I added the totals for each account separately and divided by the number of months to get a monthly average.

It was dull work, maybe the dullest I'd ever done. When I'd finished, I did the same thing only working forward from Lamont's check. After staring at the results, I expanded my efforts to twelve months to make sure the pattern I thought I saw was really emerging.

"Find anything?"

Freeze's voice, directly over my shoulder, startled me so that I almost dropped my pencil. I'd been resting my chin on my hand, scarcely six inches off the desk, as I looked back and forth from my own sheets of figures. I straightened, kneading a kink in my shoulder.

"Yeah, I think maybe I have."

I shoved my work sheets to one side. The two detectives came around to look. I pointed with my pencil.

"These are the monthly figures for what Foster put in his personal account in the six month period before that check from Lamont. These are the ones for the first twelve months after.

"Here's the monthly average before." I pointed. "And after. Notice anything?"

"There's more every month from around then," Freeze said. "We already knew that."

"More by an average of fifty-one dollars and forty-three cents, to be precise. And the check Lamont wrote was for fifty dollars."

Freeze gave me a sharp look.

"Are you thinking Foster was putting the bite on Lamont? Blackmailing him?"

"I'm saying when you look at it month by month, his deposits were always up by about fifty dollars. Sometimes forty-eight or forty-nine, sometimes a buck or two the other direction. Every month except one, when he put in forty dollars, which was probably a fluke. And..." This time I patted with my finger. "...after that one check, the deposits for the extra amount were always in cash, sometimes for the full amount, sometimes in two or three chunks."

Boike gave a low whistle. Freeze picked up my pages of calculations and scanned them.

"Lamont must have wised up. Checks every month for the same amount would have left too much of a trail."

"It's a smart amount, too," I said. "Enough to make a difference in Foster's finances, but not so large it attracted attention."

"There's no proof the cash payments came from Lamont."

"You're a pain sometimes, Boike."

THIRTY-ONE

With lights from businesses muted or off altogether these days, standing at a bus stop at eight in the evening felt like waiting at midnight. Two trolleys came and went before the one displaying the number Lulu Sollers had given me swung to the curb.

At this time of night, it was only half full. I slid into the seat behind the driver.

"Are you Pat?" I asked when we reached a stretch where stops thinned out.

The codger at the wheel cocked a shaggy eyebrow at me in his mirror.

"Now what's a pretty young thing like you asking about a worthless fellow like Pat Collins for?" he kidded.

I smiled.

"A friend told me to say hello to him."

"Ah. Well, I'm not Pat." He pulled over as the bell rang to tell him a passenger wanted to get off. "The man didn't even set foot on this bus before he went home sick as could be. One look and you knew he wasn't fit to drive. Dragging himself along, eyes all feverish. That's why some of us retirees take turns coming in. If one of the regular drivers gets sick or calls in late, we can step right to it."

The bus nosed back into traffic.

"When do you think he'll be back?"

"Oh, hard to say. Two or three days of sleep and coddling by the missus and he might be back on his feet."

It had started to drizzle. He turned on his windshield wipers. I went home feeling pretty drizzly myself at the setback where I'd hoped for progress.

***

One problem kept winking at me from the otherwise tidy theory that Foster had been blackmailing Lamont. Namely, I found it hard to imagine the less-than-flamboyant Lamont indulging in anything worthy of blackmail. Still, ordinary seeming people sometimes had private lives that would curl hair.

I let the problem have center stage in my thoughts once I'd finished reading the morning papers. Maybe Lamont had been paying hush money to cover up something unrelated to carnal misdeeds or vices. People got blackmailed for having their hand in the till. But Lamont owned his company. He *was* the till. It could be over something else related to business, though.

In that case, my chance of determining what was just about nil. Rachel and I might figure it out if we sat working elbow to elbow for however long it took, but that wasn't feasible, given the tight rein being kept on her. I spent the rest of the morning visiting other bidders for the project where Rachel's crew was working, and returned to the office without so much as a scrap of new information.

"Some policeman stopped by to see you," Heebs reported. "He needed a shave real bad. First he said he'd wait, but then he started to yawn, so he left this for you. He your boyfriend, sis?"

The note was from Connelly, of course, sealed in one of my envelopes.

See you at Finn's when you're done for the day?
You're not going to throw me over because of what I said when you dropped me off the other night, are you?
Mick

"You never answered the question about whether he was your boyfriend."

I pointed a finger at him.

"That's because it's none of your business." But I knew I was smiling.

On the off chance some of Gloria's former co-workers might have heard from her, I went to the place where she'd worked and walked along with the same bunch I'd talked to before when they got out for lunch.

"She wouldn't waste time writing to someone unless she thought they could help her," one of them sniffed.

It fit the gist of their remarks on the previous occasion.

Spending a few hours in my own chair reading through mail recharged my batteries. Jenkins ambled in to ask if I wanted to go hear a jazz trio with him and Ione the following night. The photographer gave a curious look at Heebs, so I introduced them without volunteering anything more. Not long after Jenkins left, the phone rang. Heebs told somebody that yes, I was there.

"Is this that woman detective who came around two or three days ago asking if there'd been any word from Gloria Overbrook?" a woman asked when I said hello. "This is the super's wife. At the place where she lives."

"Yes, I'm the one." I put down my nail file. "Is Gloria there?"

"No, but she called."

"When?"

"Just now. My husband wasn't here, so she had to settle for me. Had Clyde twisted around her little finger, she did. He falls all over himself for any woman that gives him a wide-eyed look."

For any woman but her, down on her knees scrubbing the floor and wearing a housedress, I thought. I tried not to be impatient over where this was leading.

"Believe me, he's changed his tune on that one, though. She ought to be glad it was me she talked to, or she'd have gotten an earful."

"What was she calling about? Did she say?" I nudged.

"Oh, you bet. No asking, giving orders, same as always. Worse, maybe. She was calling to say we better not have touched anything in her apartment, that she'd had to go out of town on a family emergency and was coming back for it. Said she still had a whole 'nother month with her rent paid up and she'd expect a refund for what was left when she got here."

"Did she say when that would be?"

"Nope."

"Give any hint?"

"Nope. It sounded to me like she didn't intend to let much grass grow, though."

Several thoughts jostled each other to be first in my mind. An address book Gloria left behind hadn't listed anybody named Overbrook. Maybe she'd been married before, or what family she had was on her mother's side of things. At the place where she'd worked, though, under Next of Kin, she'd listed 'none.'

"Have you told the police?"

"Nope. Don't much like that one in charge, the one that smokes. None of them gave me the time of day."

"You need to call them."

"Why? They were all worked up because they thought she might have been killed. Well, she wasn't."

"There's more to it. Gloria may have information that helps with a murder investigation."

She sucked in her breath.

"Well, if she shows up, I guess maybe we better let them know then. Clyde won't like it, though."

"If she does come to get her things, or even just calls again, give me a call right away, will you? There's two bucks in it for your trouble. Clyde doesn't have to know."

"I'm sure glad I let you know this time, then, and I will."

I gave her my number at Mrs. Z's, and was starting to give her the one at Finn's when she cut in hastily.

"Got to go."

The abrupt way she hung up made me anxious. Had Gloria turned up at the door? When five minutes had passed, I called her back. The super himself answered. Without letting on that I already knew, I asked if they'd heard from Gloria.

"She called and told my wife she wants what's left on her rent. Can you feature that? You saw that spilt milk, and that - that mess on the wall. I tell you, my knees just about gave out when I saw that," he said morosely.

What if Foster's girlfriend had made her phone call from the railway station? The superintendent's wife had talked like she expected Gloria might turn up in a day or two, but I couldn't shake the thought it could be in the next hour or so.

I knew it was probably desperation on my part, but better safe than sorry. I drove to her apartment and parked where I could watch people come and go. Based on the photos I'd seen of her, Gloria wasn't among them.

Finally I gave up and headed for Finn's. By the time I got there, I'd missed Connelly.

THIRTY-TWO

Monday morning things fell apart. I'd spent the last two hours making phone calls as part of the background checks on a handful of people applying for jobs at Rike's. Heebs was at the window looking out.

"Hey, sis, some guy with a briefcase just hopped out of a taxi and headed in here like his pants were on fire. Maybe you're going to have a new client."

"I don't have time for a new client, Heebs. He's probably late for an appointment with the podiatrist."

The podiatrist was the only office on the ground floor of my building. He always seemed to have patients coming and going. There was money in sore feet.

I was lifting the phone to make another call when a fusillade of knocking rattled my door. Joel Minsky followed by entering. One glance at his grim expression told me something was wrong.

"Rachel was—" He caught sight of Heebs and came to a halt.

"Heebs, why don't you walk over to the Arcade and bring me an elephant ear? Get something for yourself too."

I gave him some change. He looked from me to Joel and back at me again. The kid was no dummy. He knew I wanted privacy.

"Sure thing, sis."

Joel turned to watch as Heebs closed the door behind him.

"I didn't want to miss any calls while I'm out trying to track down things right now. He's my temporary answering service. In spite of what the black eye and such might lead you to think, he's okay. What's happened?"

The lawyer threw himself into the chair in front of my desk and tipped his head back.

"I've just come from Rachel's arraignment," he said without opening his eyes. "I'd hoped to postpone it again, but I couldn't."

"I've got gin in my drawer."

"I'd better not." He sat erect. "I've got papers to draw up that require a clear head."

"Does this mean her name in the paper?"

"Possibly. That's the least of my worries."

"Did the judge revoke bail?"

"No."

I was trying to figure out what had upset the seemingly unflappable man across from me.

"He set the date for the preliminary hearing," Joel said. "I tried to argue for a postponement, told him new evidence had just come to light on Friday. He said he couldn't wait forever for us to locate a witness, and that in view of the seriousness of the crime he'd already been lenient, which is true."

Pivoting to his feet he began to pace, one hand gripping the opposite wrist behind him. Whether the posture signaled returning composure or was merely habit, I couldn't guess.

"That means that unless I can mount a persuasive

argument by the end of the week that they've got the wrong suspect, this will most likely go to trial. I don't suppose you've come up with anything new?"

"No."

"Neither has the man we use, our usual investigator. He's shown Gloria Overbrook's photograph at every train depot and bus station here and within a hundred mile radius. Airfields too. He's come up with nothing."

"There is one possible development." I told him about the phone call Gloria had made to the superintendent's wife Friday.

"Get word to my office the minute you hear she's turned up."

I nodded.

"I'm working on one or two other things that might help too."

I didn't think a tale about kids who folded a candy wrapper like a bow tie would do much to calm him. I wasn't pinning much hope on that one myself.

"And I'm going to try and get to Cincinnati to talk to a man who's forgotten more about the law than I'll ever know. He might have an idea how to get the hearing delayed at least." Joel snatched up his briefcase. "Damn Rachel anyway. I don't know whether to shake her or defend her to the death."

"How about you do both, but in reverse order?"

That won me a chuckle, if nothing else.

***

When Heebs returned, I broke off a flake or two of the flat, crisp pastry he'd brought me and nibbled without much appetite. Gradually I became aware that Heebs appeared to have even less.

"Something wrong, Heebs?"

His shoulder twitched indifference.

"Just that I ran into Marcie. Well, saw her anyway. I started across to meet her, and she grabbed the arm of a guy she was walking with and laughed like he'd said the funniest thing she'd ever heard, and leaned up against him. Never even held hands with me."

What could you say to a kid whose heart had been broken? Probably for the first time, too.

"Some girls are just like that, Heebs. One of these days I'll bet she's sorry she didn't treat you better."

"Yeah, well I'm not going to take her back if she is. Guess I found out what she was like."

Cramming a chunk of elephant ear into his mouth, he chewed with gusto. His wounded pride, if not his heart, was mending. If only I could solve my own problem as easily.

Patience was a virtue in my game, but I'd never had a great supply and I couldn't afford it now, in light of what Joel had told me. It was time to twist tails and take a gamble or two. The only tail I could think of to twist was Lamont's. I picked up the phone.

"Mr. Lamont must have, uh, gone out without letting me know," his secretary told me a minute after she'd asked my name and invited me to wait just a moment. She wasn't a very good liar.

"When could I catch him? I just need a few minutes."

"Oh, um, his schedule … his schedule looks pretty full for the rest of the week."

He was ducking me. Putting his secretary on the spot wouldn't get me anywhere, so I thanked her and hung up. I nibbled another bite of pastry.

The monthly lunchtime confab of construction company owners was today. Phil Clark had promised to make discreet inquiries there. But I couldn't discount the possibility Clark himself was the one behind Foster's murder. No connection had come to light between him and Foster. Clark had dated Rachel, though, including overnight stays, which would have given him opportunity to pilfer the earring that had turned up at the murder scene.

Except Rachel claimed it had gone missing more recently. And, as she'd pointed out, while Clark's anger at losing to her on the bid for a project had ended their relationship, it didn't seem like enough to frame someone for murder.

Maybe sugar from the elephant's ear stimulated my brain, because all at once I had an idea. First I drilled Heebs on his part. He was tickled to finally be promoted to what he saw as real detective work. He dialed Lamont's office with exceptional care.

"Good morning, miss. The Citizen Protective Committee is checking records of private vehicles registered for use in case of forced evacuation. If you could please give me the license plate number for Mr. Winfred Lamont's automobile? Good, that matches."

I read over his shoulder as he wrote down the number.

"And that's a Buick, correct? A Dodge. See, that's why we're checking. So many got registered so fast right after Pearl Harbor that here and there the wrong thing got entered. Thank you, miss. We do appreciate it."

He sat back, glowing. Taking the receiver from him, I

dialed Cecilia, fourteen-carat secretary and conjuror of information.

"It's Maggie," I said. "Do you know the time and location for that construction owners luncheon today?"

***

The little group of locals who owned construction companies was meeting at the same restaurant it had been at six months earlier when Rachel hurled her unwise words at Foster. The Stockyard Inn was on the edge of town and had an ample parking lot. Equipped with make and license number, it was no trick to identify Lamont's vehicle. Around the time I expected the get-together to start breaking up, I hoisted my fanny onto the hood, crossed my legs and waited.

A few men drifted out, then some miscellaneous diners, then a few more men, chatting in pairs or groups of three. Here and there I got a curious look. I spotted Clark in conversation with two other men. He noticed me and cocked his head, but didn't come over. Finally Lamont and another man came out, talking.

Halfway to his car, Lamont looked up and saw me perched there. In case he didn't recognize me, I gave a cheery wave. He halted. His companion, noticing, said something. Lamont shook his head and glancing left and right, made a beeline toward me.

"Get off my car. How dare you!" His face was scarlet.

"Gee, your secretary told me how busy you were for the rest of the week. I thought coming here would make it easier for you to answer one more pesky question I have."

"I've got nothing more to say to you. I've had more than enough of you and your insinuations. Get down!"

He took a tentative step toward me, trying to figure out how to remove me from his car. A few heads had turned to watch us now. I smiled.

"Dear me. We're attracting an audience. The smartest thing for you to do is answer my one teeny question and get me out of your hair, don't you think? Otherwise, I might have to repeat it a few times, louder and louder. I think some of those gentlemen you just had lunch with might be as fascinated as I am about the reason for that fifty dollar check you wrote to Gabriel Foster."

He spun and saw the curious faces.

"The ... why ... why shouldn't I write him a check? It was for a - a fishing trip if you must know."

"A fishing trip."

"Up in Michigan. For transportation, and food and - and a guide. He put it together."

"Just the two of you?"

"No. No, there were a few others."

"Anybody from this group?"

"No. A - a dentist, I think. I don't remember. Can I go?"

It was just far-fetched enough to be true. I remembered the fishing rod and mounted fish on plaques in Lamont's office. I also recognized two very large holes.

"Funny he didn't cash the check, don't you think? For a trip that pricey?"

"He didn't...?" The color drained from his face as if I'd pulled a plug. "He told me he'd lost it, asked me to write him another. I didn't have my checkbook. I paid him in cash. He must have found it. It - it must have slipped his mind. Surely he never meant to be dishonest."

An irritating shred of plausibility clung to his stammered words. After the hours I'd spent calculating the extra money in Foster's bank account each month since that check, I wasn't willing to accept it so easily.

"Foster put together a lot of fishing trips, did he?"

"I wouldn't know. Why?"

I slid off the hood and stood nose-to-nose with him.

"Because, Mr. Lamont, after that check of yours, the same amount extra showed up in his bank account month-in-month-out. Even in the dead of winter."

THIRTY-THREE

Clark had lingered, talking with another man. The stranger thoughtfully took his leave about the time Lamont tore out of the parking lot. Clark ambled toward me. I met him halfway.

"You make a very decorative hood ornament. Lamont didn't seem to enjoy your conversation."

I smiled. Lamont had jumped into his car with his eyes bugged out like those of the dead fish on his wall. He hadn't even given me a chance to ask what Foster had on him.

"Mr. Lamont is a terribly nervous man," I said mildly. "How was your trip to Middletown? Did you buy a puppy?"

"An absolute charmer. She wailed so I could hardly stand it when I closed her in the kitchen so I could come to work."

He nodded toward the restaurant. "I'm afraid I didn't learn anything in there. I didn't want to be too obvious. The hints I dropped about hearing Foster had some kind of deal on the side raised an eyebrow or two, but nobody volunteered anything or seemed especially interested."

"Well, thanks anyway."

"Stop by and see the puppy sometime," Clark called after me as I left.

***

After supper I took a second stab at finding Pat Collins, hoping enough days had passed for the bus driver to shake whatever unpleasant malady had sidelined him. When I got on the bus, a different man was behind the wheel. Someone also occupied the seat I wanted behind him. Three blocks later, the passenger got off and I slid into place.

"Are you Pat Collins?"

He nodded, watching to make sure tokens went in the box as people climbed in.

"You must be the girl the substitute told me about. Said we had a friend in common?"

"Acquaintance, anyway. Lulu Sollers."

"The policewoman. Sure, I've talked to her a few times. Nice lady."

The door whooshed shut. He rolled on almost a block.

"Ah. Them kids," he said suddenly. "The candy wrappers. This have anything to do with that?"

"This has everything to do with that. I'm the one that told Lulu about it. I'm a detective. Some kids were out roaming at night when they shouldn't have been, in a place they shouldn't have been, and they left some candy wrappers that were kind of distinctive. I've known Lulu a long time, so I asked her to ask around."

"Huh. Well, isn't that something, a woman detective. But then Miss Sollers is plenty smart."

Like the substitute I'd talked to before, Pat conversed while keeping his eyes on the road, save for occasional glances at me in his rearview mirror.

"What did you want to know?"

"First tell me about the candy wrappers. Describe them. Then tell me about the kids."

He nodded and slowed as he maneuvered curbside for the next bus stop. Still eagle-eyed over the fare box, he tucked his hands under his arms and turned to talk.

"They throw the wrappers on the floor. That's what irritated me, got me noticing them, their dropping trash like it didn't matter. It's Whiz bar wrappers, mostly, always two of them. Once or twice there's been a Clove gum paper, too. Those Whiz wrappers, though, whichever kid drops them folds them up like bow ties first. Now if he can go to the trouble of doing that, why can't he hold onto them long enough to put in a trash can?"

The bus got underway again. I felt slightly dazed that so tenuous a thread might be leading to something.

"And the kids?" I prompted. "How many? What age?"

"Two older, fourteen or fifteen, and one a good bit younger, maybe nine or ten. The first few times they weren't a nuisance, except for the trash. Oh, they whispered a little like kids do when they're in church or somewhere you've warned them to behave. My wife says it's because they're nervous on account of they don't know quite how to act in a grownup world."

"What do they do now?"

Between what Lulu had told me about the new problem of kids roaming and what had happened to Heebs, I felt my interest sharpening, though I couldn't say why.

"They sit in that back seat there and snicker, is what they do. Snicker at passengers and whisper about them, only they don't quite whisper. They want you to overhear them, if you know what I mean. Say things to each other and then start laughing, acting rowdy. Last time, one of them said a bad word."

It didn't exactly sound like serious crime, but I could see it was a disruption. I could see boys like he was describing being cheeky enough to hide under a tarp if they risked being caught somewhere they shouldn't be.

It was full dark now. The bus moved steadily northward, past businesses closed for the day, away from the city and toward less traveled streets. The driver warmed to his topic.

"I'd just about had it then. I told them if they didn't settle down, I'd put them off the bus. Not sure I'd have the heart to do that, though. Who's going to put kids out on their own that time of night? It might do them good, having to wait at a bus stop and wondering whether the bus going back would stop for them."

"I need to talk to them. It's important. Are they on here every night?"

"Naw, just Tuesdays usually. A couple of times they've ridden another night too."

Side sweeps to bus stops punctuated our conversation.

"Where do they get on?"

"Same stop you did."

Meaning it was an easy walk from two other lines. No telling where they came from initially.

"Any particular time?"

He squinted in thought.

"Must be about half past nine. I'm due there at nine thirty-two."

"And where do they get off?"

"Now that varies. Sometimes not til the end of the line. Sometimes one or two stops before."

***

Come the following morning, I was walking back and forth a block from Market House in front of the United Brethren Building where Lulu Sollers had her office. It was still twenty minutes before she was due to come in, but catching her as she arrived was the best way I could think of to guarantee I didn't miss her. I'd been there all of five minutes before she marched into view.

"Well, Maggie, you look like a woman with something on her mind," she said in greeting.

"Morning, Lulu. I need to talk to you about those kids with the candy wrappers."

It took her half a second to sift through what must be scores of problems and situations she kept track of.

"The bus driver. Collins. He had something useful for you then?"

"Yes. It sounds like the kids I'm hunting." She'd shown no inclination to pause while we chatted. I matched her brisk pace. "Collins says they usually ride on Tuesdays, so I'm going to be on the bus tonight. I want to talk to them. I think maybe you or one of your women ought to be there when I do."

She shot me a look.

"I've never questioned kids before. I thought I might need to be extra careful, what with them being minors and all."

"You're right, but if you get their names and addresses—"

"They might lie. And Lulu, they may have witnessed a murder."

She halted in mid-step, staring at me in horror.

"Dear God!"

THIRTY-FOUR

I got some breakfast and went to the office. Heebs was poring over the lists Cecilia had typed up ten days ago, the ones with neat columns of information on all projects Rachel had bid on in the last five years.

"What is this stuff you keep under your typewriter?" he asked frowning at the sheets spread before him.

"What I keep under there is what I don't want someone to find if they break in and go through my files." I hung the robin's egg blue fascinator I was fond of this time of year on the hat rack. "How'd you manage to get those? That Remington's heavy."

He shrugged. "Not that heavy. I stand around holding bags of newspapers all day, sis. They start out heavy. Anyways, I'm not a kid any more."

For the first time in a while, I took a good look at him. He was taller, but not by a lot. Still skinny. No danger of his needing to shave for a couple more years. Blue and yellow bruises still decorated his face, but they were fading quickly and there was no swelling. His lip still had a crack I knew must be painful, but eating and talking made split lips slow to heal. His week's rent at the place I'd found him ran out today. I'd give him enough for two more nights.

"I already guessed the papers were under there so no one would find them." His tone was aggrieved as I gathered the pages together and stacked them. "What I meant, was what are all those names and numbers? I know it has to do with money, and people and square feet, which I know has to do with size. But other than that, I couldn't make heads or tails. I didn't think you'd mind me looking at them since I'm working for you. Anyways, you've put them under there right in front of me."

His reproach at my dismissive answer made me feel like a heel. I needed to pass a lot of slow-crawling hours before I got on Pat Collins' bus tonight.

"Pull your chair over," I said, his cue to vacate mine.

Heebs complied, and with him at my side, I skimmed my finger over the top sheet as I went through the basics.

"These all have to do with construction projects, office buildings and apartments and that. Here's a project, see? What the guy with the money wants built, how big, the kind of materials they have to use. These are the companies that bid on the work."

"And that's how much each one wanted to build it," he said catching on.

"Right. That one there is the one that got it."

"The one that bid lowest?"

"Right. I thought maybe I could find something useful in it. Person A always coming in second to Person B, for example. But I didn't. Look at them all you want. Maybe you'll have better luck."

Admitting that I'd been stymied by the information spread before us mollified him. His enthusiasm was dwindling too.

"Lots of finicky studying."

"Yep. That's what lots of this kind of work amounts to.

Finicky. Now scoot your chair around. I didn't finish reading the paper. Then I've got phone calls to make."

Late in the morning, I called Joel Minsky's office, intending to leave a message. To my surprise he was in.

"Do you have something?" His tenseness crackled down the line.

"No, but there's a small chance I may have. I won't know until tonight, but I might have found a witness."

His breath sucked in.

"Thank God."

"Don't get your hopes up. I said 'might.'"

"Any hope sounds good at this point. Even the prospect of a witness could help. I'm going to Cincinnati this afternoon to talk to that man I mentioned. I won't be back until late."

"Me either."

"I'll be in court on a different case in the morning. Leave a message with my secretary, one way or another. Just 'yes' or 'no' so she can send a messenger. If this goes to trial, my job is going to be much harder."

And, I thought, harder on Rachel's reputation, in business and otherwise.

***

Not more than a few minutes past noon I got a call from one of Gloria's former co-workers.

"I thought you'd want to know that Gloria called," she said in a rush. "She wanted to know if anyone had been asking about her. I said yes and tried to give her your number, but she hung up on me."

219

I'd been leaning back in my chair. I straightened.

"Did she say where she was? Is she back in town?"

"She didn't say, but she sounded muffled."

"Muffled how?"

"You know... muffled. Like she was far away or had her hand around her mouth so she wouldn't be overheard. Like that."

Not wanting to be overheard would fit with the hanging up part.

"Hey, I've got to go," said the girl I was talking to. "I'm on my lunch hour."

"Sure, and thanks. Have you told the police?"

"No. 'Bye."

For several seconds I sat listening to the dial tone.

"Good news?" Heebs asked when I hung up.

"I'm not sure."

I also wasn't sure if I should tell Freeze. I called the superintendent at Gloria's apartment building.

"No, we haven't heard from her since last time you asked," he snapped. "Now stop pestering."

I called Freeze.

"Foster's girlfriend might be back in town, or on her way." I recounted my conversation with the girl where she'd worked, and Gloria's call to the apartment building a few days earlier.

"Maybe you have time to waste on 'might.' We don't." His old sourness was back in full.

"She took off because she was scared, Freeze. It sounds like she still is."

"Doesn't mean she knows anything."

He had me there.

"Look, you've had some good ideas," he said diplomatically. "Especially that one with the bank sheets. But unless you can give me another suspect—"

"Lamont."

"What you've got there is a nice theory. Nothing else. I had one of the uniforms who's good at that sort of thing sniff around. Lamont's a Boy Scout, and his business isn't making money hand over fist, but it's not in the red, either."

"He claims that fifty dollar check was for a fishing trip."

"So?"

"For one thing, the check was never cashed, remember? For another thing, it was in the middle of winter."

That slowed him down. I heard the scrape of a match.

"It wasn't the middle of winter. November, if I recall. People fish through the ice."

***

I spent the next few hours in a very bad mood. Gloria danced up like a harem girl from Aladdin's lamp and then disappeared again. Bossy with the apartment superintendent's wife, rushed and maybe scared with her former co-worker. Had something happened in between? Would she ever appear in the flesh? If she did, would she know anything helpful to Rachel?

I kicked my wastebasket. Heebs looked up from the Charlie Chan book I'd picked up for him at the library. I glowered back. The logical part of me knew Freeze was right to dismiss Gloria and even Lamont as not worth his efforts. Since he worked in behalf of taxpayers, his efforts had to be rational, hardheaded, efficient. Since I worked for a client, and in this case a friend, I had the freedom to follow any thread, no matter how slender. And time was running out for Rachel.

Midway through the afternoon I got down my hat and started out to get the early edition. When the phone rang, I paused with the door open in case Heebs motioned me back.

"Just a minute," he said. "Let me see if I can catch her."

He pressed the mouthpiece tightly to his chest so even his strained whisper wouldn't be heard.

"It's somebody named Gloria."

THIRTY-FIVE

The voice at the other end was bold but nervous.

"You the one going around asking questions, trying to find me?"

"If you were Gabriel Foster's girlfriend, then yes."

"Well, cut it out. You wanna get us both killed?"

"Gloria, what's going on? Where are you?"

"In town, but not for any longer than I have to be. So if you want to know anything about Foster and me or those men who showed up, it's gonna cost you forty bucks. Cash."

"Forty bucks is a lot of money."

"Yeah? Well, train tickets don't come cheap."

"What about the refund check on your apartment?"

"The... You don't get it, do you? I have to leave *tonight!*"

"Okay. Where do we meet?"

"Deeds Point. Know where that is?"

"Yes."

"Nine-fifteen, and don't be late. I've got a train to catch, and some things to pick up on the way."

"At your apartment?"

"None of your business. And listen. Come by yourself, understand? No cops. Nobody else. I'll be able to watch, and if I see anyone with you, I'm gone. Same if you don't have the money."

Nine-fifteen. That meant missing my chance to nab the kids on the bus. They rode every week though, and talking to Gloria promised a much bigger payoff.

"Nine-fifteen," I confirmed. "What if I need to reach—?"

She'd hung up.

***

Deeds Point was a narrow snout of land directly across the river from downtown. You could see it from the grassy embankment where I sat sometimes to eat my lunch. On the south bank of the point, the Mad River flowed in from the east. On the western bank, the Great Miami rushed down from the north. At the tip of the point, the larger Miami met and absorbed the Mad River, growing in size and strength as it swirled on west through the city. In 1913 that convergence of the rivers, swollen by too much rain, had caused a catastrophic flood.

The point had a picnic table or two, and an outdoor privy. In the summer part of it got mowed for playing ball. Mostly it was roughly three blocks of thin grass punctuated here and there by scrubby bushes.

The landscape didn't change after dark, but like any other place in a city, the feel of it did. Everything changed after dark: sounds, rhythms, what you could see. It was what you couldn't see that you had to watch for.

I'd changed into a rougher skirt and cotton stockings for my rendezvous with Gloria. The Smith & Wesson nestled in its holster at the small of my back, rubbing as it always did but not as hot as it would be come summer. My windows were down as I drove up Main past darkened businesses.

Gloria's words and manner on the phone had made her sound scared. I took extra care to make sure I wasn't followed. I'd tried to think of someone who could wait a block behind me, just to be prudent. There was no one. Rachel's bail was contingent on her staying under the wing of a family member. Pearlie was gone. Connelly was on night rotation and couldn't just skip over and keep an eye out because I asked him to. Freeze's attitude yesterday took him off the candidates list.

Four blocks north of where the two rivers met, a small bridge spanned the Great Miami. As soon as I crossed it, I doused the lights on the DeSoto. With luck, if anyone was tracking them, they would assume I'd turned into one of the narrow streets just north of where I was headed. Those streets led to an industrial area, mostly small shops but with a scatter of houses. At least a few vehicles would be coming and going there this time of night.

Spring peepers provided uneven music as I used the feel of the tires to find an area of hard packed earth at the foot of the bridge. The shape of the car would be hidden by bridge shadow. I'd be close to the road for fast takeoff, too. I switched off my engine.

I'd seen no hint of anyone following me. Now I sat while my eyes adjusted to what seemed utter darkness. Normally the lights of downtown Dayton would be twinkling across the river. Now, with concern about air raids, most places doused their lights, or all but the dimmest. My ears hunted sounds, but the roar of the river masked everything.

Once my night vision developed sufficiently, I scanned the area ahead of me for the woman I was to meet. More importantly, I watched for anyone who might be following her, or lying in wait.

The waning moon still cast decent light. Down near the tip of the point I saw a shape that didn't resemble the occasional bushes struggling up near the river. The shape didn't move. It was getting close to the time for me to meet Gloria. Making sure my dome light was switched off; I eased out of the car, closed the door without latching it and started forward.

The shape I was watching shifted. Moonlight glinted off a pale patch on the shape. Blonde hair. Gloria was a blonde. The weight of the .38 at the small of my back reassured me. I walked slowly. When I was able to see that the shape ahead of me was a woman, my steps quickened.

Gloria had started to pace. She hugged herself protectively. She hadn't seen me yet. A dozen steps more and I was within hailing distance.

"Gloria! It's Maggie."

She turned. She took one tentative step, then two. Her progress halted. Was she having second thoughts?

"I brought what you asked for," I called in reassurance. "And I have a car. I'll give you a lift."

She took another step. As she passed the privy a few yards to her right, a figure shot from its shadows and headed toward her.

"Gloria, look out!"

Skirting a patch of scrub and breaking into a run, I reached for my Smith & Wesson. The corner of my eye caught a blur of motion close to my shoulder. Before I could react, a blow to the side of my head made me stagger. Half dazed, I tried to get at my gun. But my arms were pinned. I felt myself jerked off my feet like a rag doll. A callused hand as unyielding as steel clamped over my mouth.

In the moment my mind cleared enough to know what was happening, my assailant carried my kicking body half a dozen steps and hurled me out, out, out from the embankment. Terror hit me as cold, swirling waters sucked me under.

THIRTY-SIX

Sheer instinct made me try to kick my way to the surface. I got my head up just long enough to gasp half a breath and get a noseful of water before I went under again. I tried to swim and couldn't.

My shoes. I had to get rid of the weight of my shoes.

I pushed them off, one foot freeing the other, while my arms stroked hard enough to bring me up for a bigger gulp of air. I was swimming now, but making no headway. The current was too strong, and kept twisting me onto my back.

No. Not the current. The Smith & Wesson. It had saved me dozens of times. Now any small chance of saving myself depended on discarding it, so I did. That little bit made me more buoyant, but I'd taken only half a dozen strokes when the current spun me. The bank where I'd gone in — I thought it was where I'd gone in — seemed impossibly far away already.

A tree branch that had snapped off somewhere upstream rushed at me. In an effort to escape impact, I tried to duck under. It caught my foot. I kicked and kicked free and managed to surface, choking on water.

I wasn't a strong swimmer. I'd probably been in the water no more than a minute. It felt like a lifetime. I couldn't tell if I was making any progress or was being swept haphazardly along. I knew I was going under too often.

Both shores seemed equally distant. My arms cut through the water with every ounce of strength I had. Then the torrent of the Mad River slammed into me from the east, spinning me. I choked on waves and swallowed water. I grabbed at a limb on a dead tree floating past, but got only a scrape on my hand.

Snatches of memory shot through my head: My father smiling down at me as we walked along with my hand in his. The warmth of Connelly's arms around me.

Another log was coming toward me. My fingers wrapped around a nub of it, but it started to roll, taking me along with it. As the log rotated and the waters pulled me under for a final time, I felt infinitesimally small and alone. My last conscious thought was wondering what it would have been like to sleep with Connelly.

***

Hell was colder than I'd expected. It smelled worse, too. And it was empty... so empty... Hell was a void wasn't it? Something about darkness... Where were the screams?

The emptiness wavered. A blob. Coalescing. Looming over me. Foul, foul breath. The smell of death. The devil.

"Get back or I'll shoot you!"

Was that thin croak that passed for a voice ... could that be me? Could you shoot the devil?

I reached for my .38. It wasn't there. A figure scrabbled back from me like a crab, hands raised.

"Don't shoot, lady. Didn't mean you no harm. Just dragged you away from the water some in case a wave come, and was trying to turn you onto your side so's you could breathe better."

I blinked vision back to my eyes. I could make him out now. A hobo.

"Sorry." I started to say more, but rolled to the side and vomited river.

When I'd finished, the hobo was still waiting. Close enough I could still smell him. Or maybe that was me. Bits and pieces of what had happened began to return. I pushed up on my elbows. Everything tumbled inside me. Brain. Stomach. Gurgling like the river that had almost drowned me.

Had been meant to drown me.

I felt weak as a kitten.

I tried to sit and didn't make it. The hobo reached out an arm, which I grabbed gratefully, and held as I eased myself back to the ground in defeat. Goose bumps covered my body from chill night air joining forces with sodden clothes.

"Let me try this again," I said after several minutes had passed. Or maybe I'd nodded off. The hobo offered his arm again. This time I succeeded.

It felt good to be upright, even though everything around me rocked as if I were still in the water. After a moment the sensation ebbed, though it didn't vanish completely. I sat and concentrated on breathing.

"Help me back to my car and I'll give you two bucks," I said. "I keep a couple hidden there for emergencies."

Along with my automatic.

"Lady, you ain't fit to walk anywhere, help or no help. I thought you was dead when I first saw you." The hobo sat on his haunches, eyeing me curiously. "Sure is a wonder you're not, lying more in the water than out the way you was. Current must of washed you in, same as it did that ol' log that was there beside you."

A tilt of his head indicated direction. I looked and in the dark could make out the shape of a log twice the size that I was. My head hurt.

"Lots of driftwood gets washed up on that shingle, 'specially in spring," he was saying. "Good for fires. Only it has to dry out first, and I don't have no matches."

My eyes kept wanting to close. I had to get someplace safer.

"Where are we?"

"Don't know what you mean, 'zackly. City's called Dayton."

"No. Where ... in Dayton?" What little energy I had was dwindling fast.

"Oh. Well. Just north of downtown, then, right past where the two rivers come together. Deeds Point's right across there."

So I was across from where I'd gone to meet Gloria. Across from where I'd been thrown in. The Great Miami had carried me downstream and the current of the Mad River joining it had hooked me east.

"Emmet Street?" I croaked.

"Emmet's over there a ways."

I hadn't gone far in the water, but it had been more than enough to drown me. It was a miracle I hadn't.

My shivering intensified. Now it came as much from realization of how close I'd come to dying as from the chilly evening. I pushed the thought away and tried to think. Had the time in the water affected my brain?

"...blanket up under them bushes," the hobo was saying. "If you can make it up there, you can wrap up in it and keep warm while I go for the police."

"No police." They would give me a ride to the station and I'd be warm, but they'd want endless explanations. Right now all I wanted was to dry off and sleep. "Thanks on the blanket, but I want my clothes to dry out." *And to not get lice.*

Matt and Ione Jenkins lived in a small Moorish style apartment house not far away. I'd spent more than a few nights on their couch when the three of us sat up late drinking and talking. They had a car, and because of his work on the paper, Jenkins was used to being roused in the middle of the night.

"Is there anyplace open where you can make a telephone call?"

"Little beer joint that doesn't always close when it's s'pposed to. Reckon they might let me use theirs."

He sounded uncertain.

Ever since I'd been on my own, I'd carried a two-dollar bill tucked into the cup of my bra for emergencies. A discreet shift of my arm assured me it was still there, plastered against my skin. Turning away, I extracted it.

"Make it worth their time to let you use it. Get yourself a beer. The rest is yours too." I held it out. "Make the call before you have the beer, though. And you'll have to remember the number. I don't have paper."

He repeated it back.

"Oh, and my name's Maggie."

I thought I managed to say it before my eyes closed, but I wasn't certain.

THIRTY-SEVEN

I awoke to the feel of water sloshing over me again and yelped.

"Shhh," a voice soothed. "I'm washing your hair. Keep your eyes closed."

The voice was familiar. The water was warm. My face was well above it.

Softness enveloped me. I was wrapped in a cloud. I was warm. I felt safe. Somebody spoke to me, but I couldn't answer. I drifted.

After awhile the cloud parted. Something cold and round moved over my chest as I muttered a protest. A pair of stubby fingers opened my eye and shone a light in.

Murmurs.

The cloud closed around me again.

My leg got cold. A needle stabbed into my bottom. A faint laugh. Blissful sleep.

***

Click click click clickity-clackity click click clickity-click.

Rhythm. Nice rhythm. Happy rhythm.

Hearing sound, recognizing it, drew me into consciousness. Or maybe I'd been waking anyway and heard it. I needed to relieve myself. I managed to sit. My head felt thick and hot. So did my eyes. I recognized my surroundings, though. I was sitting on the couch at Jenkins' apartment. Somewhere in the apartment Ione was typing away at one of the stories she sold to magazines.

"Maggie?" Her face swam into view. "Good heavens, you're sitting."

"I need to go to the bathroom."

The next time I woke, Ione was shaking my shoulder.

"I need you to drink some water. Now, take these." She handed me two tablets. "Try and finish the water. You've got a fever."

I obeyed meekly. Ione wiped my face with a cool washcloth.

"There's a lovely old doctor who lives on the floor above us. He looked you over and gave you a jab to protect you against some of the nasty things you might have gotten exposed to in the river. He's rather worried your fever might turn into pneumonia, so don't you dare let it. My reputation as a nurse is on the line."

***

The next time I woke, it was to someone poking me. Not a gentle touch like Ione had used several more times to give me water and tablets, this was a poke.

"Ah, you are awake," Jenkins said cheerfully.

A lamp glowed somewhere in the room. Daylight crept through a nearby window, but its paleness told me it was evening. I sat slowly up. For the first time I discovered I was wearing very nice tailored pajamas. They must be Ione's unless Jenkins went for pale pink sateen.

"What day is it?"

"Wednesday. How are you feeling?"

I took a drink of water from a glass on the gate leg table set up beside me.

"I had to toss my shoes. I had to toss my gun. I almost drowned. I'm mad as hops is how I feel."

"Oh, good. She's better."

Ione materialized with a cup of tea and a saucer holding a single slice of toast. My thoughts stuck on the dawning implications of losing my gun.

"Anything metal's hard to come by now—"

"Well, don't get any ideas about melting one of my cameras down to make one. One of the cops you know's bound to know how you can get a replacement."

"They probably have a drawer labeled 'Guns Maggie Sullivan has taken from crooks'," Ione said. "Now drink your tea."

They pulled up chairs.

Tea had never tasted so good. One simple joy of being alive, even though I was still hot with fever.

"Someone pushed you into that river, didn't they?"

Jenkins leaned forward intently, hands dangling between his knees. All signs of his teasing had vanished. Behind his wire-rimmed specs, his eyes were somber.

I chewed some toast. "Yes."

"Were you meeting someone over there at Deeds Point?"

I nodded.

"A witness I'd been hunting."

I told them about it.

"So, which one of you was the target? Did you walk in on something you shouldn't have, or was someone after you?"

The question, or something akin to it, had bumped its way into my consciousness a time or two.

"I don't know."

The following day, my fever began to go down. The doctor I didn't remember stopped by again and promoted me to broth and a coddled egg. While Jenkins and Ione had supper that night, I took a bath. I was back on the couch when Jenkins ambled in with a handful of eight-by-ten photos. He hitched up a chair and perched like a satisfied grasshopper.

First he told me some things he'd told me before but I'd only half remembered. That he'd driven Ione to retrieve my car and return it to a spot in front of Mrs. Z's. She'd also popped in to tell my landlady I'd been taken ill and was staying at their place. Jenkins had spun the same story for Heebs and called Finn's to spread the word there so they wouldn't worry. Thanks perhaps to his press card, he'd managed to have a brief word with Joel Minsky to relate as many details as he knew about what had happened to me.

Then he showed me the pictures in his hands as he explained them. He'd returned to Deeds Point and found a set of footprints next to the privy, the point from which someone had rushed out toward Gloria. He'd followed them back to tire tracks from a car that had been parked in a brushy area two streets over. Two sets of footprints led to the car, the ones from the privy, and a second set that had come from a gravel area near the park entrance. Those had come from a man considerably bigger, wearing shoes squared off at the toe, like a work boot.

Hawkins.

***

"If you wanted to swim, Mo has a pool at her place she'd let you use."

I chuckled. It was Rachel. When I opened one eye from my mid-morning drowse, she was standing above me with arms crossed.

"I'll put this in the kitchen." Ione, the soul of discretion, gestured with a jar she was holding and left.

"Mama sent you some soup." Rachel sat on the edge of the couch. "She says if what we've heard about you nearly drowning is true, I'm to bring you home so she can take care of you. I have to admit there's no better nurse."

I sat up and scrubbed at my face to banish the cobwebs.

"Tell her thanks, but I'm just about back on my feet. I thought I'd have Ione drive me back to my place this evening."

"Maggie, what in the name of—" Rachel broke off, shaking her cloud of dark hair. "Give me the high points, if you're up to it. Joel wants to know."

Her dark eyes had a dangerous sheen when I finished.

"Well. Joel said tell you that while he considered your float down the river a bit extreme, it was just what he needed to get a postponement. Attempted murder of his investigator. Subsequent loss of a crucial witness. Things along those lines." She had her lighter out, rotating it in her fingers, but not lighting up.

"But I *lost* her!" I said in frustration. "I don't know if she's alive or dead. I don't even know if the woman who called and set it all up was really Gloria. She talked as if she'd taken off, which Gloria had, and she sounded nervous. The super's wife where she lived had gotten a call from her a few days earlier saying she was coming back and wanted a check for her unused rent. The woman who called me wanted money, so that fit too."

I paused.

"I've been set up before, Rachel, but never when the person I was meeting demanded money."

"Maybe you turned up where someone wasn't expecting you."

"Maybe."

"I need to be on my way." Rachel got up. "Mo and Esther are waiting for me in the hall, and I don't want to tire you."

"In the hall—"

"They don't mind. The whole family's concerned. So's Pearlie. He called today and I told him." She hesitated, then bent and brushed a kiss on my forehead. "Call if you need anything."

**

"You haven't mentioned whether you liked the sewing machine," I said as Ione cleared away the bowl that had held Mrs. Minsky's wonderful chicken soup and a sort of Jewish dumpling I'd had once before and found delicious.

"Good thing you didn't ask when I had you in the bathtub that first night. I'd have finished what those people who tried to drown you bungled."

I meant to laugh but mostly coughed instead. Ione thumped my back.

"I don't know what the man was thinking. I suppose I

might be glad of it someday, if it gets to the point where we can't buy new things. *McCall's* magazine already says there won't be anything wool, or girdles or brassieres either once whatever's in stores now is gone."

"You're not telling me you might make a girdle on that thing."

"Of course not. That would take rubber for one thing, which is why we won't be able to get them in stores. The fact is, I couldn't make anything on it. I don't have the faintest idea. My mother would be glad to have it if hers broke, though, so I'll gnash my teeth quietly. I need to run out and get some veal for dinner. Be a good girl and nap."

I heard the front door close behind her. Almost immediately, it opened again.

"My, but you have an admirer! This was outside the door." She set the largest box of chocolates I'd ever seen on my lap. "No having one yet, though. Your poor tummy would rebel."

Adjusting her hat microscopically, she left again. I sat staring at the foil box, which was nearly as deep as it was wide. It didn't seem like the sort of gift anyone I knew would send, and not that many people knew I was here. Someone in Rachel's family?

An envelope waited under the blue satin bow. I slid it out. The letters forming my name were printed and didn't call to mind any I recognized. Sliding my finger under the flap of the envelope, I broke the seal and opened the plain white note card it contained.

You'll like the bottom layer best.
It's a better size for you.

There was no signature, not even initials. Wary now, I examined the box from all angles. Finally I undid the ribbon tying the box and lifted the lid.

Chocolates. Fine quality. What was I going to find on the bottom layer?

Using both hands, I removed the stiffened cardboard supporting the top layer. As it cleared the edge of the box, I stopped so abruptly a chocolate tumbled off to the floor. Along the edges of the bottom two layers, several rows of chocolates remained at the ready in their cardboard wells. The center rows had been removed. Nestling in the resulting space was a .38 Smith & Wesson. It was shorter than mine, a three-inch barrel, but it was a dandy.

Only one person I could think of would have sent it.

Pearlie.

THIRTY-EIGHT

Ione pressed me to stay one more night at their place, but I suspected having me around was deterring her and Jenkins from making whoopie. I argued that getting back to Mrs. Z's on Friday night when most of the girls were out on dates would mean fewer questions. She relented. Back in my own bed I slept on and off for most of the weekend. By Sunday afternoon I was sitting up reading. On Monday I got into my DeSoto and inhaled deeply, in charge of my life again.

When I opened the door to my office, I stopped in surprise. There, enthroned behind my desk, was Heebs.

"Boy, sis, are you a sight for sore eyes!" He sprang to his feet. "Here, sit down."

"Heebs, what are you doing here? I'm pretty sure I sent word that you could go back to peddling papers."

"Yeah, that camera guy from the paper came and told me. He said you were real sick. It didn't seem right just to walk out, with you in the midst of a big case and all. Not after you stepped in and looked after me and saw to it I didn't get sent to that orphan asylum and all.

"And guess, what, sis? Those sheets with all the numbers and columns, the ones about bidding? I found something in them."

I sat down faster than intended in the chair he'd vacated. My chair. I held up a hand.

"Wait a minute. Let me catch my breath."

Oatmeal had once again proved its amazing restorative properties at the first real breakfast I'd had in days, but I needed a minute to stabilize before my brain could process whatever it was Heebs was throwing at me. I was a person who drew strength from the familiar. I needed to sit and look at my office. I needed to see my Dad's picture in his police uniform, and the oak filing cabinet on which I knew the history of each scar and dent. As I looked at the Remington on which I'd typed countless reports and the stapler with which I'd once threatened a man, healing flowed in.

Heebs was fidgeting. I leaned back in my chair and looked at him.

"Found something, have you?"

"I think so."

"Good, because I'm spinning my wheels." I motioned for him to tilt the Remington. "Get them out and show me."

It felt good to sit after driving and walking, even though it hadn't been far. Heebs spread the typed up lists on which I'd spent so many fruitless hours. He stood next to me as he talked.

"You can't exactly see it looking at these. You have to count what everyone got. That's what I did. About halfway through these, this one guy, Lamont, started getting half again as many bids or contracts — is that what you call them? — as he did before. See—"

I held up a hand. "Wait. Give me a minute."

Lamont. If I understood what Heebs was telling me, there'd been a point at which Lamont started getting more contracts. It was before he started shelling out to the late

Gabriel Foster though. Had he been doing something crooked that got him more contracts only to fall prey to blackmail when Foster somehow learned about it?

"Heebs, are you sure about this?"

"Yeah, sis, I am. Pretty sure, anyway. Here's where I counted up the six that got the most."

The sheet he handed me wasn't typed like the ones from Cecilia. It was tablet paper on which vertical columns were marked off with a ruler. The hand printed names were passably neat and had hatch-marked groups representing numbers following each. I realized the columns represented years.

"Heebs, I'm impressed. How did you ever spot this?" *And why hadn't I?*

Heebs squinted in thought. Only a bruise under one eye and a crack on his lip remained as evidence of his beating.

"It wasn't so much a matter of spotting, sis. I ran out of things to do. I'd stared and stared at those pages and I understood them, but they didn't tell me anything, if you know what I mean."

"Yeah, I do."

"So I started wondering how much money guys that did this made, and I totaled up that. But then I got thinking that didn't necessarily mean they got the most jobs, because once you'd pointed it out to me I knew the jobs were all different. So then I thought why not see who got the most jobs? That's where I started to see a pattern. On this." He stubbed his finger proudly on the sheet with the hatch-marked totals, then paused uncertainly. "It is a pattern, isn't it, sis?"

"It certainly looks like it."

"Does that mean I've broken the case?"

"By rights it ought to. The trouble is, it wouldn't exactly be accepted as proof. It gives me something to work with, though. I just need time to think.

"Now I owe you some money—"

The phone rang.

"This is Bess, the super's wife. She's back. She's up in her apartment."

I sat up so abruptly it jolted my spine.

"Gloria's back? Have you seen her?"

"She had her hand out demanding that refund as soon as I opened the door. I told her his nibs was out and he had all the money."

"Don't let her leave, Bess. I'll be right over."

Thirty seconds or so elapsed as I weighed things. I didn't know if it had been Gloria at Deeds Point or not. I did know I didn't want to be jumped again. I was dialing Lt. Freeze when I remembered Heebs. I looked around. He was nowhere in sight.

The good lieutenant's voice grated in my ear.

"The manager's wife just called to tell me Gloria's in her apartment. Since I was good enough to tell you, how about swinging by and giving me a lift? The wife doesn't think much of you or Boike, so if you go there on your own, you're likely to find nobody at home."

His struggle to decide was almost audible. Unaware of how depleted my energy was, he was thinking if he turned me down I might beat him.

"Be down in front of your building, then, and don't take time to powder your nose."

***

"Give me ten minutes alone with her before you come in," I said from the back of the unmarked car used by the detective bureau.

"Did I miss out on why you're giving orders?" Freeze lighted a cigarette and dangled it out the window while Boike drove.

"What I said about the manager's wife not warming to you? That's pretty much how all the women you've talked to on this feel. Her, the girls who worked with Gloria. You're a cop, you're a man, and I hate to say it, Freeze, but you don't exactly have a winning way. Some of them don't like me much either. I have a feeling Gloria won't. But I pick up on little things. I recognize ways to get their goat, or make them trust me enough to spill things. It's a skill, Freeze, like working a silk stocking up your leg."

He snorted.

"Okay. Five minutes."

My patience snapped.

"Dammit, Freeze, I said ten and I meant it! You've been playacting with me this whole case, all of a sudden listening to my ideas like you thought they had merit, sharing bits of information. Not because your opinion of me has changed. Oh, no. It's all because you think I might know things I'm not sharing!"

"Hey, now—"

"Well maybe I do, and *if* I do, it's because I've dug for them, same as you do. Only I dig deeper, Freeze, and okay, maybe you can't. Time constraints, cops leaving — I get that. But maybe, just maybe, now and again you could at least play fair with me. Because I've helped you plenty, and we both know it. I even went to meet someone who claimed to be Gloria, and got tossed in the Great Miami for my efforts. I have earned every one of those ten minutes, and I intend to have them!"

Boike let out a sound of dismay when I mentioned the river. It didn't slow me or my anger. I swung the door open and hopped from the car before it came to a full stop in front of Gloria's apartment building.

THIRTY-NINE

I rapped on Gloria's door with the fleeting thought it might be satisfying to give Gloria's nose a tap or two as well when she opened it. If she opened it. There was no response from inside. Before I knocked I'd caught a sound or two, and the manager's wife, who was keeping vigil in the downstairs hall when I arrived, assured me the girl hadn't left.

"Gloria, I know you're in there. You can either talk to me or talk to the cops. Or waste enough time and you might get a chance to talk to the men who roughed you up last time. Take your pick."

A dollop of silence melted away. Then footsteps whispered across carpet. The door opened just enough for me to shove my foot through it if needs be.

"Who are you?"

She was my height, made an inch or so taller by high heels. Her blonde hair looked natural. She was pretty enough to cause envy among girls in a small office, but not much more. Apart from a hint of petulance, her eyes lacked animation.

Shelving thoughts of a pop in the nose, I managed a mild tone.

"My name's Maggie Sullivan. Ring any bells?"

"No, should it?"

I waited. Her petulance deepened into a frown.

"I didn't work with you. I never saw you before in my life. You must be looking for someone else. Now hit the road."

This girl was the authentic Gloria. The superintendent's wife had recognized her. Now I also knew she wasn't the one who had called me last week and led me into an ambush. The blonde who was barring my way had a lisp, albeit a slight one. Whoever had spoken to me on the phone didn't. I pushed my way in.

"Hey! Get out or I'll scream for the super."

"He's out right now, remember? The quickest way to get rid of me is to answer some questions. I'm a detective." I tossed her a card. She fumbled it. I tossed her another. "I'm trying to find out who killed your boyfriend — and who slammed you into the wall back there."

"I don't know anything!"

"What were they hunting? Who were they?"

"I don't know!"

"What did they look like then?" Dropping onto her couch, I crossed my legs and leaned back, suggesting I'd stay all day if necessary. "You might as well start answering. Either that or pop into the kitchen and make us some tea."

Her mouth opened and then closed again. She looked around helplessly. Not in panic, though. There was a strange indifference about her. I wondered if she saw most things in terms of herself.

"How do I know you're what you say you are?"

"You don't — but I haven't roughed you up like the others did."

She processed that, while I tried not to think about

seconds ticking away from my five minutes. Ten minutes if my outburst had worked miracles and spurred Freeze to some semblance of fair play.

"I don't know what they were looking for, or who they were. It was something to do with Gabe's work." Without taking her eyes off me, she edged onto the arm of a chair. "Some kind of receipt, I think."

For blackmail payments? She had to be lying. But she was speaking again.

"They... I think they called it an invoice."

Now she had my attention. "For what?"

Her head shook. "I don't know. Honest. They kept yelling at me about had I seen it, where did Gabe keep things, where would he hide it. But I was blindfolded and they'd tied my hands, and that was after one of them had banged my head on the wall to make me talk." She swallowed. "I was too scared to think."

That admission was the first time she'd seemed human. It was also the point at which I decided she was telling the truth.

"You said what they were hunting had to do with Mr. Foster's business. What made you think that?"

"I don't know."

"Think."

She gave a sigh of exasperation.

"It just seemed..." She broke off as a thought occurred. "It had something to do with building things, that's why."

From down below I caught the murmur of voices. Freeze and Boike. I ground my teeth.

"Bids? Contracts?" I pressed.

"No, no. Things you use. Shingles. Or maybe lumber. Or

pipe. Yeah, I think it was pipe. No, lumber. I think."

A key clattered at the lock. Gloria sprang from her perch. The door opened, admitting the two detectives.

"Everything okay in here?"

"Dandy," I said through my teeth. To be fair, the time I'd spent with Gloria was probably closer to what I'd asked for than not.

Freeze was temporarily sans cigarette. His mouth gave a tic, which was probably meant to be a smile.

"Miss Overbrook? I'm Detective Freeze. This is Detective Boike. We've been worried about your welfare."

Gloria looked from the men to me.

"You said if I talked to you, you wouldn't call the cops!"

"Don't you want them to catch whoever killed your boyfriend?"

"Well, yeah, sure. But it won't bring Gabe back, will it? I gotta think about myself now, so all of you clear out."

Freeze's gaze slid over to meet mine.

"She's heartbroken," I said.

"Yeah, I see that." His index finger made a circular motion as he spoke to Gloria. "You might as well sit down."

"But—"

"The men who roughed her up were hunting an invoice for lumber," I said. "Or maybe pipes. Tell the nice policemen what you told me."

The blonde glared. Flouncing into the chair she'd perched on earlier, she crossed her arms and repeated her story.

"And you'd never seen these men before?" Freeze asked for the third time."

"No! I already told you. I mean, I didn't even get enough of a look to know. I opened the door, and the first one — he filled the whole doorway — before I could even ask what he wanted, he smacked me so hard it knocked me down and my head went woozy. By the time it stopped spinning, he'd rolled me onto my belly and was tying my hands. He told me Gabe was dead and if I tried to scream, I would be too. Then he blindfolded me."

"What about the second one? You said there were two."

"He had on a hat. He was standing to the side, though, out in the hall. That's all I saw."

"What kind of hat?"

"I don't know... snap brim, I think."

She didn't remember anything useful about their voices, timbre, pitch, words they used. The one who'd tied her up and slammed her against the wall so hard she'd cut her head sounded 'tough.' The other one sounded 'mean.'

Freeze had hitched up a chair while she talked. When she finally ran down, he leaned forward. He gave her a hard look, but his words were uncommonly quiet.

"Why do you think they left without killing you?"

Gloria's eyes shifted. It was her first sign of nervousness.

"I-I told them there was somebody who might know where they could find what they wanted. It was a lie though, see. Gabe had this old girlfriend who sang at a club up on Salem. I don't even know if she's still there or not, but I said he'd gone out to see her one night and told me not to be jealous, he just needed to drop something off to her." She swallowed. "The one who did the talking said if they found out I was lying, they'd be back.

"I didn't have much to lose. I figured if Sally — that was

her name — if she was still working there, they'd have to wait until she took a break and then grill her. If she wasn't there, they'd put the screws to whoever ran the club, same as they did me. Either way would give me enough time to stuff some clothes in a suitcase and get to the train station, so that's what I did."

***

"You buy what she told us?" asked Freeze as the two of us walked to his car. Boike was watching Gloria until a uniformed unit arrived to take her to a holding cell so the cops could get a formal statement and Joel a deposition if he wanted one.

"That she'd sic her attackers on some innocent woman to save her own skin? Sure."

"I was thinking more about her busting out of the bathroom and using a kitchen knife to cut the ropes around her hands."

"It's just a thumb latch on the bathroom door. She might have scraped her chin, but she could maneuver the lock around with it like she said. And using the knife to saw through the ropes? Sure. Half of getting out of a pickle like that's keeping your head."

"Voice of experience?"

I shrugged.

"You looked like you might have an idea who one of the men might have been, the one she said was big."

"An idea, no proof. One of the workmen on Miss Minsky's project is the size of a boxcar, and he doesn't like her."

"Enough to pin a murder on her?"

"For money. He's not the sort who could plan it all out. He'd be muscle for someone."

"Still think that would be Lamont?"

"Who else? If Gloria's right about them hunting a bill or an invoice, it fits nicely with blackmail."

"Over shingles or lumber? Why?"

"Billing for more than you get? I don't know. Rachel may have some ideas." I shot him a sideways look. "Yeah, I know. I need proof."

What starch I had left in me was evaporating. Frustration at knowing more than I had before, but not how or where to plug it in didn't help.

Steering with one hand, Freeze scraped a match with his thumb and started a cigarette.

"Lot of lumberyards in this town. If you want to go looking for a needle in a haystack, be my guest."

I started to smile. There was looking in haystacks, and then there was burning a few down to see what was left.

FORTY

I called Rachel.

"We need to brainstorm. I need to ask you some things about construction and materials. I'm not sure where it's going to go, or maybe even the questions to ask, but it's important."

She didn't speak for a moment.

"Let me see if Mo can pick me up and chaperone."

"You'll need to come to my office. I'm not up to any more running around this morning."

"Wait a minute." A voice murmured in the background. "Mama says if Mo's not available, she'll come with me. We'll call a cab."

"She doesn't like the way you drive?"

"Joel confiscated my car as part of his initial deal with the judge."

"Ah."

"Regardless of which it is, don't expect us for forty-five minutes. We'll need time to get properly attired."

Either she was signaling that one or more of them were still in their nighties, or her kin thought coming to my office was a dressier occasion than could be satisfied by their current togs.

While I waited, I put my feet up and closed my eyes for ten minutes to get my starch back. Then I thought some.

Though all claimed to lack the capacity to take over Foster's project, any of the other three unsuccessful bidders could potentially benefit if Rachel was out of the game. There might be others, but none with a connection I'd turned up so far. Moreover, both the developer financing the murdered man's project and the one behind Rachel's had despaired about other local construction companies of any size already having their hands full. The fact the men who'd threatened Gloria were hunting a paper related to construction materials — even if she couldn't recall what kind — appeared to eliminate a grudge unrelated to that world as a motive for murder. As to why Rachel had been framed, learning why Foster had been killed, and by whom, might lead to an answer there as well.

Clark. Jones. Lamont. My money stayed on Lamont as the primary suspect. He'd enjoyed an unexplained increase in contracts awarded him, followed by what almost certainly had been blackmail. Grabbing at the most obvious explanation wasn't always smart, though.

Time to burn haystacks.

Where to start was the question. Shingles, lumber or pipe?

I called Phil Clark first. His secretary must have gone to powder her nose. He answered the phone.

"Mr. Clark? Maggie Sullivan."

"Miss Sullivan?" he repeated after several seconds. "Yes. Sorry. Good to hear from you."

"Did I catch you at a bad time?"

"No. No, I just had someone in my office. They're gone now. What can I do for you?"

His voice was returning to normal, but I hadn't imagined

that initial note of... what? Strain? Disorientation? Abruptly I changed my mind about asking what I'd intended.

"You told me you'd run into Foster and his girlfriend once at a club. Which girlfriend?"

"Pardon?"

"He had another girlfriend before the one he promoted to mistress."

"He what? That sly dog. No. I'm afraid I don't know which it was."

"You didn't get a name?"

"No."

"Remember what she looked like?"

"No. Blonde perhaps?" His outward breath held mild impatience. "Is it important?"

"Possibly. What about the club? Do you remember the name?"

"I'm afraid I can't help you there either. Was there anything else?"

"Would you happen to know where Foster bought the pipe for his buildings?"

"Pipe? The plumber he subcontracted to would supply it. That would be in his paperwork."

He didn't ask why I wanted to know, and since his answer led me to think I could scratch pipe off the list of things Gloria had mentioned, I saw no benefit in prolonging our conversation.

***

"You and Rachel are the only women in the family who drive?" I asked Mo when the two of them arrived.

"It practically makes her a fallen woman," said Rachel.

"Rache, that's not fair. You know Joel tried his best to get Judith to learn." Mo was looking around my office with an expression I couldn't quite read. I thought there was interest somewhere in it.

"I brought a book." She produced it. "I can take a chair into the hall if you'd like privacy."

"We're not going to talk about anything salacious, unless there's a side to the construction business I haven't come across yet."

"In that case I'm glad I brought the book."

Mo showed promise.

I sat down at my desk, but Rachel moved restlessly around the room.

"How are you feeling, by the way?"

"Not perky, but holding my own."

I told her what Gloria had said about a bill or invoice. When I'd finished, she came to rest in the client's chair in front of my desk. Her crossed leg swung, an outlet for the rapid turning of her mind.

"You're thinking it's proof of a swindle of some sort Lamont had going."

"Yes."

"Which fits with Foster blackmailing him if he found out."

"Also with Lamont's sudden increase in successful bids."

I slid Heebs' handiwork across the desk for her to examine. As its import sank in, her mouth hardened.

"He was getting a break on materials somewhere. A crooked one by the sound of it. I'd bet a hundred dollars Foster not only blackmailed Lamont, but cut himself in on the swindle. That would explain how the s.o.b. managed such a low bid on that contract I spouted off about, and why Lamont looked so mad that day."

"It would also mean you were close to the truth when you accused Foster of cutting corners to keep down his cost. Close enough to make the killer think you had the proof, so he knew it existed."

"And tore up my office hunting it."

"And framed you for Foster's death."

"Lamont?"

"Or whoever was working the swindle with him. The supplier. Or someone who, like Foster, caught wind of it and wanted to cut himself in. Is that a possibility? Would enough be at stake?"

Rachel slumped into the chair, pigeon-toed with her hands between her knees. She was thirty-one, three years older than me, but right now resembled a forlorn kid of twelve.

"Yes, depending on the swindle, it could be enough. With business uncertain as it is now, it would very well be worth someone's time — or the blackmail alone could, making for a much bigger field."

"Not necessarily. We've got an end to pull at now that we know more or less what the invoice covered."

"Lumber, shingles, pipe — which it wouldn't be, by the way, because—"

"The plumbing subcontractor would supply it. I've already learned that."

"If we assume the girl's even remotely right, there could be half a dozen other construction materials it might have involved. Gravel, concrete, steel beams — those would be the expensive ones."

Her low spirits were palpable. She got up and walked to the window.

"I need a cigarette."

She opened the window and smoked. I sat at my desk. Mo appeared to be reading.

"All right." Rachel made a good show of strutting back with her old verve. "Let's look at the biggest costs in a project first."

She talked. I listened and questioned. In terms of materials, the three most expensive were lumber, steel joists and beams, and concrete. The first two had gone up in price since the war started, and were increasingly hard to get for civilian construction.

"Black market?" I asked.

"Not yet, and not likely ever. Firms like mine will have to switch to military projects, new buildings at Patterson Field for example, or to much smaller ones like four-plexes where we might be able to get enough of what trickles out in the way of materials."

"Let's rule that out, then, since Lamont began getting more contracts a good two years ago. That means the swindle would probably be along the lines of billing Lamont the full amount for beams, say, but selling them to him for less and getting a cut of that difference? Is that how it works?"

"Yes. Or charging for a certain number but delivering fewer." Her mouth gave a sideways twist. "There are probably ways I've never heard of, and it could involve all the other supplies we've talked about, not just the top three. There are dozens, no, scores of people who could be Lamont's partner. We're back to square one."

"Not necessarily."

FORTY-ONE

Despite my show of optimism for Rachel, I didn't have the least idea what to do next. I'd already burned down the Phil Clark haystack with nothing to show for it. My next option was to confront Lamont without so much as a decent bluff about knowing the particulars of his swindling, which I didn't want to do. Apart from that, I'd have to pick through a lot of straw.

I did have one germ of an idea but my recent dunking had robbed me of stamina. A couple of phones calls, a spot of typing, and I went back to Mrs. Z's where I slept away most of the afternoon. When I woke up, there was just enough of it left to call Joel Minsky's office.

"Mr. Minsky got the envelope you left," reported his receptionist. "He said if you called to tell you he'd gone to talk to the witness you found and will call you tomorrow if anything new comes to light."

The grandfather clock ticking away in the downstairs hall by Mrs. Z's phone stand told me the smartest thing I could do with what remained of the day was go to Finn's so people would know I was still among the living.

***

"Saw you come in, love." Rose slid a freshly pulled Guinness to me as I neared my usual spot at the bar's far end. "We heard you were sick."

"Yeah, but the devil didn't want me. Thought I'd better come in and let everybody know I'm okay."

All stools in the area where I ordinarily found a spot were occupied. Only a few faces at the bar were familiar.

"We get more and more in who've arrived to do factory work," Rose murmured noting my gaze. She set another Guinness next to the tap while its foam settled. Farther along the bar, an unfamiliar customer clinked his empty grass impatiently. Rose filled her hands with drinks to deliver. "Mick's back by the wall," she called over her shoulder.

Connelly sat alone at a table next to the back partition. He looked up when I was halfway there.

"This seat saved for anyone?" I asked pulling the chair across from him out.

"Just my hat. You're a sight better company."

He put his patrolman's hat on the table. The sight of him there across from me, solid and reassuring, brought flooding memories of the fear I'd felt there alone in the river. Guinness didn't still them.

"You okay?" Connelly was frowning.

"Just tired. I've been under the weather."

"Yeah, Rose said."

The dark, cold current rushing through my head wouldn't stop. With the same desperation I'd clung to the log in the river, my eyes now clung to the familiar sight of the man across from me. The steel blue eyes that could tease; the hard yet mobile mouth with its perfect masculine shape; the last face I'd thought of alone in the water.

I could take care of myself.

I'd managed to ever since my dad died. Even before.

I could take care of myself.

I'd escaped the river. I was sitting here. Why, then, did I feel so desperately glad for Connelly's presence? For the resonant baritone of his voice and the faint, faint scent of his morning shaving cream? The feel of his leg against mine was proof of my safety.

"When I first came in, I thought I might have turned into the wrong pub," I chattered. "How'd I miss Wee Willie?"

"Don't know about Willie. Seamus has night rotation. Maggie..." Connelly's frown had deepened into a mask of concern. "Maggie, you're acting strange." He chose words carefully. "You're not worse sick than you're letting on, are you? On my way home after Rose told me why you hadn't been in, I stopped by Mrs. Z's to see if I could bring you anything. She said a friend was looking after you. I thought you might be in hospital."

At the worry pinching his features, the tenderness in his voice, I started to tremble. I tried to take a sip of stout. It sloshed to the rim, almost spilling. Setting the glass down, I fought to discipline my shaking lips into shaping words.

"I wasn't sick. Someone threw me into the river."

"Maggie!"

The word he breathed was so filled with anguish that tears started in my eyes. I willed them away. I hadn't cried since my dad's funeral. I wasn't going to sit here and bawl where people could see.

"I washed ashore and a bum found me. Jenkins and Ione took me to their place." Tears kept squeezing out. My trembling progressed to full-blown shaking. "I almost

drowned, Mick! I don't know how I made it out. I...
almost... drowned!"

Connelly enveloped my hand with his, warming my
fingers and holding them tightly. His free hand reached
across and his thumb wiped a tear away, its touch warm
and strong and so infinitely caring.

"Let's have a walk, shall we? Get a breath of fresh air?"

Unable to speak, I nodded. We left my pint barely
touched and his half finished. By the time we reached the
sidewalk my breath was coming in tiny gulps, silent sobs I
couldn't control. Connelly's arm slid around me, holding
me close.

"There, Maggie, it's all right. It's all right." He kissed my
hair. "You're safe, love."

Three doors down from Finn's was the kind of alley
Connelly called a 'close.' A few steps into it was the
entrance to a shop that made picture frames. Connelly
steered me into the arch of the shop, away from the curious
gazes of passersby. Wrapping his arms around me, he
tucked me under his chin. He stroked my hair, soothing
and petting me as if I were a child, while my silent sobs
spilled out tears. When at last they diminished, his soft
cotton handkerchief dried my face.

"Better?"

I nodded.

"You hadn't told anyone, had you? How truly scared you
were?"

"Stupid of me going on about it now. It's over. I made it
out."

"And I'm glad, *mavourneen*. So glad. I don't think I could
bear it if anything happened to you."

His voice throbbed with emotion. He kissed my swollen eyelids gently. For several minutes we simply stood there with his arms around me while I leaned against him listening to traffic and footsteps and murmurs of conversation as the city headed home from the workday.

Tipping my face up, Connelly brushed my lips with his. The tenderness softened memories of being alone in the river. It hadn't been so much the fear of dying. It had been the loneliness, my insignificance. Fierce hunger, need, an urgency to seize what I had almost lost surged inside me. I drew back far enough to see his familiar face.

"Is that invitation to come up to your place still good?"

***

His room was as quiet and unassuming as the man himself. There was a three-quarter bed against one wall, a wardrobe, an armchair and reading lamp. That was all I noticed.

Like two who had gone too long without food we wound together.

"I thought this day would never come, Maggie. Christ but I love you."

His Sam Browne belt with its service revolver dropped onto the chair. With one accord our clothes came off. After all these years, it seemed both natural and dreamlike. We moved to the tune we'd been waiting for since we met, and one as ancient as the hills.

FORTY-TWO

"I always knew you'd have freckles."

"And bragged you'd see them one day, as I recall."

Connelly chuckled. Not fully awake but far from drowsing, he traced the place where the freckles resided, the inner curve of my breast.

It was four in the morning. We'd explored each other, talked, slept for an hour or two, then done it all over again. Now we lay with my head on his shoulder. I'd never been so content in my life.

"This feels like it might have come from a bullet." My open palm slid over a patch of satiny skin on his chest.

"Mmm. Nicked a lung. Another reason why the Army didn't want me, I think."

We drifted, each with our own thoughts. Dawn would arrive soon.

"You know anything about construction?" I asked.

"I can mend a gate, put up a lean-to, replace rotting stairs on a porch. That's about the extent of it." Rolling over, hands braced on either side of me, he smiled. "Why? Have I flunked my first test?"

"There's always the chance you could get an A elsewhere."

He did.

When I awoke again, it was to his whistling. He was dressing for duty. For a while I watched him, enjoying the neat economy of his movements. Finally I stirred.

"Guess I'd better get going too so your landlady doesn't see me and throw you out for having a woman up here."

"Do you always wake up worrying, Sunshine? The dear woman's deaf as a post." He sat on the edge of the bed, blocking my exit. "Anyway, she's away for the week visiting her nephew. And if she did throw me out..." He dropped a light kiss on me. "...it would be worth it."

He resumed dressing, donning his puttees.

"Why did you ask about carpentry? Does something at Mrs. Z's need fixing?"

"No, I want an opinion on something at a construction project. It wouldn't be smart to involve you in it anyway."

"It wouldn't help Lt. Freeze's opinion of you if he thought you had me wrapped around his finger like you have him."

I laughed.

"That's a different gun than you had before." He nodded at where it lay on the table.

"You took it out of my purse?"

"You put it there when you got up to visit the loo. Don't you remember?"

"It wasn't exactly topmost in my mind, and yes, it's new. I had to ditch the one I had to stay afloat. Someone left that for me. I think it must have been Pearlie."

Connelly turned abruptly.

"Pearlie Gibbons. The man who drives for your friend Rachel and used to be a junior gunman for Two-Finger Louie in Cleveland?"

I didn't like what I was hearing, or the sound of it. I sat up, wrapping the sheet around me.

"I don't know his last name, and I don't know anything

about his previous employment, but yes, I'm talking about the man who drives for Rachel. Or did. He left town." But had he? "Why?"

After a minute the stiffness melted from Connelly's manner. He drew a breath, then shook his head.

"When push comes to shove, anybody who looks out for you is okay by me. Just be careful, will you, *mavourneen*? A man like that can be a magnet for the same kind of men. And he doesn't always change his spots completely."

"But sometimes he does."

Connelly had killed at least one man in Ireland, caught in bitter conflict between Republicans and Free Staters that tangled the lives of so many. Whether or not he knew what was on my mind, he smiled faintly.

"Yah, sometimes they do. I'd better be off. Day shift's hoping to nab a pair of purse-snatchers who've been after women cashing their factory checks. See you at Finn's?"

I stepped up into the kiss he was bending to give me.

"Can't. I need to talk to someone who does know about construction when he gets done for the day. Then I plan on doing something you're better off not knowing about."

"Maggie—"

"It's not dangerous, just something a respectable policeman shouldn't be expected to ignore. And at half-past eight I need to take a bus ride."

"A bus ride."

The day before I'd left word for Lulu Sollers that I'd been detained the previous week but intended to have a crack at catching up with the kids on the bus tonight.

"Come over after that then?"

"It could be late. I may have to spend some time with Lulu Sollers or one of her policewomen."

"Ah. That business with the candy wrappers, is it?"

"Yes."

"Late doesn't matter." His eyes were twinkling. He swayed me side to side as if dancing. "I guarantee I'll make it worth your while."

***

The curtained tub-shower at one end of Connelly's room was cramped but adequate. For once I didn't buy a paper before settling on a stool at McCrory's for breakfast. When I went to get one afterward, the sight of Heebs back on his corner put a spring in my step.

"Hey, sis. You look lots better today."

"You too, Heebs. Any trouble getting your place back?"

"Naw. The kid that was here backed off like he was scared of me. Guess I must have a reputation for holding my own. Paper, mister?"

Things were starting to feel normal again, or as normal as they'd been since Pearl Harbor. I spent the morning making futile phone calls to shingle, steel and lumber places. Each one left me more convinced that Morris, the workman with the droopy eye at Rachel's work site, was my best hope for putting the last nail I needed in Lamont's coffin. Lamont might not be the one who'd actually murdered Gabriel Foster, but if I could confront him with what the swindle he had going involved, he'd squeal like a baby pig pulled off its mother's milk.

Lack of supper on the previous day, not to mention the night's very pleasant exertions, had left me ravenous. I went for an early lunch at a diner I liked where I topped off a blue plate special with rhubarb pie á la mode. With a potentially lengthy evening ahead of me, I went back to Mrs. Z's and repeated my afternoon nap of the day before.

At five o'clock I drove past Rachel's construction site to see if the men were leaving. They weren't. The big machine with the bucket in front that had almost smashed me into oblivion the night this whole business started was parked at the edge of the site now. Its presence puzzled me since it looked to me as if all the digging or whatever they did with such machines was already finished.

I parked two blocks farther away, toward where Morris had indicated he caught the trolley, and hoped the gorilla Hawkins didn't come the same direction. Everything I'd seen about Morris made me trust him, and think he'd go a mile or two extra to help the woman he worked for. Everything I'd seen about Hawkins made me think he'd trip her any chance he got.

About forty minutes after I'd parked, Morris came striding down the sidewalk. I leaned across the seat and called out the passenger window.

"Morris! Want a ride?"

He looked around, spotted me, and came over. Bending down to see me he grinned.

"Thanks for the offer, but no. By this time of day I smell pretty ripe."

"I've been ripe a time or two myself, and I want to talk to you about helping with something that might get Miss Minsky off the hook."

"Sure, anything."

"Get in."

He was right. As the door closed behind him and I pulled into traffic, his sweat made its presence known. I'd smelled worse things. I thought about the bum who'd dragged me up from the edge of the river.

"You've worked construction projects long enough to have a feel for the materials, right?" No point pussyfooting.

Morris frowned. "I'm not sure I understand what you mean."

"Say the steel beams or lumber or shingles or something wasn't up to snuff. You'd be able to tell that."

He rubbed his chin in thought.

"Lumber, probably, since framing and sheathing is what I work on mostly. Shingles, maybe. On some projects I've helped with roofing; other times not. As for the beams, they'd have to be rusty or something just about as obvious for me to guess anything was wrong. Concrete... it might take something like rust for me to think it wasn't right. Other companies come in and pour. I've never paid any attention to it until it's set." His puzzlement showed. "You think that's why the man got killed? Because something we've been using wasn't right?"

"Not something your crew was using, something at the dead man's project. Which way to where you live?

It turned out to be a tidy white frame house with a not-quite-as-tidy addition in back. He lived with his sister and her family.

"Pick you up at seven," I reminded as I let him out.

We'd agreed it was time enough for him to shower and eat his dinner, with plenty of daylight left for him to look around at our destination. He nodded and started into the house, then spun back.

"What do we do if they have a guard?"

I grinned. That part was the least of my worries.

"I have a plan."

FORTY-THREE

"Why's that big machine with the jaws that used to be in Rachel's equipment yard where you're building now? Aren't you done digging?" With Morris beside me, I circled the project Gabriel Foster's company had been in charge of before his death. It looked to be deserted.

"Another outfit's breaking ground a block over. Miss Minsky's renting it to them, but the other outfit needed to leave it at our site a couple of days. It's called a bucket loader."

I found a parking spot on a cross street and sat for a minute watching Foster's site and the streets around it to make sure I hadn't missed anything. This wasn't a residential area like where Rachel was building. It was a commercial district that had seen better days. The mostly small offices were closed for the day. A cinder block garage, its gas pump slumping forlornly in front of it, was closed for good. We got out and walked casually toward the building project with its three-floor skeleton.

"If anyone comes along, I'll be the giggly girlfriend. I'll go on about how you love looking at construction and I told you nobody was going to care if you took a peek."

Morris nodded absently.

"And if they act like there's a chance I might look familiar, I'll say where I'm working now looks a little iffy and I was wondering whether this job might be taking on workers. Got it."

His shirt and trousers weren't the ones he wore on the job, but they were just as crisply pressed. He was already eyeing the structure in front of us. I sat down on an overturned bucket and concentrated on looking demure. A few cars passed. Their occupants must have bought the little tableau I'd tried to create. There weren't any shade trees around, so there weren't any birds save for plucky sparrows that seemed to thrive anywhere.

A sandwich shop that, like its neighbors, was closed for the day tried to splash out cheer with a window box of petunias. It lost the battle to drab business fronts and concrete. The evening breeze rippling over my skin was pleasant, though, and the surroundings felt peaceful. My new .38 was tucked in my purse in case they proved otherwise.

My aim would be slightly off because of the shorter barrel. I needed to go somewhere and practice. I thought about it during the thirty minutes or so Morris spent inspecting things. First he circled the building's perimeter, where sheets of wood already were starting to cover uprights at ground level. Periodically he stopped and stood looking up. Then he stepped through an opening destined to be a door, and I couldn't see him.

I started to fidget, hoping I wouldn't missing the eight-thirty bus; hoping the kids I was hunting wouldn't be on it yet if I didn't. Morris reappeared. The confidence in his steps as he strode toward me brought me to my feet.

"I think I've found something," he said. "Want to see?" He turned and retraced his steps without awaiting my answer.

Inside, he led the way to a wall where sheathing wasn't up yet. Light still flooded in from outside.

"Look at this board, and at this one." He indicated one four feet away. "See the difference?"

After staring and looking at each of them up close, I shook my head.

"Feel then. Can you feel it?"

I ran my hand along the two boards like he did, but more cautiously for fear of splinters. Again I shook my head.

"This one is grade one framing stock. This one is grade two, still good, but not as good. Not quite as strong or long lasting. You'd use it for a house, but not for commercial construction." He spun, indicating the wooden skeleton around us. "Except where there's an extra board for doors and that, every fifth stud in here is grade two."

"Twenty percent."

"Give or take."

"I take it there'd be a significant difference in price between the two grades?"

"I don't know about significant, but there'd be a difference, and more than pennies. Don't forget, there's lots of lumber goes into a building, too, so it would add up."

"Could the difference in price be enough for a company to bid lower than their competitors? Even if the lower grade only accounted for twenty percent of their lumber costs?"

He started to frown. I was pushing him out of his depth.

"Maybe."

I already had the answers I needed, though. I knew from wading through the data on projects Rachel had bid on that every project specified the grade of the various materials to be used.

***

The eight-thirty bus was just pulling to the curb as I neared the bus stop. I broke into a run.

Collins, the driver, didn't notice me as I got on. When he'd closed the door and started off again, he caught sight of me in the mirror.

"Well, well. So you did decide to take another ride with me, eh? When you didn't come last week, I thought maybe you'd lost interest."

"Got sick," I said.

He nodded in sympathy. "I hope it wasn't that same bug I got. It sure flattens you."

We chatted some. The kids in question hadn't been on the bus last week either, it turned out. That worried me. Maybe a neighbor or sibling had gotten wise to them and put an end to their nocturnal wanderings. On the other hand, when I initially talked to the driver about the kids, he'd said they usually got on around nine-thirty. It had been my choice getting in place early in case they varied their pattern, so I was content to ride along and exchange a few words with Collins from time to time and think.

As half-past nine approached, I slid forward and spoke into Collins' ear, briefing him on the arrangements Lulu Sollers had helped me make in hopes the kids showed up. I moved to a spot two seats up from the back bench where they usually sat.

At the nine thirty-two stop, two kids with dun brown hair and one with black curls climbed on amid the arriving riders. Two were fourteen or fifteen. One of the brown-haired ones was considerably younger. I didn't need Collins' tug at his earlobe, a touch he'd insisted on, to tell me these were the kids I'd been hunting.

They settled in and exchanged a whisper or two. There was a soft snicker. A candy wrapper rustled. I peeked around. I couldn't read the name on it, but the wrapper was the right color for a Whiz bar.

The next stop for the bus was directly in front of the neon sign of a liquor store. I made sure I was the first one off and ran inside. Jostling past a customer, I rapped the counter to get the clerk's attention

"Call the policewoman." He looked up and nodded.

The bus doors closed behind me as I clambered back on board. I wondered if Collins had been forced to wait for me, but I didn't think so. The bus was half full now, but the place I'd occupied was still vacant. I slid back in.

"She must have needed booze real bad, jumping off and getting right back on like that," the older of the brown hairs whispered.

"Dummy, she couldn't buy anything that fast."

"Maybe she called ahead and they had it for her under the counter."

They snickered.

"Maybe she's the driver's girlfriend and that's why he waited."

More snickers.

They weren't bad kids. Probably no worse than Wee Willie and I would have been at that age if we'd been unsupervised. But these kids *were* unsupervised. They were testing limits where none existed, flirting with fire.

Half a dozen rows ahead of me, two women gabbed away, not loudly enough to be nuisances, just night music.

My pulses were jittering, filled with expectation of what might be learned from the threesome behind me. Within the hour it could be dashed, but every little scrap I could snatch for Joel — for Rachel — mattered now.

The bus began to nose to the curb. Here and there passengers left. Half a dozen others dropped their fares in the box at the front and began to take seats. Among them was a blonde about my age whose bearing and composure marked her as the policewoman, even though from this distance the small badge pinned to her bodice might just as easily have been a pretty brooch. I went forward to meet her.

"Are you with Lulu?"

Her head inclined. "You must be Maggie."

We shook hands.

She qualified as fresh faced if you overlooked the alertness in her eyes. They were fixed on the boys in the back seat. She spoke to me under her breath.

"Let's take opposite sides of the aisle, shall we?" She sat down just in front of the boys and half turned to face them. I followed suit.

"Good evening, boys. I'm Policewoman Perkins and this is detective Sullivan."

Her voice was mild. Behind us, our fellow riders read papers and continued conversations, unaware of the drama. The boys' mouths dropped open. They stared. The eyes of the youngest one flicked to her badge.

"Police?" The older brown haired one recovered first. "Why? We haven't done anything."

"How about littering?" With considerable satisfaction I pointed at the candy wrapper tossed on the floor. Not only would it qualify as litter, it was folded into a neat little bow tie.

The one who had spoken smacked the younger one on the back of the head.

"Pick it up, stupid! Look at the trouble you got us in."

"Actually, you've done a dandy job getting yourself in," Perkins assured him. "I expect you're already sorry, though ... what's your name?"

"Benny. Benjamin. Yeah, I'm real—"

"What's your mother's name?"

"Hattie. Hattie Rose. Why?"

"And your mother?"

The one with black curls had figured out where this was going.

"Angela Carmichael. She's not home, though. She's working."

"At Univis with our mom. We don't know what they make, though, 'cause it's secret. But it's for the war." The little one spoke up proudly.

Benny raised his hand to deliver another back-of-head smack. A look from Perkins discouraged him.

"That's certainly an important job," she said to the little one. "We wouldn't want to call your mothers at work and make them come home to sort this out, would we? Let's have a little chat downtown instead, shall we?

"Miss Sullivan, would you pull the cord to let us off? We should have transportation waiting." She glanced out the window. "Ah, yes. There it is."

It was a patrol car.

FORTY-FOUR

"Now, boys." Lulu Sollers folded her hands on the desk in front of her and looked at the trio across from her so sternly they squirmed. "Suppose you tell me what you saw and heard at the construction site you were at the end of last month?"

We were upstairs at Market House. A block away, the UBB building that housed the Bureau of Policewomen was closed for the day. Marching the boys past a duty sergeant and into the detective squad room, where a few men were working the night shift, probably loosened their tongues more anyway.

"What construction site?" Benny made another of his periodic stabs at being a tough nut.

"The one where you hid under the tarp," I said.

"What makes you think—"

"The candy wrappers your brother left."

His arm twitched but he managed not to raise his hand.

"Dummy," he muttered.

We'd been through the preliminaries. The little one was named Tom. The one with curly black hair was Ian. Lulu had scared most of the stuffing out of them by first asking sternly what they knew about recent petty thefts and broken windows by boys their age. They'd fallen all over themselves pleading ignorance, which was probably true.

"We didn't see anything." Ian piped up now. "Just their shapes, anyway, and that they had a car. But nothing about what kind of car, or what they looked like. When we had to run, we were too scared to look back at their faces."

Lulu's fingers tensed.

"You ran? The men saw you?"

"Not our faces, 'cause like I said, we were too busy running to look back."

With saintly patience, as Perkins took notes and I listened, Lulu coaxed out details in bits and pieces. Their mothers gave them spending money as a reward for looking after themselves and going to bed when they were supposed to. They spent part of it riding buses all over town. If they saw something that looked interesting, they got off to 'explore.' They'd been poking around Rachel's site, seeing what there was to see, when a car swung in with its lights off. Caught off guard by the sudden appearance and fearing discovery, they'd hidden under the tarpaulin that covered the lumber.

"They took this big thing out of the trunk." Little Tom's eyes were huge. "And when they unwrapped it... it was a dead guy!"

"You couldn't tell he was dead," scoffed his brother.

"Yeah, you could, the way they dragged him around," said Ian.

Lulu silenced them with a lift of her hand. They quit their squabbling and more or less took turns telling the story.

"They brought him over like they were going to put him close to where we were, only then they didn't."

"They were arguing, see. The one in charge got real mad when the other one went to get something out of his pocket and it wasn't there. That one, the big guy, said it must've fallen out and he'd go look in the truck."

"But the one in charge said they didn't have time. He called the big one an idiot."

"And the big one said he'd had a bellyful of the other one spouting off, and if he called him stupid again he'd clip him a good one and leave him to do his own dirty work."

"Then they picked up the dead guy and moved him farther away and we couldn't hear what they said."

The trio hadn't been able to see much, either. It was dark. Afraid to raise the tarp more than a crack, they'd crowded together, Tom lying on top of his brother, all of them trying to catch just a glimpse.

Instead they'd heard a shot.

"Then he — the one with the gun — looked around and started right toward us."

"We were scared he'd seen us, so we ran!"

"And he did see us then, and he shot at us!"

"And Fraidy Cat screamed."

"So did you!"

"But we kept running."

Two shots. With a pause in between. Just as Willa Lee had described.

Lulu asked more questions, but the answers didn't amount to anything.

"Think really hard," I said when she paused for a minute. "Did you hear any names?"

The boys on the hot seat jumped. They'd forgotten my presence. One by one their heads shook.

"Anything else they said to each other? About why they'd come to that particular place?"

Again their heads moved left to right. Tom's halted suddenly.

"Before they started arguing they were talking like they might be planning to kill someone else."

Lulu sucked in her breath. I held mine.

"No, they weren't."

"They could have been." Ignoring his brother, Tom addressed himself to Lulu and me. "The one who was giving the orders, the one with the gun, he said something like, 'If this doesn't make that pipsqueak play ball, a visit to his buddy on Springfield Pike will.'"

FORTY-FIVE

When I slipped into bed beside Connelly, I realized he was awake, and probably had been from the moment I tiptoed in. Buoyed by my success with Lulu, I kissed him soundly.

"You appear to be in a good mood," he said shifting to accommodate me.

"I am in a very good mood."

"Perhaps we should take advantage of it."

A few minutes later, as my fingers caressed his face, I froze.

"Is that a puffy eye?"

I pushed up on my arm to look. In the dark I couldn't make out details, only the shape of his head.

"We managed to nab one of the purse snatchers. The other one got away. My walking delight took exception to being arrested and I didn't duck fast enough. Turns out he'd done time for assault, so he's well off the street. Anyway, the swelling will be gone by morning, so you needn't fret." He pulled me back down. "A kiss would make it better, though."

Toward dawn we sat with our backs against the wall and the sheet draped over us and talked. He told me about apprehending the purse-snatchers. I told him about the boys hiding under the tarp the night Foster's body was dumped.

"Why the shots if Foster was already dead, then?" Connelly asked.

"I'd guess they were both unplanned. They'd picked up the casing from wherever they actually killed Foster. They meant to leave it along with his body so it would look like it came from the slug in his head."

"Only it got lost on the way."

"Right. So they fired a shot, into the ground, probably, so the cops would find a casing."

"The angle and that would be wrong."

"They didn't have any choice. But the shot spooked the kids. They'd seen Foster's body. When the killer started walking in their direction, probably hunting the casing to make sure the cops would find it, they thought they'd been spotted and bolted."

"And the killer did spot them then, and fired the second shot."

"Which is when little Tom let out the scream Willa Lee heard, poor kid."

"The killer realized someone might already have been awakened by the shots and he and his pal better take off."

"Yes." I leaned against him with a sigh. "This is nice, sitting and talking."

"You seemed to think what we were doing before we fell asleep was okay too."

I chuckled.

"I know what you mean about the talking part, though. Seems like the only familiar faces I see any more are Finn and Rose. You once a week if I'm lucky. It's even trickier connecting with Seamus what with us on different schedules and those always shifting."

We sat in silence. Enough dawn light was coming in now for me to make out a thumb-sized swelling beneath his left eye. He stroked my hair, both of us drowsy and lost in thought.

"When we're married, we can have the best of both," he said. "The talking and the other too. And when the war ends, we'll be able to find a proper house. Our schedules will settle. Seamus will be able to retire and can mind the kids when we need him."

I felt my breath catch. I cared for Connelly in a way I'd never cared for anyone else. Maybe I even loved him, though it was a question I was afraid to explore. But sharing his bed hadn't been a commitment. He sensed my change in mood.

"Not that we have to rush it if you don't want," he said hastily. "I know you're skittish because of how it was with your parents. But now we've seen it can work, haven't we? We can leave it like this for a bit. Take it slow."

I'd been a fool not to see that coming here, being with him like this, would encourage expectations on his part. Expectations which I couldn't meet. Even continuing as we were now, I would lose some vital part of myself. At the back of my mind there would be the weight of knowing I held his happiness in my hands. It would change me. In some moment when I needed to make a split-second decision, I might hesitate, knowing how the loss of me would affect him.

I reached for my slip.

"We both need to get going," I said. "It's late."

***

"If a contractor used a lower grade wood on twenty-percent of what he was building but billed full price, would the difference be worth enough to set up a swindle?" I asked when Rachel came to the phone.

"You dragged me out of bed to ask me that?"

The intensity of her snarl stunned me. The clock on the wall of my office told me it was half past ten. I'd already been to Market House to see if Freeze was going to do anything based on Lulu's report from the night before. Both he and Boike were out. I'd called Joel's office, but he was in court, so I'd spent more time typing a summary of the new information from the boys and my visit to Foster's worksite with Morris. It wasn't exactly the shank of the morning now. I decided on lightness.

"I thought you'd be up and around, Sleeping Beauty. I know you're not an early bird, but you're usually at work by ten or eleven."

"I don't have any work to get to, do I?" she snapped.

I cleared my throat and waited.

"Yes, it would be worth plenty." Her words stretched tight. "Is that what this is about? That weasel Lamont was cutting corners and killed Foster to keep him from squealing?"

"I'm not sure it was Lamont who did the killing," I said carefully.

"Then who? Who? Why are you sticking up for him?"

I'd never seen her like this. It alarmed me.

"I'm not sticking up—"

"So what if he didn't pull the trigger? He knows who did. Hired them probably."

"Rachel—"

"And made *me* look guilty!"

I heard something hit the wall and shatter at her end.

"Rachel, simmer down."

"When I've done absolutely nothing to him! Absolutely *nothing*! Oh, I suppose the fact I win a contract now and then is grievance enough in his eyes. It justifies getting me out of the picture along with Foster. I didn't know my place. That's what he thinks. That's what they all think!"

She was a powder keg, needing only a spark. I trod carefully.

"Rachel, we're getting near the end of this, I promise."

"You promise? What a joke! You're never going to get the tidy little package of proof you need to make this go away. You're just like Joel — another damn Goody Two Shoes!"

I held the receiver away from my head in time to avoid a damaged eardrum as she slammed down the phone.

***

For several minutes I stood with my forehead pressed to the window and my hands clenched, seeing nothing. Rachel was unpredictable. She could also be dangerous. I had to act. I returned to my desk and got out the phone book. Three lumberyards were listed on Springfield Pike. I wrote their locations and phone numbers and started out.

The first one had been replaced by a manufacturing firm. The second had a tall wire fence around it, office and all. A gate at the front stood open, but there was no place inviting cars. Maybe the boss and whoever else worked there parked in back, but I'd already checked, and there was no alley. All comings and goings would have to be through the front entrance.

Across the way sat two machine shops with a few houses and a little café with fresh blue paint edging its single window. Ten feet from the door to the café sat a phone booth. A panel truck with most of its paint worn off was nice enough to vacate the spot it had occupied along the asphalt shoulder and leave me a parking place. I had a slice of pie at the café to get me through, then walked to the pay phone. Dialing the lumberyard across the way, I tried the story I'd concocted.

What sounded like genuine bewilderment, coupled with a suggestion I must have the wrong lumberyard, rewarded my efforts. I went back to my car and sat half an hour in case anyone came running out. When that didn't happen, I drove to the last possibility on my list, thinking hard.

The remaining lumberyard was farther out on Springfield, shortly before Gaddis angled off to the south. It was the largest of the three places, and like the one before it, had a sturdy wire fence surrounding a wood-sided office building, stacks of lumber and a good-sized corrugated shed visible at the rear. Here, however, there was a gravel area big enough for half a dozen cars in front. A Pontiac with about three years on it sat on the gravel. Continuing for a block, I spotted what I was after, a phone booth wedged up against the side of a warehouse.

Doubling back, I parked and took a breath. Then I went to the phone booth, dropped a nickel in and dialed.

"Trowbridge Lumber," answered a faintly harried male voice.

"Oh, hello. This is Mr. Lamont's office," I chirped. "I'm

supposed to check on an invoice from you, but I'm new here and I don't remember who I was supposed to talk to. Can you help me out?"

"Hang on," said the harried voice. He leaned away and spoke to someone else. "Lamont Construction, they usually deal directly with the boss, don't they?" Indistinct murmuring followed. "Mr. Trowbridge handles all the orders from your place," the man who'd answered reported. "Used to date Mr. Lamont's sister, something like that."

"Gee, thanks. Thanks a million. Could I talk to him, please?"

"Agnes. Put this through to the boss. Somebody from Lamont asking about an invoice."

I heard the click that signals you'll be transferred with another click, or that someone had muffed it and lost the connection. Fifteen seconds or so elapsed. Another voice came on, this one cautious.

"Who is this again?"

"Nancy, at Mr. Lamont's office. I'm new and the woman who's showing me how to do things is out sick and—"

"What is it you wanted to know?"

"Oh, um, when you sent that last invoice. We can't seem to find it."

He swore. "Tell your boss I'll look it up and give him a call."

He didn't give me a chance to say anything else. I hung up and scurried back to my car. I'd barely closed the door before a man came barreling out the front door of the lumberyard office. He was clearly worked up about something. And I'd seen him before. It took a second or two before it clicked. He'd been in a photograph. A picnic scene hanging on Lamont's wall the first time I went there. He was the man who'd been wearing the stiff Katy that sat so comically atop his bushy hair.

FORTY-SIX

I reached over to turn the key in my DeSoto, then paused. Instead of getting into the car parked in front of the building, he headed for the telephone booth I'd just vacated, breaking into a trot to beat it across in front of a truck coming down the street. The truck horn blared.

Leaning back, I watched him place his call. His arms began to wave in agitation, or possibly anger. The booth's confining sides kept him from pacing. He did the next best thing, turning this way and that, limited even there by the black cord tethering the phone.

His conversation lasted less than two minutes. Now, I thought, reaching toward the ignition again as he stomped back toward the lumberyard and the car parked in front. Again he surprised me. Without looking left or right, he went back inside.

Now what? I'd eat my second-favorite hat if he'd been talking to anyone other than Lamont. If I was right, they both now knew my phone call had been a trick, and that someone was onto them.

There'd been times through the years when I wished I had a partner. Now was one of them. When people have rolled in the mud and don't want it to show, they start to do things — anything. They start to panic. Either Trowbridge would make a move now, or Lamont would. It was a coin toss which one it would be, and I couldn't watch both of them. My choice was to stick with Trowbridge or risk losing both of them. I stuck.

It was almost the lunch hour, a good time for two men to meet somewhere without attracting notice. If Lamont came here, I'd see him. If Trowbridge left, I'd follow. But Trowbridge stayed put and the only ones who came and went were customers, and an empty flatbed truck with the Trowbridge name on the cab. Two men in work clothes dangled their feet from the tail of the truck. It pulled around back, where I guessed they would break out their lunch pails. Forty-five minutes later, the truck, or one like it, came out stacked with boards and two-by-fours.

The afternoon trickled away, punctuated by sounds of a power saw and lumber slapping together in back. Blending with street sounds came the occasional drone of large propellers. More planes were flying into Patterson Field now.

My bladder had started to protest. My backside was numb. I'd noticed a beer joint up the street next to a tool and die place. It was farther away from my car than I liked, but the front window would give a decent view of the lumberyard entrance.

"Say, could you let me know if any vehicles come in and out at the lumberyard while I run powder my nose?" I asked when I'd ordered a beer. I gestured with the clipboard I'd brought with me. "Helping with a local report for the War Production Board in Washington."

The old fellow manning the bar looked impressed.

"One of those volunteer auxiliary girls, are you?"

I nodded vigorously.

"Good for you, honey. All of us need to do our bit, right? Sure, I'll keep an eye out."

My luck ran out when I asked if they served any food there. The only thing he could offer was peanuts. At least they were fresh, so I sat by the window and shelled some peanuts and took small sips of beer. From time to time I wrote down 'car' or 'truck' on the nice printed sheet I'd bought at an office supply store.

What was I missing? Why wasn't anything happening?

Both Gloria and the boys who'd hidden under the tarp had described one of the men they'd seen as big. That had to be Hawkins, didn't it? Unless he suddenly turned up here, my certainty in the matter was useless. I'd wasted almost an entire day now and had nothing to show for it. I felt like beating my head on the table.

It was getting near quitting time for most people. Trowbridge and Lamont would be leaving their respective places of business. I needed to keep track of both men. Mo Minsky drove. If I could get her to come here and watch, or to call Joel...

"Want another beer, honey?" the white-haired bartender called.

Half a dozen customers had arrived without my noticing. I jumped up.

"No thanks." I went to the bar and leaned forward, inviting him to confidential conversation. "The woman who's supposed to relieve me is late, and I'm in a bind. My kid sis is supposed to go into labor any time now, and I promised I'd come when she did. Will you keep an eye out for me again while I run to that phone booth and make a couple of calls?"

"Oh, you don't need to do that," he protested as I slid him a two-spot.

"It's for all those peanuts I ate." I winked.

A minute later I was in the phone booth dialing Mo's number.

"Mo, it's Maggie—"

"Thank God! I've been calling your office."

"Why? What's wrong?"

"Rachel's disappeared."

"When? How?"

In my mind I heard again the ready-to-burst-the-dam fury in Rachel's voice that morning.

"I dropped her off at her hair appointment. She was supposed to call a cab and come straight home. She called Mama to say she was on her way, and the desk girl at the beauty salon says she called a cab. But that was an hour and a half ago. She hasn't shown up. Mama called to see if she'd come to see me, to - to get away and talk. I hoped maybe she'd come to see you..."

I found it hard to speak for the speed of my thoughts.

"Should we call the police?" Mo was asking.

"You've checked with your other sisters-in-law?"

"Yes. And her secretary in case she went to her office. No one's heard from her."

"No, don't call the police." The awful certainty I knew where Rachel had gone and what she might do began to crush me. "Call Joel," I said. "Don't do anything before you talk to Joel."

I needed to get to Rachel before she made matters worse for herself.

FORTY-SEVEN

Dryness filled my mouth as I maneuvered the DeSoto numbly and as quickly as possible toward Lamont's office. My arguments this morning hadn't persuaded Rachel someone other than Lamont might be responsible for Foster's murder. She saw only that she'd been accused. Confined. Humiliated. Denied control of her own life, which was at the core of what she did and who she was. This morning I'd seen the cracks forming in her, but I hadn't been able to act fast enough. If, as I suspected, she'd gone to Lamont's, if she did something rash there, a chunk of the blame — maybe all of it — would be mine.

Lamont's rectangular white office building had a CLOSED sign on the door when I arrived. The space marked off by railroad ties was empty of cars and the fenced area with supplies was padlocked for the night. On the unfenced side of the building a worn down dirt track led around to the back. I followed it. Lamont's car was there, the one I'd perched on when I lay in wait for him after his business luncheon. The only other vehicle was an old gray pickup.

My initial reaction was relief. Rachel's car wasn't here. Then I remembered that Joel had confiscated her keys. She'd called a cab from the beauty salon where she'd had her hair done. Once she got in, it would have been simple to have the driver bring her here instead of her home address. Sliding out of the DeSoto, I closed the door with minimal noise except for my heart pounding.

How did I play this? Once I got inside, should I call "Yoo-hoo" to distract her? I didn't think she'd shoot Lamont in front of me. If I was in time. But if she looked around at the sound of my voice, Lamont, as scared as he was, might lunge for her gun.

Ridiculous. She didn't have a gun.

Or did she? Rachel was a woman of secrets. I crept to the back door.

The door opened easily when I tried it. At first all I heard was silence. Then I caught the murmur of voices in Lamont's office. Two voices. Both of them male. Whoever was here, it wasn't Rachel.

I frowned. Trowbridge? Could he have slipped out somehow? Did a road or access of some kind that I hadn't noticed squeeze between the railroad siding and the back of his lumberyard?

Because I hadn't had time to practice with my new Smith & Wesson, I'd put it under a pair of coveralls I kept in the trunk of my car, resolved to leave it there until we became more familiar with each other. Meanwhile, the automatic I kept as a backup was in my purse. I took it out, set my purse in the hall, and edged along the wall to Lamont's office.

The door stood open a foot, but I couldn't see anything. The voices had stopped. A radio, maybe? Keeping the gun out of sight at my side, I nudged the door open. My breath stopped. Winfred Lamont sprawled sideways with his head on his desk and one hand reaching toward the telephone.

There was a bullet hole in his forehead.

"Ah, the clever Miss Sullivan. If you were a dog, I'd be impressed by your performance as well as your form," said Phil Clark stepping into my line of vision. He leveled a gun at me with steady confidence.

As he spoke a vise caught my shoulder, smashing me against a file cabinet so hard I lost my grip on the automatic. I snarled as anger followed pain.

"Another yell like that or any fast moves and your friend in the closet gets a bullet," Clark warned. "A painful one. I won't kill her until Dougie has some fun with her. He doesn't like her much."

I didn't need to see the man who was pinning my arms and clamping a hand across my mouth with force enough to snap my jaw. It was Hawkins. Both of them being mixed up in Lamont's swindle and whatever else he was guilty of made no sense.

And then it did.

Clark was fueled by ambition, by the need for success. So much so that he hadn't been able to stand it when the woman he was dating bested him on a bid. He hadn't cared about taking over Foster's project. He'd wanted in on the scam with the two grades of lumber, a scam which would give him an edge. Or maybe just leverage in securing a source of lumber as military construction commandeered the bulk of supplies.

And Hawkins? Hawkins was the cousin he'd mentioned. The one who'd kept him from getting roughed up when they were kids.

"Take your hand off her mouth," Clark ordered. "She's got brains enough to know I meant what I said about her friend, and it looks better if she doesn't have bruises."

The departing twist Hawkins gave my lips made my eyes water.

"Let me see Rachel. How do I know she's still alive?"

Backing up half a dozen paces, Clark half opened the door to Lamont's coat closet. I saw a pair of legs, tied at the ankles. They kicked.

"Bring her here and use the rest of that rope to tie her up like the other one." He nosed the gun in his hand toward the closet a couple of times, his eyes on mine. "Don't forget what I said about shooting her."

With a gun between me and Rachel and her trussed up, I couldn't see any options. Given Hawkins' size, it might take more than one shot to bring him down. Odds were against such an opportunity.

"What happened, Clark? Did you start to worry the cops weren't buying the idea Rachel killed Foster so you dragged her here and killed Lamont to pin this on her too?"

"What happened was you — your sniffing and meddling. If you'd drowned the way you were supposed to, I could have calmed Lamont down. When he called this afternoon in a panic because the man supplying the lumber for their scheme had gotten a call about invoices, I knew the spineless twit presented a risk."

Hawkins jerked me around and started tying my hands behind me.

"You've killed the Golden Goose, though."

"Not necessarily." Clark's smile was unpleasant. "If Lamont's arrangement with the man supplying the lumber—"

"Trowbridge."

"Of course. You had to know his name to call him, didn't you? There's no reason to think the police investigating Lamont's death will discover their scheme. Trowbridge may decide it's in his best interest to enter into a similar arrangement with me. Either way, I have two competitors out of the picture."

"And either way, you get the satisfaction of having evened scores with Rachel. You punish her for beating you fair and square when she got that contract."

"That ain't true!" Hawkins yanked the rope around my wrists and spun me to face him. "Wasn't anything fair and square about it! That bitch has had everything given to her, just like all dames. Phil's fought to get where he is — fought every step of the way! Dames don't have to fight for what they get. You don't even know how to. All you know how to do is strut around and give orders and act important. But you're not giving orders now, are you, huh?"

He raised his hand to belt me.

"Don't!" Clark said sharply. "I told you I don't want any marks on her. I need you to keep your temper now, Dougie, so I can think."

The childish form of address for the hulk holding me made the whole ugly scene bizarre.

"She's thrown a wrench in things coming here," Clark told his cousin. "We're going to have to change plans. Get a gag in her mouth and finish tying her. Then put her in with the other one. Make sure those knots are tight, too."

"Other people already know how Foster cheated with the lumber," I said. If Clark started to worry he couldn't knock enough dominoes down to make himself safe, he might cut his losses and run.

"They know Foster did, maybe. No reason they should connect anything about it to me. Or to Trowbridge."

Hawkins stuffed the pressed and folded handkerchief from Lamont's jacket into my mouth. I tried not to notice the speck of blood on it. He secured it in place with another cloth of unknown provenance.

"When you've finished with her, go get her car and park it somewhere down the street. By that bar we noticed." Clark was thinking aloud. "I'll move Lamont's car and meet you at the truck. We'll wait til it's dark to come back for them."

"What do you mean come back?"

"Weren't you listening? I just told you we have to change plans."

Hawkins tied my feet, running his hand up the length of my thigh for good measure. Then he carried me across the room like a rolled up carpet and dropped me into the closet, fully aware that tied as I was, I had no means of breaking my fall.

FORTY-EIGHT

The closet door banged. I lay in darkness. I'd landed on something softer than floor, but uneven. Several seconds elapsed and I realized it was Rachel, lying on her side with knees drawn up, maybe in an effort to cushion my fall. I eased off her and we both slid back to sit on opposite sides of the closet so we could see each other.

On the other side of the door, Clark told Hawkins to look for my purse, and something about the car. Their voices started to fade. They were leaving. Or pretending to.

I nudged Rachel's knee with mine in reassurance. After a moment, she nudged back. In what little light leaked in beneath the office door, I could see her eyes were glistening. They had tears in them. As petulant and vile tempered as she'd been that morning, Rachel wasn't one for self-pity. The tears were for me. For getting me involved.

When enough time had passed for me to believe we were really alone, I drew up my knees and tried to get my chin against them to scrape my gag off. Rachel caught on and tried the same move. It soon became apparent neither of us could make sufficient contact with our knees for long enough to succeed.

Blocked on that idea, I searched my mind for another. I thrust my shoulder forward and nodded at Rachel. She frowned. I repeated it and she understood. Scooting forward, she angled her shoulder toward me.

As small as the coat closet was, it didn't take much maneuvering on either of our parts. It was barely wide enough for us to sit with our legs stretched out and deep enough for us to fit in side by side. I could get the top edge of cloth down over my mouth but I couldn't work it down any farther. Hawkins had done a dandy job with that assignment.

Suddenly Rachel pulled away and began twisting and grunting. She rolled onto her knees. Unable to balance or push with her hands, she braced her head and shoulder against the closet wall. With sheer determination as much as anything else, she managed to totter onto her feet. While I sat wondering what in the name of sense she was doing, she began to ram her head into hangers and lift until she knocked a few down.

As soon as she got it across to me what to do, her idea proved its cleverness. She maneuvered a hanger until I could clamp it between my drawn-up knees. Then she tilted her head, worked the edge of her gag over the hook of the hanger, and pulled and tugged. There were setbacks, most notably when the hanger slipped free of my knees, but after fifteen minutes we were free to talk.

"I'm sorry," she said with her first breath. "All the things I've said to you, getting you into this to begin with—"

"It's okay, Rache. What happened?"

"I was at the beauty shop. When I came out I hadn't gone ten feet before I met Phil. Clark. He came up like he meant to wish me well or some such and stuck a gun in my ribs. Told me very pleasantly that they had Cecilia, and that if I didn't come with him, her kid wouldn't have a mother."

"They don't have Cecilia. Mo talked to her when they started hunting you."

She told me the rest. Hawkins had been behind the wheel of Clark's car in a nearby alley. Clark knocked her over the head. When she woke up, she was bound and gagged. They bundled her into the trunk and brought her to the meeting he had scheduled with Lamont.

"Poor Lamont. He thought he and Phil were going to be putting their heads together to find a way out of the mess they realized they were in after your phone call. When he saw Hawkins and me, he knew something was off and was terrified. Phil kept asking him what he'd told you. Lamont kept saying nothing, that he didn't know how you'd learned about Trowbridge. After five minutes or so of that, Phil shot him. No warning, just ... shot him."

As she talked, we'd both been working to loosen the ropes that tied our hands. There was no way we could help each other with that task. The fibers of the rough rope scraped into my skin like sandpaper as I picked and pulled with my fingers and seesawed my wrists, but I began to feel a small gap. It might amount to only a quarter inch, but once I could work my thumbs under, I could make serious progress.

"They were about to shoot me, make it look like suicide in a fit of remorse, when they heard you drive up outside."

"If Clark had been fast on his feet, he would have shot me then and there, made it look as though I'd walked in and found you with the gun in your hand."

"Allow me to say I'm quite pleased he didn't."

"Me too. He's a planner. I don't think he's good at

making things up as he goes." It might be the one advantage we had. "He thought he could pin Foster's murder on you because of the argument the two of you had, and the rumor Foster spread. What makes him think the cops would fall for the idea of your killing Lamont?"

"My volatile nature." Her voice was bitter. "He said everyone I'd had dealings with knew how quick-tempered I could be."

"Ah." There was no disputing that part. "How close are you to freeing your hands?"

"Not very. I can wiggle my wrists, though."

It was dark in the closet now. I had no sense of time. Clark and his enforcer could come back any minute.

"Unless he's changed plans, it sounds like he plans to take us both elsewhere to dispose of us."

"Agreed. If I were in his position, I'd try to maintain the fiction that this was all somehow related to Foster's death, in which case I'd take us to either my office or the Drinkwater site."

"That's what I was thinking. He's smart enough to know we'll be easier to control if he separates us. He'll either make two trips with my car or he'll use Lamont's too."

"To make it look like I killed Lamont, used his car, and lured you wherever."

"Yes."

I told her about the .38 hidden under the dirt stained coveralls in the DeSoto. If they used my car twice and I didn't get a chance to use the gun, she might.

Hawkins was wrong in his estimation of women, and not just in the slighting term he'd used, either. When something that mattered to them was at stake, women fought.

Rachel and I lapsed into silence. We weren't the type for false assurances. We knew the odds that either of us would get out of this alive were long, odds of both of us making it even longer. Nor did we waste words on declarations of friendship. They were unneeded. Thinking of Rachel's friendship called up thoughts of Connelly and the raw emotion in his voice when he'd said he couldn't bear it if anything happened to me. I hoped he would forgive me. I hoped he would see I would never have been right for him.

Rachel's voice interrupted.

"I wish I'd fired that s.o.b. Hawkins six months ago." Our laughter blended, muted and sad.

Out in the hall there were sounds. No bugle played, so it wasn't the cavalry come to rescue us. Instead I heard Clark's voice.

I'd managed to work my thumbs under the outer loop of the rope and slip one side over, giving more play. Now I hooked my thumbs around the rope a different way and applied tension. If Clark or Hawkins tested the rope but didn't look closely, it would still seem secure.

"Get your gag up," I whispered to Rachel, then used my tongue to pull the outer band of cloth up a couple of times to a tenuous covering of my mouth. The handkerchief that had been stuffed under it had long since gotten shoved beneath a topcoat knocked to the floor in Rachel's attempt to get hangers.

She swore, an indication she couldn't get the gag up even though I'd made her practice the move half a dozen times. Curling into a ball she turned her face to the wall, hiding her face as she pretended to sleep.

The closet door opened.

"Take the detective out first," Clark ordered. "When she's in, pull her car away and back Lamont's car up to the door."

Hawkins' paw wrapped around my arm and jerked me upright.

"Aw, ain't that a pity." He sneered past me at Rachel. "We're gonna have to disturb Her Majesty's beauty sleep."

FORTY-NINE

As soon as the trunk lid slammed imprisoning me, I started to work at the ropes on my wrists again. By the time the car was in motion, I was back to where I'd been before. The joints of my thumbs were sore. Hawkins had given the rope a hard yank to test it. He hadn't noticed my hard-won two inches of slack, but my thumb joints had strained to maintain an appearance of tightness.

The next part was tricky. I could slip one hand under a single strand of the rope that encircled my wrists several times, but when I tried to pull the other hand free, the loops remaining tightened. On my fourth attempt I succeeded and the rest went quickly. The first thing I did was feel beneath me for my folded-up coveralls with the Smith & Wesson.

It was still there.

Tucking it into my waistband, I began to work at the ropes around my ankles. The tips of my fingers were raw. My nails dug into the crevices of the knot again and again, desperate even as I coached myself to stay calm. If I couldn't free my feet by the time they opened the trunk, I didn't have a chance. I might put a bullet in one of them, but I'd be a sitting duck for the other one.

I thought about Rachel and how her family would suffer if Clark's plan succeeded. They wouldn't believe in her guilt, but they'd never be able to clear her name either. People they knew, as well as strangers, would believe the worst of her. I, along with a chunk of metal I hadn't yet tried, was the only hope that they had. That Rachel had. I clawed feverishly at the unyielding knot.

You*'re wrong, Hawkins. Dames fight plenty. Dames fight harder than men because they've had to their whole lives.*

Even if I couldn't free myself, even if I had to do so from the confines of the trunk, I would fight the two men holding us captive. I would shoot whichever one opened the trunk, and when I ran out of bullets I would keep fighting. I would fight them as long as I had breath in my body.

The knot began to give. It parted.

The car swayed, turning, and gravel crunched under the tires.

I kicked and tugged, unwinding the rope. The DeSoto stopped. What mattered now was to be prepared. I eased the .38 into a steady grip, getting a feel for it in my hand. Lighter than my previous one because of its shorter barrel. Agreeable, though.

As best I could in the cramped space, I positioned myself. When the trunk lid started to raise, belatedly, I realized a loop of rope still clung to one of my ankles. With no time to remedy the situation, I fired at the shape that raised the trunk lid and then fired again. It was Hawkins.

He'd leaned to the side as he lifted, so shots meant for his chest hit closer to his shoulder. He stumbled back with a howl, lost his balance and fell. He wasn't out of commission. He made a grab for my ankle as I scrambled out.

If he noticed the rope around my foot he would grab for that next, and catching it would be easier. Aware of precious seconds sacrificed, I hopped on the other foot and kicked free. Hawkins was already on his knees, surging up. He lunged. I turned and ran.

"What's—? Stop her, you fool!"

Two weeks had passed since Easter. The moon was near its darkest phase. What light the sky above shared came mostly from stars, and as my eyes picked out shapes I recognized where I was — and that I was running in the absolute worst direction.

We were at Rachel's building project. In my disorientation I had headed toward the back of the lot, which was barricaded by a high wire fence. Immediately to my left was the gravel pile. In the other direction was the loathsome front loader with its dangling bucket. If I veered harder right, I'd be trapped by the building going up and the now diminished pile of lumber where the kids with candy wrappers had hidden.

"I'll cut her off this way!" Clark's voice was low and intense. The sound of a bullet whined behind me.

With no bullets to waste, I couldn't shoot blindly behind me. If I looked back long enough to pinpoint Clark, I would become a stationary target myself, or Hawkins would pounce.

I zigzagged. Something caught at my blouse, jerked me back. Hawkins. Using all my weight, I threw myself forward. Cloth ripped and I managed two steps. He caught me again. This time he had me by the wrist, squeezing it in his viselike grip as he tried to force the .38 from my hand.

"Get out of the way, Doug! Doug! Get out of the way!"

But Hawkins was as enraged as a bull with an arrow lodged in its shoulder. His left arm hung useless, glistening with blood from the damage I had inflicted. Intent on nothing but evening scores, he swung me back against the waist-high gravel pile. Resorting to playground tactics I flung a handful of gravel in his face.

He yelped and jerked back. I rolled. The sideways motion, or maybe sheer luck, pulled my hand from his startled grip.

The Goliath aimed a kick at me as I hit the ground. I managed to dodge, but his toe connected enough to send the Smith & Wesson spinning out of my hand. Drifting clouds blotted out stars. The sudden disappearance of shapes worked for me as well as against me. On my knees, I sucked in oxygen and held it. Hawkins' furious breathing told me where he was. I had no sense at all of Clark's location.

As quickly as they'd interfered, the clouds parted, but only long enough for me to glimpse two things: the underbelly of the bucket loader I'd taken refuge behind, and beneath it a glint which might be my gun.

Dark again. As silently as possible I scrambled around to the other side of the loader.

Where was Clark?

Starlight returned, this time to stay. I saw Hawkins' legs on the other side of the loader. And yes, my gun. Flattening myself, I crawled under and stretched my arm until I could pull the .38 to me.

As I backed out and knelt, a shot pinged into the dirt beside me. It came from high in the skeleton of the structure that was going up there. Clark, who had started in the lowliest jobs in construction and worked his way up, Clark who could walk a beam with the best of them, stood silhouetted and steady on framing for the building's second floor. Another shot slammed down as I flattened myself against the side of the loader.

The next sound I heard curled the hairs on the back of my neck. The metal monster next to me rumbled to life.

"I've got her!" Hawkins yelled exultantly. "I've got her!"

The machine lurched and its heavy, merciless jaws began to swing in my direction.

I tried to flee, nearly lost my footing on a scrap of construction debris, then stopped. I'd played this game before. I wasn't going to play it again.

Turning toward the machine, I ran forward the few yards separating us. With momentum propelling me now, I leaped. Grabbing a fistful of Hawkins' shirt, I hauled myself up.

I was on the side with his injured arm. It flailed at me ineffectually. I hooked my leg over his shoulders and straddled him, riding piggyback for my life. He started to grab at me with his good hand, but as it left the controls, the loader jerked and he gripped them again. I rammed the .38 against his head.

"Turn it off."

"You want a ride, girlie? I'll give you one!"

The machine beneath us started to vibrate with a force that rattled my bones.

"Turn it off!"

He laughed.

I pointed the gun toward the back of his good hand and fired. With a muffled howl he started to call me every name in the book, hugging his hand against him. The loader sputtered and stalled.

"Drop the gun and come down, Clark," I yelled with my .38 once more pressed to his cousin's head.

His answer was a shot that showered sparks as it skittered along a piece of metal inches from me.

Then another shot split the night, this one a loud crack. Clark's shape, outlined by the starlight, stood motionless before it pitched earthward in an almost graceful fall.

The noise of the loader engine had stopped. For thirty seconds or better I sat too drained to move. Then I slung my leg over Hawkins' pain curled shoulders and dropped to the ground. The big man was keening softly.

A thin, erect figure strode into view, her rifle lowered but ready. It was Willa Lee Cottle. Judging by the nightgown billowing under her raincoat, she'd been roused from sleep, just as she'd been on the night Foster's body was dumped here.

She detoured to nudge Clark's shape with her toe, then came toward me. Her jaw was squared.

"I heard shots over here. Saw your car." She gave a single, satisfied nod. "Guess those policemen who talked to me last time may decide there's nothing wrong with my hearing, or my eyes either."

FIFTY

"You haven't asked me what was in the envelope."

Rachel and I were walking up Patterson toward my office after lunch together. Though we'd passed each other in hallways, and managed a word here and there, the past four days had been a blur of talking to the police, snatching sleep, being called back to answer more questions, then going through it all again with Joel. Today was the first time since our night as captives that we'd had a chance to really see each other and talk.

Hawkins, now under guard in the hospital, had claimed he was at the construction site hunting his lost wallet. The fact the arriving cops had found Rachel still trussed up in the trunk of a car belonging to a dead man on the other side of town gave his story the credibility of a fairytale. It also, when added to evidence that came to light in various places, removed all suspicion that Rachel had known anything about Foster's murder.

"I figured if you wanted me to know what was in it, you would have told me," I said.

"It was poems. Love poems, mostly."

She smiled, a sad, sweet smile unlike any I'd ever seen from her.

"I was twenty. I wanted to be an architect. My father wouldn't hear of college and sent me to Paris with cousins

312

I'd never met instead. They were shocked to find I wasn't content to traipse around in a group to predictable tourist sites. I scampered off on my own and met Andrew. He was studying law. We were going to change the world together.

"He came from New York, a very progressive family, he said. Not quite as progressive as he thought, it turned out. When we got back and told our families about ... us ... it quickly became clear we'd have to choose between them and being together. For two years we exchanged letters, biding our time, believing they'd change."

"But they didn't?"

"One day I got a letter from a friend of Andrew's saying a gas line had exploded where he was working and he'd been killed. About the same time, an uncle of mine was headed for prison. His weasel of a son had gotten Uncle Hy's construction company mixed up in something crooked. Rather than testify against his own blood, Uncle Hy went to prison too. He was desperate to sell to provide for his wife. I had a small inheritance. I bought him out — and hired Pearlie, to help me convince my cousin's old pals I wasn't open to backroom deals."

I was silent. It explained the lingering rumors Rachel's business was shady.

"Have you heard from Pearlie?"

"Briefly. He said he'd call me at the office this afternoon if he could get to a phone. I'm headed there now."

We'd reached my building. Rachel reached for my hand and gave it a wordless squeeze. I watched her bustle off back toward her car. Her rose pink suit was a welcome sight after the drab hues she'd worn when she was a suspect and penitent.

That afternoon's mail brought an envelope whose return address was an army post in Kentucky. Intrigued, I opened it and unfolded the sheet of paper inside. A photograph fluttered out.

It was Pearlie. In an army uniform.

I expect you wondered why I took off right when Rachel could have used me around. I figured I owed something to my country just like everyone else, so I signed up. They'd told me to report right before that mess happened, and the army doesn't take it too well if you don't show up like you should.

That new .38 work okay for you? Sounds like it did. Rachel will have my address. If you want to write or anything.

Pearlie

I folded a clean piece of paper around the picture and put it in a drawer until I could buy a frame. For the rest of the afternoon I lost myself in paperwork. When it came time to head to Finn's, though, I walked to the river instead.

I hadn't been to Finn's since my wild ride at the construction site, and I hadn't been back to Connelly's. I wasn't ready to say the words I needed to say. Sitting on a bench with a warm breeze stroking my face, I wondered how I could still find pleasure in watching the river dance past, bejeweled with sunlight. I'd been terrified out in its dark waters. It wasn't the river that had tried to drown me, though. It was men.

I felt a presence and looked around as he spoke.

"I thought I might find you here." Connelly slid into place beside me. He had a shadow of beard. He was newly off duty. "You haven't been up."

"I needed time by myself."

"When you don't, I'll be waiting."

I shook my head slowly, wearily.

"It won't work, Mick. Us."

"It did. It will again. We can make it work."

"No. We can't. The other night, when I thought those yahoos were going to kill me, the hardest part was thinking how much you'd grieve."

"And I would. But it's a risk you take when you care—"

"*I can't do it, Mick!* I can't bear knowing I matter that much to someone."

"But you will matter that much, regardless of what you do. You can't change that."

I caught the hand he touched to my cheek.

"No, but you can. You have to. Please, Mick. Those nights we had together — I cherish them. I always will. But if you truly care for me, for what we've had, accept what I'm saying. I want you to move on. I want you to find someone else."

A tear I couldn't explain slid down my cheek. His thumb, ever gentle, wiped it away. He kissed the top of my head.

"I love you, Maggie."

"I know."

He was silent, waiting for words I couldn't say. If I told him I loved him, gave voice to it, that would make it true.

"If I could change myself ... if I could be the way I want to be ... I would. For you. But I can't, Mick. And I want you to be happy. I want you to have a home and family like you came from. Like you miss. Like you deserve."

More tears I didn't want to shed blurred my vision. After a moment his hand found mine. Our fingers intertwined;

gripping hard because we knew when we let go this time it would be forever.

Our words were all used up. Only the ache in our hearts remained. We sat in silence, watching the river twist and flow. Watching our lives.

The End

If you enjoyed this book, please leave a short review on Amazon or Goodreads to help other readers discover it. Just a few lines is fine and will be greatly appreciated.

Get a FREE Maggie Sullivan short story, exclusive tidbits, and early word on new releases when you sign up for Ruth's newsletter. Your email will never be shared and you can unsubscribe at any time.

READ ALL THE MAGGIE SULLIVAN MYSTERIES

No Game for a Dame (Maggie Sullivan #1)

When a stranger who threatened her and wrecked her office winds up dead, 1940s private eye Maggie Sullivan finds herself facing a crime boss.

Tough Cookie (Maggie Sullivan #2)

A high stakes swindler Maggie is hunting is found floating in the river. Now someone wants to silence her – and the corpse is strangely active.

Don't Dare a Dame (Maggie Sullivan #3)

A 25-year-old murder jeopardizes Maggie's future as a private eye as well as her life when it points toward people with political connections.

Shamus in a Skirt (Maggie Sullivan #4)

Murder and theft at a posh hotel pits Maggie against well-heeled suspects fleeing the war in Europe.

Maximum Moxie (Maggie Sullivan #5)

Kidnapping, murder and a child's plea draw Maggie into a new case days before the attack on Pearl Harbor.

OTHER NOVELS BY THIS AUTHOR

The Whiskey Tide
At the height of Prohibition, three sisters in a genteel Massachusetts family smuggle liquor by sea to save their home.

A Touch of Magic
A savvy sleight-of-hand artist pits her skills – and nerve – against a master terrorist.

Say 'hello' to Ruth online. She loves to hear from readers! Website Blog Facebook Goodreads Pinterest Twitter BookBub Email mruthmyers.words@gmail.com

ABOUT THE AUTHOR

M. Ruth Myers received a Shamus Award from Private Eye Writers of America for the third book in her Maggie Sullivan mysteries series. She is the author of more than a dozen books in assorted genres, some written under the name Mary Ruth Myers. If you shine a bright light in her eyes, she'll admit to one husband, one daughter, one son-in-law, one grandson and one cat – all of whom she adores. She lives in Ohio.

99349287R00193

Made in the USA
Columbia, SC
07 July 2018